DARK ROSALEEN

MICHAEL NICHOLSON

The History Press Ireland

ACKNOWLEDGMENTS

I am indebted to my lifetime friend Robin O'Connor for his patient labouring through the first proofs. To Billy Patterson, a meticulous and humorous second filter; to John Conway of University College Cork and Senan Seclan and his eye for the smallest error; to Dr Paul Rouse of University College Dublin for checking the historical accuracy; and to Ronan Colgan who had the good sense to commission *Dark Rosaleen*.

I was inspired by two of Ireland's greatest writers of the famine, Liam Flaherty and Walter Macken. I am indebted to the historians, among them Cecil Woodham-Smith, Christine Kinealy, Tim Pat Coogan and Treveylan's biographers Jennifer Hart and Robin Haines. First-person accounts written at the time include Gerald Keegan's *Famine Diary*, Asenath Nicholson's *Annals of the Famine in Ireland*, Robert Whyte's *Famine Ship Diary* and the writings of the Quaker James Hake Tuke.

AUTHOR'S NOTE

This novel tells the story of the Irish potato famine of 1845, 'the Great Hunger', out of which came the militant rebels who fought to free Ireland from English rule and the man who gave rise to the Fenians. Nothing in these pages, not the people, nor the life they lived, is wholly fictional. Almost all of what I have written happened in real life.

In order to turn history into a novel, an author is obliged to dramatise, to put words into mouths that might never have been spoken, to lay blame that perhaps was not wholly deserved. But little here is exaggerated. There is no need. The truth is appalling enough. If you find descriptions of people, events and their outcome hard to believe, then go to the history books and be convinced.

Sebec Lake
Maine
12 August 1934

It is recorded in the register of the coroner's office in the County of Limerick that my mother drowned escaping the English in 1848. She was a fine English lady and, at that time, would have been twenty-four years of age. It is also written that the authorities waited a month or more for the sea to return her body but it did not.

I am an old man and her only child and before I die I wish to correct those records in Ireland. For unless I do, the lie will forever remain the truth.

The English did not kill my mother, nor did the sea swallow her up. She is buried on the coast of Maine in a grave I helped dig myself.

Even now, I can hear her story in a voice as clear and as close as when she first told it, speaking in her fine language of a land of savagery and sadness, of a people who suffered for their patience and died from their hunger.

And I cried as a child, although I could not know why. I knew nothing then of hunger, or suffering or dying. Nor even anger.

CHAPTER ONE

The coals were white hot. The face of the child was ringed by flames. Soon it would be engulfed by fire, soon it would die, soon it would be ash. She could do nothing but sit and watch. It was a small gaunt face, cursed by innocence, its eyes full of melancholy. Its image scorched her.

The tip of the flames touched his face but his eyes stared resolutely back. She looked for a name and a place but she dared not reach out, the heat too fierce. It troubled her, she who cared nothing for distant calamities that befell others. Why now was she suffocating? Why now this something she had never felt before, this guilt? What was one death among so many?

Until this moment she had been consumed by her own self-pity, wretched at her father's selfish ultimatum, furious at his imposition dressed up as duty. Did she care that Irish peasants were hungry because they had lost their potatoes? Why should she waste a moment's thought on brutes too lazy to feed their litters, too drunk to dig for their own food? How dare they disrupt her life so suddenly and so completely, forcing her headlong into a hostile land she despised, that filthy country of saints and savages they called Ireland?

He had told her so casually. The government, he said, was to provide aid to the Irish and he had been given the authority as Relief Commissioner to oversee its distribution. Soon he must leave for Ireland, and she was obliged to go with him.

The flames licked at her fingers. The heat scorched the skin of her forehead but still she could not move away. Sweat soaked the hair around her temples, the salt from her tears stung her cheeks and stung again as they eased into her cracked lips. Yet she remained close, compelled to share something in those final moments.

She waited for the flames to cremate the last of the image and in that waiting, as a hot poultice slowly draws out pain, so the fire gradually evaporated her anger. She was subdued. She felt only sadness, grief and something more, something she had never before known in all her young and very privileged life. She felt uncertain and afraid.

တ

Kate Macaulay's life that day changed as abruptly as the weather. The warm, bright early October morning sun had surrendered to a grey afternoon and by the time it was dark, the barometer had dipped further. The wind, stirred from the east and blowing unhindered from the Urals, swept across the North Sea to the Anglian Fens and froze all of Lincolnshire. It shook the house, piled snow against its walls and windows and forced smoke back down the chimneys, blackening the mantelpieces and spreading soot across the rugs.

She had become more furious by the hour. She had argued with her father at breakfast, at lunch and again at dinner. She had refused to eat and, in an attempt to offend him more, had barely touched her supper. Now she was hungry and defeated. She had tried every trick she knew but the cajolery that had won him over so often in the past had failed her. He was deaf to it and instead, addressing her as if he was speaking to one of his junior staff, reminded her of her duty, his duty and the duty of the government, so that it seemed to her that all of England was a slave to duty and that all pleasures and recreation, most especially her own, were to be entirely forfeited in the Queen's service.

To quieten and comfort her, he promised that they would not be away from England long and that he expected his work would be over before next year's summer ended. Then they would return to Lincolnshire or to their house in London, whatever suited her. He would retire from government service and they would travel north together to cousins at their Northumberland estate and perhaps go further still into the Highlands for the shooting. To dry her tears he told her that Irish society was almost as interesting as English society, with country estates as vast and as sumptuous as any she had known. She could have her own mare and she would not want for company. There were many of her own sort there.

Kate was accustomed to being soothed by promises. She had never had to wait long for something she wanted but he was offering nothing she did not already have. She would not be bargained with. She would not be pacified, refusing to believe his promises even though she had never known him break one. Her friends were here in Lincolnshire and London and she was in no mood to seek out new ones for her father's or even Queen Victoria's convenience.

She had fought him all day but she had not won a single concession, not even the compromise of a further few months' stay so that she might enjoy her Christmas and New Year in England. He cared nothing that she would miss the Belvoir Hunt weekend with Colonel Arden-Walker, who had been so generous and so attentive since the last. She would have to send her apologies to the Earl of March for not attending his Goodwood Ball and to Lord Abercrombie, whose night of fancy dress and charades at London's Ritz so glamorously and entertainingly welcomed in the New Year.

Her year's social calendar had been painstakingly planned. There was never a weekend when she was not the centre of somebody's attention, never an evening in the London season that was not filled by one or other of her many adoring young suitors. Now, without warning or apology, it was all to be cancelled. She was being forced to leave behind people who were both dear and necessary to her simply because of something despicable far away. The prospect appalled her and all day she cried tears that for once she had no way of stopping.

In one final attempt that evening she had screamed at her father deliberately in front of the servants, demanding her independence, threatening to leave the house and never return. She was twenty-two years old and she would not let him re-arrange her life. She was not a minor, obliged to do his bidding. She could leave him as she pleased, go wherever she wanted with whoever she chose, even marry if that was her whim. The law was the law and that was what the law allowed. The servants took refuge in the kitchen. They had cosseted her since she was a child and knew well enough her moods and contrariness. But they had never seen her in such a state before and they were all agreed that when her father left for Ireland, he would have no choice but to leave her behind to do as she pleased. They were wrong.

Sir William Macaulay was a long and faithful servant of the Crown. He had served with distinction as Commissariat General of the British Army, had seen action in the Peninsular Campaign, had been with Wellington at Waterloo and had been knighted for devotion to duty during the Canadian Rebellion. As the man in charge of army supplies he was a devoted cheesepare, ready to save a penny wherever a penny could be saved. It made him ideally suited to oversee the distribution of aid to the starving Irish.

He was about to embark on the last great challenge of his career and was concerned with more urgent matters than his young daughter's hysterical obstinacy. He was a gentle and patient man and loved her more intensely than he had ever had the courage to show. Her tears and tantrums had been painful and made him relive a part of his life that still haunted him, memories that he had for so long been trying to erase, memories of the wife he loved, of the day she had given birth to Kate and that final, fateful day when she had left them both. Even now, all these years on, he could not remember that time without his fists tightening, the muscles of his jaw hardening and a pain in his chest so severe it left him breathless. And he cursed the God that made her go.

That day, he had returned from London after an interview in Whitehall with the austere, pious and powerful Sir Charles Trevelyan, Secretary to the Treasury. Despite a title that suggested he was of a lesser order, he controlled all government expenditure. He was a young and handsome man of rigid integrity, a devout evangelical, impatient, blunt, arrogant, uncompromising. He considered himself to be always on the right side of a question and many of those who dared cross him found their careers blighted soon afterwards. As guardian of the nation's coffers, his guiding principle was balancing humanity with practical economics. It was he who would steer the course of Ireland now.

He sat upright at his desk and, as was his practice, made no effort to acknowledge the presence of the man he had summoned. He made no gesture towards the chair opposite him, so Sir William stood to attention, as he had done all his military life in the presence of superiors.

Trevelyan spoke, as ever, to the point.

'I waste no time on courtesies, Sir William. I am familiar with your record of public service and know you are more than capable of the employment I am about to charge you with. I break no confidences when I tell you that Prime Minister Peel is alarmed by events in Ireland. It would appear that this year's potato crop has failed there as it has in England, Scotland and almost every country in Northern Europe. We understand the disease comes from America but it cannot be identified. What we do know is that it is more thoroughly destructive than anything before. You may have read of this?'

'Yes, Sir Charles. I have read much about it. It is a serious matter.'

'Serious indeed. Unlike the peasantry in England, the Irish are entirely dependent on their potatoes. It is their entire diet. Monday to Sunday, January to December, they eat nothing else. Without potatoes they starve.'

'So it appears, sir.'

'Yes Sir William, it is exactly as it appears. For that reason and with commendably swift decision, the Prime Minister has authorised a Commission to oversee relief and the distribution of food in the affected provinces. You, Sir William, will head it. There is to be no delay. He expects you to sail to Ireland within the week. Your headquarters will be in Cork.'

'Must it be so soon, sir? A week is no time at all for me to settle my own affairs. To be away for so long without preparation— '

'You assume too much. It need not be long. The Prime Minister believes the worst will be over by the summer. It may or may not be. God alone will decide. But be assured of this. We will do what is necessary but no more than that. The Irish peasants are perverse and prefer to beg than borrow; they would rather eat free English food than labour for their own. It would be unjust and unwise to pamper them when our own people are pleading for assistance and I do not intend to transfer famine from one country to another. You understand?'

'I fully understand, sir. It makes very practical sense.'

'And one last thing, Sir William, before you go. As I understand it, you no longer have a wife but you have a daughter?'

'I do, sir. Her name is Kathryn.'

'Then the Prime Minister would have you take her too. She will need to accompany you on the official functions that, as the Queen's representative, you will be expected to attend.'

༄

Kate counted the twelve slow chimes of the clock on the landing outside her bedroom door. The house was silent. The wind had dropped. The last of the servants had gone to their attic beds and, in his bedroom, her father had stopped the soft coughing that always ended his day. She looked down at the remains of the fire. The image of the child had been consumed and all that was left was a wedge of paper ash. She watched as bit by bit it was drawn up the chimney to be broken into tiny flakes and scattered across the rooftops on that white winter's night.

She was exhausted. Her tantrums had won her nothing. On the rug at her feet were the few remaining pages of the *Illustrated London News*. Her father had slid it under her door, hoping she might be tempted to read something of the land she was about to sail to and the tragedy she was about to witness. In her fury she had stamped on it, ripped it apart, thrown its pages into the flames and stirred the coals to make it burn faster. But she could not touch the drawing of the boy, thin and almost naked, standing defiantly by the bodies of his mother and sisters. His face held her until the fire had finally devoured him.

The room was cold. She shivered but it was not from the chill. Again she felt the same sensation, a surging fear that, despite herself and her shrill threats of defiance, she too was about to become a casualty of Ireland's Great Hunger.

CHAPTER TWO

Sky and earth were one black sprawling mess. It was raining the first day when they landed in Ireland and it had been raining ever since. Kate had now been in Cork for a month and seven days and she had not yet seen a blue sky or the tip of a mountain or an expanse of sea. It was like living under a vast, dripping shadow, everything saturated by clouds that hung low, still and moody. People told her it might stay that way all winter. They said it cheerily, as if that was how they preferred it to be, curtained off, captive.

She felt so captured. What a perfect prison this Ireland was to her and she was condemned to live in it for as long as its people were hungry. Or perhaps longer. However absurd it seemed to her, the notion kept repeating itself, the fearful conviction that she was about to become entangled in the misery of this land, that its suffering would make her its prisoner.

For those first five weeks, she had stayed within the house and, for most of the time, within her own rooms. To venture out into the gardens, to inspect the stables and yards would be to admit an interest and she was determined to show none. She ignored the daily respectful formalities from the staff and the curtsies of the chambermaids. She kept silent but, to her outrage, her father was too busily involved in his new task to notice. It was the arrival of the mare he had promised that finally ended her stubborn resistance.

She rode her most afternoons but she could not go far. Her father had pencilled a perimeter on a map of the countryside surrounding Cork and warned her that if she crossed it, he would have her ride with an armed escort. Drenched in Ireland's autumn, she longed for a dry breeze and a clear horizon. On every ride she searched for higher ground, thinking that if she could climb the tracks that wound up through the mists, she would break through and find blue sky and a little warmth. But the paths were too narrow or strewn with too many boulders and the mare stumbled too often. The sun was always beyond her.

One day, ignoring her father's orders for the first time, she rode along the banks of Lough Mahon, past Monkstown and Ringaskiddy, searching for a horizon, to see the land fade into nothingness the way it did in the Lincolnshire Fens as the dykes ran the length of the sea. But here, as she stood by the mare's side, the air was so heavy and the light so grey that she could not see the river's mouth at Roche's Point, which they said was only a mile across the water.

High in her saddle, how safely distanced she felt from those who passed below her on the tracks. How poised and perfect she felt herself to be in her trim riding habit as she cantered through their villages. Men dropped their heads in respect, women were careful not to catch her eye and dirty, half-naked children hid behind their mothers' skirts. And always they were silent, as if to be heard speaking within earshot of her was an insolence. How she loathed the smell of them, the dirt of their bodies, the decay of their lives, their squat mud-and-branch hovels humped together, littered with the rotting debris of human waste.

∾

'It's natural Kate, hungry or not, it's what they prefer. Cuddling their pigs comes as naturally as hugging their wives. Not that they do that often. They show such little love that I wonder they have so many children. Such filthy hags too. God knows what gives them the passion.'

Kate laughed. She had not laughed since she had left England and had been ready to believe she might not again until she returned there. The wind had turned abruptly, it was a warm and sunny winter's day and she had company. Edward Ogilvie was with her, with her father's permission. They had ridden all morning, crossing the river at Inishannon, following its meandering course until it met the sea.

She kicked her mare, reined hard and followed him down the steep side of a hill with the sea on either side of them. He pointed to a lighthouse, far off in the distance, painted in red and white stripes, which he said stood on the Old Head of Kinsale. They dismounted, he unfurled a horse blanket and they sat and picnicked on poached salmon and cold beef. She watched a distant rain cloud scudding across the water like a rippling cloth. The breeze was fresh, bringing with it the smell of salt and seaweed. She breathed it in and was happy and thanked her new companion for it.

Edward Ogilvie was young and heavy limbed, a powerfully built young man. The seams of his jacket and breeches were stretched, barely able to contain the muscles within. Long, unkempt ginger hair touched his collar and matched the sideburns he had trimmed to hide the red blotches on his cheeks, birthmarks that were his greatest aggravation.

He was known by his tenants as a 'Half-Sir,' he being the son of the landowner, Lord Kinley, whose estate began at Cork and stretched more than fifty miles west towards Bantry Bay. Lord Kinley was an Irish Protestant who had left Ireland on his twenty-sixth birthday and, forty years on, had yet to return, preferring to lavish his income on the splendid, if expensive, aristocratic rituals England alone provided. The estate had since been run by a succession of managers, men whose ability was rated by the amount of rent they collected. But none matched the young Edward, who, in the ten years of his management, had multiplied his father's income twice over and, as such, was respected by those of his own rank, who did their best to copy him.

They knew him as a great horseman, hunter and renowned boxer. In Dublin on his twenty-first birthday, he had won a hundred guineas in one fight and that same night, for a wager of half as much again, drank three bottles of whiskey without seeming to take a breath. When things went well for him and he was among his own peers, he was considered a likeable fellow. But among the ranks below, among the thousands of tenants and labourers on the estate, he was feared and loathed. He was a bully with a vicious and barely controllable temper. Anger was always his first refuge.

On his father's land he had no time for rules that were not of his own making, nor any law that did not place the landlord's interests paramount. Nor would he countenance any discussion about a tenant's rights, as they were considered to have none. Those who disagreed suffered his own justice at the end of a bullwhip, which he used often, accurately and with terrible effect. From its stock to its tip, it was eight feet long and tied to its end were six small chamois leather pouches loaded with buckshot. Edward Ogilvie's bullwhip was law and there were many men, women and even children whose bodies were scarred defying it.

Following the customary exchange of letters of introduction, he had presented himself to Sir William offering to act as Kate's riding escort. She readily accepted, relieved to listen to another's conversation after months of her own company. She found him no more or less dull than the dozens of his kind she had known in Lincolnshire and London. She had heard nothing of his cruelty because there was no one to tell her of it except those who had suffered, and they were ever silent.

He had tempted her with a thimbleful of whiskey. It was new to her and she could feel it swirling and rising through her body. She was content to lay back on the thick horse blanket and listen to the surf breaking on the beach below. His chin shone with beef fat.

'You'll discover, Kate, that there are three Ps to the Irish problem: population, priests and potatoes. If we could rid ourselves
of them all, and empty this cursed land, we could make it worth
a living. Leave it to them and it will remain a stinking bog and a
hive of Popish mischief.'

'Edward, why are they so dependent on the potato? Father
says they are hungry because of the blight but the crops have
been ruined in England and Scotland and France too, I'm told.
Why is it so bad here?'

He bit into his beef and wiped the grease from his lips.

'The Irish are always hungry. They're always screaming that
there's a famine here, a famine there, just so they can scramble
for free handouts. It comes natural to them because they are
scoundrels and wasters and always after something for nothing.
Let me tell you, Kate, it's not our food they need but a little
order, not more English corn but a few more English Fusiliers.'

'They seem to expect charity as if it was a right,' she said.

'And we farmers have none. Nor should we. We own the land
and these peasants must pay us to live on it. That's the rub, Kate.
They will always find excuses not to. They'll blame their favourite saint or not enough rain for their barley or too much rain for
their oats. Then they plead poverty. But I make them pay their
gale even if it's with a pike up their backsides.'

'What is a gale, Edward?'

'It's what we call the rent they owe us. They're supposed to
pay it every six months but few of them can ever make it. The
trick is to leave it hanging, let them owe it, leave it in arrears.
That way they are in continual debt. It's called the hanging gale
and it means I can throw them out whenever I like and there's
not a magistrate who can defy me. That's the law. Pay the gale or
get out. That's the landlord's right, a sacred right to deal with our
property as we choose.'

Kate turned onto her stomach and looked out to the sweep
of country across the bay. The clouds made a sudden opening for

the sun. The sky was brightening and in the clean sharp light she could see how neat and tidy the land was, the slowly rising hills, their smooth humps dipping into gentle valleys and, here and there, sprawling bundles of woodland. The slopes had been crafted into terraces by labouring hands over many centuries, line upon line of them, like a vast regiment of graves, the potato mounds, now putrefied by the blight. Yet the land looked lovely in its every shade of green and brown, with rocks scattered across it, bleached by the sun and salt air. It was all so rich and lush, so properly tied together.

Ogilvie took another swig of whiskey.

'You ask why the peasant loves his potato. It's because it gives him so much spare time. That's why it is called the lazy crop. He banks them up in spring and then has all summer to drink and sire another child or two. What he needs is more labour to tire him and send him back to his cabin panting. Then we might see more industry and fewer babies.'

He laughed loudly at his wit again. Saliva dribbled from his lips, glistened on his chin, fell and settled on his waistcoat. He pulled himself across the blanket, closer to Kate. She could smell the drink and the meat on his breath and she turned her head away towards the sea. In the curve of the bay she could see a small boat, a fisherman standing at its centre, so stiff and still he might have been a mast. She waited for him to move, to throw a net or pull an anchor but he stood as if he had been frozen rigid.

She did not speak and hoped the silence would create space between them. She felt uneasy. She was not used to such familiarity. He touched her arm.

'You have wondrous hair, Kate. In this light it's the colour of this autumn. And eyes so blue, I wonder if you haven't a little bit of Irish yourself. But it's a determined chin you have and I'll wager you've a touch of English arrogance when it's called for. You're damned pretty with it.'

She did not reply. He took her hand. His was wet and warm with sweat and grease.

'I reckon the man who marries you, Kate, will spend half his time in heaven and the other in hell and it would be a damned fool who didn't find that more than a fair division.'

The whiskey was draining from her. The ease and contentment had gone and she was angry that he had put an end to it so abruptly, so crudely. She was suddenly aware of the lighthouse and its lamp glinting pale orange behind its glass.

'We must go,' she said. 'It'll be dark very soon.'

He hesitated for a moment, then stood and, still holding her hand, pulled her to her feet.

'You have a man's grip, Kate. And a man's head too I think.'

She moved away from him. 'But a woman's heart,' she replied. 'And I think that makes a powerful mix.'

He cleared his throat and spat out the phlegm. 'And a dangerous one too, Kate.'

He rolled up the blanket and followed her to the horses. He touched her again, resting his hand on her shoulder.

'I know very little of you yet but it's comforting to have you on our side. You'll make a fine ally. Mind you, you'd make a damned desperate enemy.'

They mounted and trotted back the way they came, the sea either side of them. She undid the ribbon that tied her hair and let it fall to the wind. She had not met a man like him, whose sheer size was so oppressive and threatening and who spoke with so little sympathy.

'Why do you talk of enemies and allies, Edward?'

'Because that's how it is becoming. Your father is here to feed them with corn but that's only the start. Trouble will follow.'

'Does my father know this?'

'Your father may not know it yet. Relief Commissioners do not ask questions of men like me, men who know this land and the scum who scrounge off it. But tell your father ...' He paused as if he was uncertain to continue. Then, 'Tell him he will need more than a few padlocks on his warehouses to keep his corn safe. Soon he will be asking for a battalion of Redcoats.'

For the next hour they cantered easily, retracing their tracks along the river bank, staying with the fields until they came upon a stream that bypassed the little town of Bandon. There Ogilvie turned north towards a neighbouring landlord's lodge perched on the top of Coughlin Peak. There he had arranged a surprise dinner party for his new friend, the most attractive daughter of Ireland's Relief Commissioner. He had a plan and this was his set piece.

He reasoned that as Sir William was a stranger to Ireland and its many problems, he would need advice and guidance. Discretely offered, the Commissioner would be grateful and there was advantage to be had in such an exchange of favours. He knew, as all the landlords did, that if the hunger lasted through the winter, as it most certainly would, all but a few tenants would be unable to pay their gale. Those that could not would be forced to abandon their farms and soon their holdings would be overgrown with gorse and bramble. Yet without their rents, the estate's income would suffer and that could not be allowed to happen. It would be a poor manager who let a potato blight reduce the value of his land. Men might die but men could be replaced. But let ten shillings drop on the price of an acre though and it might take ten years to raise it back again. A landowner had a duty to protect the integrity of his land by whatever means; that was the law of property.

So another source of revenue had to be found and Ogilvie knew what that was. Those like him, who had seen famines come and go, knew that whenever cheap or free grain was on offer, there was always a profit in it for someone. And no one would be nearer to that profit than the man who had the ear of the Relief Commissioner. There was much to be gained in this new association. A profit and perhaps a marriage too. His father had been wise to send his letter of introduction to Sir William. It was a clever manoeuvre and he would make the most of it.

They saw the torches long before they saw the men carrying them. The procession of flames was a giant snake winding its way, dipping and weaving, through the lanes. Then Kate saw the riders at the front. Ogilvie was suddenly excited, shouting at her, 'It's a tumbling gang. I didn't know they were already evicting here. What luck, Kate, what luck.'

She stood in her stirrups to see better. 'Who are they, Edward? What are they doing? Who are they evicting?'

'We are tumbling their homes, Kate, pulling them down. It's our day of reckoning. Remember what I said? They pay their rent or they get out.'

'They are your men with the torches?'

'No, not mine. My bailiff employs them. Ruffians mostly, with plenty of muscle and not afraid to hurt or get hurt. We sometimes have convicts sent from your own English prisons and good hard men they are too. Come Kate, we'll follow them. It'll be good sport. You'll not have witnessed this before.'

Never had she seen anything more frightening. The torches of oiled peat gave those who carried them the look of men gone mad, wild men, their faces distorted by drink and the pleasant prospect of violence, so sinister they could have been the Devil's own army. Shillelaghs of hardened thorn tree were stuck in their belts. Some carried slings and pouches full of pebbles, others held pikes of pointed steel. Behind them came two huge grey horses already harnessed, as if they had just that moment been taken from the plough.

Then in the dip she saw why they had come and she was afraid.

'Edward, let us go now,' she whispered to him. She turned but he grabbed her reins.

'No, Kate, not yet. You'll never forgive me if I let you miss this. You'll see it on your father's behalf so you can tell him how we administer justice on our land.'

The man and his wife were together at the door of a low cottage made of mud bricks and straw thatch. He had his arm around her and Kate could see the curve of a child in her belly. Their home had been whitewashed clean. There were plants still flowering by the door and more below the single, shuttered window. At the side was an apple tree stunted by age, festooned by washing still drying. It was the neatest little home she had yet seen.

The leading horseman dismounted and with two ruffians by his side went and spoke to the couple. Kate could not hear but she saw the horseman raise his arm and the man shake his head in reply. The woman then fell sobbing at her husband's feet.

It did not take long. Iron hooks tethered to ropes were thrown over the thatch, the harnesses hitched and the horses whipped. They reared as men struck their hind legs with sticks to make them move. As they strained forward, the roof collapsed and the cottage seemed to explode. Men came running forward, towing parcels of flaming peat, which they swung onto the straw. Then everything was ablaze. An old sow came running out, squealing, smothered in fire. The horses reared again.

In the light of the flames Kate saw children in a ditch nearby. Only their heads showed, their faces smeared in tears and soot and twisted in fear. Above them, coloured orange by the fire, their mother now lay still, her arms curled around the legs of their father. The pig on fire ran in circles and the father moved to save it but there was a shot and it fell dead. The man with the gun laughed, danced around it and from the smoke came the sickly sweet smell of burning blood.

It was over quickly. The men mounted their horses, the plough horses were led away and the tumbling gang stood still, warming themselves by the fires. Great bundles of flaming thatch soared into the black sky as the last of the mud walls collapsed in a heap of suffocating smoke. An order was shouted, the men turned and shuffled away back down the lane the way they had come.

Ogilvie let go of Kate's bridle. He was grinning. 'It's all over and a more efficient tumbling you're not likely to see, Kate. And don't look so glum. They'll survive. They always do. They'll be off on the road come morning, begging, stealing, selling their children for sixpence. They'll manage to live or they'll manage to die and there's not a lot of negotiation in between. This is justice as we know it, Kate. The way it's always been. We win or they do. To prosper we have to put down those who wish to defy us.'

He saw her face in the firelight and did not wait for a reply. Instead he turned his horse and trotted off towards the column of men. Reluctantly, she pulled her reins to follow. She looked back. The man, husband of the woman, father of the children, was now on his own, standing as straight as a ramrod, shrouded in blue and brown smoke, the pig smouldering at his feet. He looked back at her. There was defiance in his face but no fear, no fear at all, not even anger. And she could not understand why.

She hesitated, wondering if there was something to be said, some gesture to be made, some little charity to be offered. There was money in her purse, a silk scarf around her neck, rings on her fingers. She waited, not knowing what to expect from him. Then she kicked hard into the mare's belly and rode as fast as she could towards the high dark shadow that was Coughlin Peak.

CHAPTER THREE

Six months had now passed since Kate had come to Ireland and the events of every day had been written into her diary, each new page more despairing than the last. Her father had promised they would return to England in the New Year, by summer, he said, at the very latest. Trevelyan had told him so and he wanted to believe it. But the calamity that was now beginning to engulf him told him otherwise. He now lived, week by week, in fear of the future.

The roads began to fill with the wretched, the hungry, the evicted. From the bogs of Erin to the mud cabins of Mayo, they tramped from village to village, from town to town and back again, searching for food and charity. Both were scarce. The lanes and tracks were crowded with searching, scavenging bands of hostile wanderers. They squatted in ditches or built shelters in shallow trenches roofed over with sticks and turf, to brave the winter's rain and cold. And they waited.

As the lush fields of summer green turned brown and the trees and hedgerows became their naked winter selves, she remembered the early days when villagers would step aside as she rode past and men would bring a forefinger to their foreheads in a salute of respect. Now they shook their fists and women shrieked their curses.

Soon she stopped her riding excursions and used the cold winds as an excuse to stay indoors. Her mare remained in the stable, unseen by her, cared for only by the yard boy. Why should she ride? There was no adventure now in the lanes and mountain paths, no excitement at the sight of the sea. How foreign it

was again and how foreign it promised to remain. That thought
tormented her. There were times, alone in her room, when she
felt as if her hands were tied to some shackle on the floor, times
sitting by candlelight when the walls crept closer, tighter, threatening to envelop and crush her.

There were nights when she could not sleep and nights when
she would not. In her dreams images tormented her like a spinning carousel in her mind. Often she saw the ink drawing of the
ragged boy, his eyes direct and as resolute as she first remembered him in the burning grate of her Lincolnshire home. She
would reach out to save him and when their fingers were almost
touching, the flames would burn her and she would wake trembling, holding her hand as if it was on fire. In another, she was
surrounded by the shrieking women, grabbing at her, pulling
her from her horse and stamping her into mud. She relived the
night of the tumbling, marching with the gang, swinging her
flaming peat into that neat and whitewashed home as the pig
danced on fire and the pregnant mother clung to the man who
had no anger in his face. And she would wake up almost retch-
ing with the stench of baked blood.

She told no one of her nightmares nor the guilt that drenched
her. There was no one she could talk to. Who was there to listen?
All within her father's house appeared to accept the inevitability
of the tragedy that was unfolding, as if nothing could be changed
by interfering. Yet she did interfere. It was unexpected, unpre-
pared, and it came at the most unlikely time and place.

৩৯

Christmas was ten days away and Sir William's house was full of
holly, tinsel and festive bustle. The kitchen was busy with new
sounds and smells. There were never-ending visits at the trades-
men's doors and the cook had been allowed to employ two
extra girls to help. The under-gardener was digging out the root

vegetables and the head gardener brought up the orchard's fruit, stored since the autumn in the darkest, coldest corner of the cellar. Having washed and polished them, he displayed them in pyramids on the sideboards in the dining room. The tree in the hall stood ten feet tall, so tall the silver angel's wand grazed the ceiling. Messengers delivered party invitations embossed in gold leaf and the Mayor of Cork, a butcher himself, sent Sir William his largest turkey with a note pinned to its breast, reminding the cook that it weighed twenty-five pounds gutted and would need at least twelve hours turning.

Christmas in England had always been the season of indulgences, of endless nights partying, of crowded, glamorous balls, of dancing and parading in the arms of admiring young suitors. Christmas here was so crudely out of place. It was as if the clock had stopped and the house was in limbo and nothing happening inside its walls bore any relevance to what was happening beyond its front door. Never had a Christmas seemed so unnecessary, even vulgar. Perhaps it was this feeling that unsettled her that particular evening and gave her the spirit to do what she did.

Every week on a Friday, her father held a dinner in the long, narrow, beech-panelled dining room. It was his favourite room. From the window of his house in Montenotte, he could see the lights of lower Cork, Blackrock Castle and below it the ships busy in the harbour. It gave the impression of contented, orderly prosperity and it pleased him. He invited his senior staff to wine and dine, to end the week's work and plan the next. At the lower end of the table sat his own locally recruited agents who were organising the distribution of the British Government's relief supplies. Next to them were the civil servants from Whitehall who kept a tally of the cost of it. At the top table, either side of Sir William, sat the Protestant clergymen who did their best to dictate who should get aid and who should not, men of the cloth notorious for their hatred of the

Catholic peasantry. The Reverend Doctor Greville Martineau, of Huguenot stock, was their senior and most uncompromising leader.

Dr Martineau blamed the Irish Catholic poor for their own wretchedness. As he considered their poverty and starvation were self-inflicted, he saw no Christian reason to help. Nor did he believe that what he was witnessing was simply an agricultural accident. For him it was a visitation of God, divine intervention, and therefore irreversible. He preached that the peasant's decline from starvation to death was of God's making, severe and complete and it had a single purpose: to cleanse the land of its papist evil and reduce its population of wrongdoers. He would quote passages of the Bible to endorse all he said and it comforted those who listened.

Kate was obliged to attend her father's Friday dinners to provide attraction and light conversation. For those few hours she was expected to distract these men from the labours of their working week and entertain them by being frivolous, witty and amusing until the cigars and brandies were brought to the table. That was the signal for her to rise, for her hand to be kissed a dozen times by as many lips and for her to depart the company so that government business and merry chit-chat could commence.

That evening was the last of the weekly dinners before Christmas and was more convivial than usual, aided by Sir William's many helpings of Yuletide Amontillado. He was in good humour, pleased with the team of helpers and advisers he had so quickly put together. They had an immense task ahead, supervising the import of grain, establishing the depots to store it, making them secure and sending it out to where it was most needed. Whenever he felt harassed by bureaucratic bungling he would console himself that such things were inevitable because nothing on this scale had ever been attempted before. There simply was not the means to cope with the rapid spread of the distress and if food was not reaching the starving quickly enough it was simply because Ireland's roads were not fit for wagons to travel on.

He had written his first progress report to Sir Charles Trevelyan, stating that he expected the worst would be over by the summer. He did not believe it himself, nor did any of his staff, but that was what Sir Charles wanted to hear.

Midway through dinner, as they were feasting on roast leg of lamb, ham hock and every variety of winter vegetable and before Moran the butler arrived with the decanter of port and the cigar box, the conversation unexpectedly and to the dismay of many turned too soon to the famine. It had never been Kate's intention to speak her thoughts so publicly and certainly never in the company of these men. Had it not been for Dr Martineau, she might never have done so.

She was listening to the youngest and newest of her father's relief agents, the slim and fair-haired Captain John Shelley. He had taken voluntary leave of his regiment purposely to help in the relief effort and had sailed from Liverpool on the same ship as Kate and her father.

To the older men who would prefer not to hear he said, 'Is it not possible to persuade the landlords to postpone payment of the gale until people can harvest next year's potato crop? They might then be able to buy a little food to tide them over.'

Primed with claret, his listeners jeered and thumped the table.

'Without rents,' they shouted, 'where is the landlord's income? If the tenants fall another year in arrears how could they ever expect to catch up on their debt? Why should landowners, and especially the Church, forfeit even a penny of their income for what is after all a natural, even a divine, catastrophe?'

Captain Shelley said, 'But surely more can be done to alleviate the effects of the famine. People are dying from hunger, yet there is food in the markets. I've seen it. The Church is doing so little when there is so much it could do. Let us provide at least some ration of Exchequer money to see them through the winter.'

In the babble of protest, Dr Martineau held up his hand, clearly angry that someone so young, so English and knowing so little of the situation had dared question both Church and government policy.

'We will excuse your young nonsense, Captain,' he said. 'You still have much to learn about our country and its people. But you must believe that all that can be done is being done. Do more and we will destroy what little spirit remains in these people to cope for themselves. Remember that God rewards the industrious and never forget that these Catholics are the architects of their misery. They are getting no less punishment than they deserve and far more charity than they have a right to. If food is scarce it must be made to last a longer time. It is the only criteria by which consumption can be controlled. I recommend, young man, that you take the time to read a few chapters of that great economist Malthus and his dictum that if the land cannot support the people then the people must perish. So leave well alone and let matters take their course. As Malthus so wisely observed, life and death must balance. A problem such as this is best solved nature's way.'

The diners were pleased with that. They nodded and murmured their assent and raised their glasses to toast the Reverend's wise words. The shy Captain Shelley, seeming to regret his impetuosity, bowed his head and said nothing more.

Kate then heard herself speak, her words echoing as if she was at the end of a very long and narrow corridor, words almost stifled by the rage inside her.

'And by natural means we must assume, Dr Martineau, that you are advocating death by starvation, death by disease. Entire families evicted from their homes and left to freeze to death in the ditches.'

Sir William choked on his wine. 'Kathryn, you will please remember who you are and whose company you are in.'

But Martineau held up his hand once more and spoke to the wall above Sir William's head as if he was addressing a congregation.

'No! Sir William. Forgive me but we are among the young and impressionable and it would be entirely wrong and even dangerous for Miss Kathryn to be encouraged by Captain's Shelley's false illusions. We have a duty to enlighten them both.'

He turned his chair to Kate so that her father might not see the menace in his eyes. Already he knew of her riding excursions alone into the countryside and what she was witnessing on the roads and in the villages. His Church was a network of spies and informants, ministers and vergers and all those who could be relied on to listen and watch for any suspicion of treason to God or government and report it directly to him. He lowered his voice as if he wanted only her to hear.

'The greater evil we have to contend with, young lady, is not the physical evil of the famine but the moral evil of the selfish, perverse and turbulent nature of the Irish themselves. We are not God but the servants of God. We cannot divine a solution. Only He, in his mercy, can do that. But the law is man-made and the law demands that rents are paid and the landlords quite properly, within that law, must use whatever force is necessary to evict those who will not or cannot pay.'

He leant nearer. She could smell eau de cologne and saw he had dabbed face powder on his cheeks to hide the mass of blue veins. A gold crucifix swung like a pendulum across his purple vest. It was hypnotic. His nearness suffocated her. She asked him in almost a whisper, 'Even if it means they must live in holes in the ground and eat rats?'

Martineau smiled. His voice now was soft and comforting, almost seductive. 'Kathryn, it is possible to hear this tale of sorrow too often. Nothing changes in Ireland, nor will it in our lifetime. It is the old habitual mass of want, the fixed tide of distress that never ebbs. The Catholic peasant is always hungry, whether the potato fails or not, and the rogues are famous for offering a multitude of reasons why. What is important, my dear, is that they should not be deprived of knowing that they are suffering from an application of God's providence and I trust their priests are making that very clear to them.'

Then, so abruptly it startled her, he turned and, raising his voice, addressed the table guests again.

'We must not exaggerate the number of evictions. There are mischief-makers enough who will have you believe what they want you to believe and they will happily add a dozen noughts to any number you care to mention. The Irish knave is the best practised liar in Christendom. Rest assured, gentlemen, and I have it on good authority, that there are no more and no less evictions than is normal at this time of the year.'

'You lie,' Kate said loudly.

Sir William rose from his chair. 'Kathryn, your behaviour is abominable. You will leave us now, at once.'

She did not move. 'It's a lie, Father, and you know it is. I saw the report on your desk this morning. I know what it says. Tell them what it says.'

'Go, Kathryn. I order you to leave this instant.'

'I saw it, Father,' she shouted. 'From your own men in Moyarta and Carrigholt. They said that so many tenants are being evicted it is a disaster. They said that over a hundred homes have been tumbled this week alone – this week, Father, the week before Christmas! Dozens of families have been thrown onto the road to live like wild animals without food and shelter, while we sit pigging ourselves. And here in our pantry we have the largest turkey in Ireland.'

Sir William rose unsteadily to his feet, kicking his chair aside. But Kate had already run to the door, pushing past Moran and his silver tray before her tears began. She slammed it shut on a shocked and silent room of men who knew well enough the truth of what she had said. And, with one young exception, were committed to keeping it a secret.

ಬಿ

It snowed hard that night, and all the following day and night too. No one, whatever their age or fondness for exaggeration, could ever remember such a fall. On the fourth night the river froze and ships' crews had to hack their way through ice in the Mahon to reach the deeper water of the outer harbour. People said it was coming straight from Russia and predicted a ferocious January. For the first two weeks of the new year, 1846, it snowed without pause.

Kate had been confined to the house by the weather and, since the embarrassment of the dinner, by her father. He had called the doctor, who was pleased to confirm Sir William's suspicion that she was over-tired and stressed, which helped explain her quite out-of-character behaviour. If she could not sleep, the doctor would prescribe a draught and if she continued to be depressed, he suggested company. He had a daughter of her age who would be delighted to come in the afternoons and play cards.

Kate sat by the window of the drawing room that overlooked the long sweep of the south garden. Its delicately cultured divisions, the herbaceous borders, the box hedges, the manicured lawns and the gravelled drive had all become one, the gardener's long summer labours now submerged in a prairie of white.

She might once have thought it beautiful. Now she could only look at the fine line of oaks and firs that marked the edge of the estate and think of the misery beyond it.

'They will die out there, like sheep trapped in a wintry ditch.'

Kate turned to the voice behind her. She was not alarmed. It was not strange to her. It belonged to her new and only ally, the young Captain John Shelley. From the night of the dinner's commotion, over three weeks before, they had become secret friends and since she had been forbidden to leave the house, he was now her only source of comfort and information. They had been careful not to show their bond in her father's presence and met only at times when the house was empty of all but the servants. They were sure that no one knew of their alliance but they were wrong. The Reverend Martineau had them watched. The young captain had shown himself to be emotional and provocative. His sympathies were in doubt and the Reverend had made it a priority to establish the young Englishman's allegiances, one way or the other.

Captain Shelley said, 'Yes, Kate, they are already dying out there, more and more every day. Three cartloads of them were brought into the city yesterday. I was called to register them. Their homes had been tumbled and many were decent properties. They were barely clothed and so weak they could not walk.'

'Where are they now?'

'In the workhouse. But I doubt they will last the week.' He sat by her and took her hand. He was pale and his eyes were red-rimmed.

'Kate. You must be the first to know this. I am about to resign my position. I cannot do what I have to do any longer. I see the reality and I write my reports on what I see without exaggeration. My God! There's no need to embellish what's happening here. The truth is harsh enough. But the truth is not reaching England. What I write is being rewritten, my reports are being reworked so completely it is impossible for the government to know the extent of this tragedy. It is being hidden and I do not know why. On Monday a priest came to me. He had been called to give comfort to an old woman whose cottage was to be tumbled. She was dying inside. He appealed to the gang to wait until he could administer the last rites. But they ignored him and he had to drag her out even as they set the place on fire. She died in his arms, watching her home reduced to rubble. As she closed her eyes, the last she heard of this life was their bawling laughter. I reported it to the Commission but they refused to list a complaint against the landlord.'

'What will you do?' she asked. 'Return to England?'

'No! I cannot go back. Not yet. I think maybe there are other things I can do here, Kate, other ways to help. I am not a godly man, nor am I a sentimentalist but I cannot do nothing now that I know so much.'

He let go her hand and stood. 'I'm sorry, Kate. We have known each other for such a short time but we were allies and with your help I thought for a while that I might have the will to fight them and turn them our way. But they are too many and too strong and their minds are set against the very people they have been sent here to help.'

He paused. 'I do believe we English know more about the furthest corners of our Empire than we do about Ireland? I'm sorry. I cannot expect you to understand.'

But she understood. How she longed now to burn her skirts and do what only men could do. How she had begun to despise her pretty lace and perfumed shackles and all the niceties of her privileged life.

She stood. 'When will you leave?'

'I am obliged to serve this month out but on the first day of February I will deliver my notice. Tomorrow I must ride south beyond Kinsale to a place called Skibbereen. The hunger is especially bad there and until now we have sent them nothing. I am taking eight wagons of corn and if the snow stops, we might be there in time to save them.'

'Let me come with you!' she pleaded, already knowing his answer.

'Kate. Do you really want to help?'

'Of course. Do you think it suits me to sit by a drawing-room fire, tinkering with embroidery and sipping tea from bone china?'

'Then let us be real allies, you and me. You cannot come to

Skibbereen but you can be more help to me by staying. I can expect to see the worst down south and I shall report what I see. But I know for certain that it will never be read by your father. It will never reach his desk. So let me send you a copy by another route. I will tell you everything I see. Make sure it is known in England. I don't know how you can do it but let them know a little of this horror.'

So the pact was made. As he left he went to take her hand but instead she took his and pressed it to her cheek and then kissed the palm of it. She had never done such a thing to anyone before but in this cold and captive country she had finally found someone warm and open and she was grateful. He smiled, leant forward and put his lips gently to her forehead.

'Goodbye, Kate. You are like a sister to me. Be my conspirator too. It will be worthwhile if we can find a way. You will be my secret agent.'

From the window she watched him go down the steps to his carriage. He looked up at her to wave his goodbye, his dark cloak already turning white, his face speckled with flakes. She wanted to run to the door to stop him, to make him stay longer, to speak more to him. It was as if she never expected to see him again.

∞

The winds that came from Russia blew colder by the day and more of the hungry began to freeze to death. A month before, Sir William had reported to Sir Charles Trevelyan that thousands were affected by the famine. Now, had he the courage, he would have reported them in their hundreds of thousands. At the Cork workhouse, there were queues a mile long of people, half-naked, young and old, waiting in the snow for someone to die inside the walls so that they might take their place. It was reported from Leitrim that two wagonloads of boy orphans had been turned away from the workhouse gates. They had been found the next morning abandoned and frozen to death. The magistrate reported he had counted thirty-two bodies and ordered they should be buried together in lime.

Captain Shelley had been gone a fortnight and still Kate had not received his promised letter. She asked after him as often as she dared and as discretely as she could but no one could or would tell more than she knew already. February the first, the day of his resignation, passed without any further news and she became more and more anxious. Her father mistakenly interpreted this as her impatience at being housebound and promised that just as soon as the weather broke and the thaw began, he would ask Edward Ogilvie to call again. He would have liked to involve her more in the Commission's work, but the Reverend Martineau reminded him of his daughter's emotional lapses and pointed out how much concern it would cause in London should her sympathies and opinions ever become public. Sir William agreed.

His work was at a critical stage. His relief programme was now into its eighth month and he still wanted to believe that it would be finished by late summer. But Trevelyan was, as ever, introducing further complications. He was insisting that it was not the government's intention to freely give food to any but the truly destitute. It was his opinion that the Irish peasant was not so poor as to be unable to buy food if it was cheaply available. With that in mind he had persuaded Prime Minister Peel to authorise the buying of shiploads of maize from America to sell on the Irish markets.

This enraged the Irish grain merchants and their bankers, all disciples of free trade, who feared cheap imports would undercut the market with a consequent loss of profit.

They had no need to worry. The Corn Law and a British government brimming with contradictions ensured the market stalls in Dublin, Cork and Waterford would still be heavy with oats and wheat and the butchers would continue to hang out their hooks of beef and lamb and pork and every sort of wild fowl, so that a stranger with a full purse might wonder who it was who was hungry. But those with empty pockets and empty stomachs knew well enough. Everything they owned had been pawned to the gombeen man, the wandering pawnbroker who went about the countryside with his donkey and cart, swindling the last penny from a hungry man and taking the shawl off a suckling child for less.

There were times, especially in this cold weather, when Sir William, who was not by nature a hard man, wondered whether his government might not be more generous. In one moment of rare courage he had even suggested it in a letter to Trevelyan, but was brusquely told that the government had set a ceiling on the amount of money allocated to Irish relief and it was already over budget. What was being provided was considered enough for the poor to survive one famished winter. The devout Sir Charles reminded his Commissioner that conscience was not always the best guide and that God and market forces were on the same side. To interfere was tantamount to economic blasphemy. Sir William was careful not to mention his concerns again.

∞

Kate had made a pact with Captain Shelley and already he seemed to have abandoned it. She had waited for his letters and the waiting had meant so much. Imprisoned by snow, their alliance promised liberation, his message would revive her spirit. He would tell her what she must do to become part of what was happening. But he had left over a month ago and there had been silence since.

The thaw began in the third week of February. The wind turned around from the east and, for the first time in this new year, the snow clouds split apart and there was blue in the sky and the promise of sun. Everything began to drip, snow turned to slush, roads became rivers and the fields slow-moving lakes of brown water.

It was evening and she was eating alone at the dinner table. Taking advantage of the milder weather and the forecast of still better to come, her father, with Dr Martineau and his retinue, had ridden to Dublin for a meeting with Lord Clarendon, the Lord Lieutenant.

She had snuffed out all but a single candle, preferring in her mood to eat by the light of the fire. She remembered the night at this same table when she had so brazenly declared herself and she thought yet again of the young man who had sat opposite, the captain who had braved the anger of his superiors and exposed his humanity. Where was he now? Why had he forgotten her?

'Miss Kathryn.' She turned as Moran the butler came into the room.

'I didn't call,' she said. 'And I shall need nothing more tonight.'

'Thank you, Miss Kathryn. There's a fire in your room. But I've come to give you something. It came by special messenger two days ago but I thought it would be unwise to bring it until your father had left. I hope you will forgive my caution but this may help you understand.'

He placed a small parcel on the table, bowed his head and left the room. It was wrapped in moleskin and for a moment she thought it was the present Edward Ogilvie had so frequently promised her. It was sewn together and with the cheese knife she carefully cut the threads apart. There was no writing on the envelope but even as she unfolded it she knew who it was from and why he had sent it so disguised, so secretively. She went to the fireplace, knelt and held it to the light of the flames.

My dearest Kate, sister, conspirator. You must have despaired of me. Perhaps you thought I was playing a game with you. Forgive me but once you have read this you will see how difficult it has been not only to conclude my business here but to arrange that this letter reach you and no one else.

These are evil times and I have discovered that people are not always what they seem to be. But you must trust whoever passes this letter to you. He is part of what I want to be and maybe you too one day.

When you have read this, find ways to dispatch it to as many people in England as you think will act on it. A Member of Parliament, a newspaper editor, whoever can create a flood of disgust at what is happening here. I have witnessed such scenes as I cannot relive.

I am at Schull. Once it was a thriving centre of farming but no longer. Would you believe that the market has food for sale and I hear that ships all along the coast are sailing away laden with Irish grain and Irish livestock, yet starvation is worse here than at any place I have yet seen? Yes! There is food here but people are starving. They are stripping the beaches of seaweed, and many I have seen on the roads have green saliva running from their mouths from eating nettles and any number of weeds.

Women and their children climb the sheer face of the cliffs searching for seagull's eggs. Yesterday, I heard that three children and their mother had fallen to their deaths and no one cares. Today an old man, little more than a skeleton, came crawling towards me on all fours along the beach with his dead son tied to his back. At the tide's edge he scooped out a shallow ditch, lay the boy in it and covered him in sand. The surf soon showed him again and the tide then took him away. That was his burial. It is for hundreds here.

To buy food the fishermen have sold their boats and everything to the gombeen men, who tramp the countryside in their carts, preying on them like vultures that soar over the battlefield of the dead. Today I saw fisherfolk on the beach. They were sucking the wool of their jerseys, looking at a shoal of herring only a few hundred yards to sea and they could do nothing. I even saw them breaking up sea shells to eat.

I cannot believe what I saw, even now, all these days on. I can smell their diseased bodies, I can hear their babies croaking like wizened old women. The dying wander among the dead. These people have not eaten properly in five months. I stood and prayed for them as I pray now.

God help them and do not blame us for all that is happening.

And pray for me dear Kate.

John

CHAPTER FOUR

Moran the butler was a quiet man. Many thought him wise. For half a century he had served in the houses of some of Ireland's oldest families and his loyalty and attention to his responsibilities were considered impeccable. In the drawing rooms and at the dining tables of the rich and powerful he had listened to them talk of Ireland's perpetual calamities and knew by heart all their random, brutal remedies. Yet he had stood as still as a statue, awaiting the beckoned call or the snap of a finger, an obedient, discrete and utterly trustworthy servant, seemingly deaf to it all.

He had been born into service. His mother was a scullery maid to Lord Bessborough, his father was His Lordship's senior groom. From the cradle Moran had known only his mother's warmth and love. He was a stranger to the pangs of an empty stomach. As he grew older, he knew little of the world outside the estates. He would listen to the kitchen staff tell of the hunger among the poor but, hearing the contrary from his employers, preferred to believe them. To him, kitchen talk was grossly exaggerated gossip and he reminded the storytellers that among the Irish there was considerable verbal licence. He seemed to care nothing for his country's ills. Until the day the English hanged the son of his sister, his only nephew, Liam.

The boy had been a month short of his nineteenth birthday, an innocent in Ireland's mayhem. He was a simple boy who snared hares for a living, content to pass the time of day with anyone who offered a smile. But he shared a cottage with men who lived very differently, men who lived violently, men prepared to kill for a living. In time they were caught and sentenced to hang and Liam was sentenced with them.

Outside the walls of Dublin's Newgate Prison, Moran watched the three climb the steps to the scaffold, the killers shouting their defiance, kicking the air until their last breath. He saw the noose tighten around Liam's neck, the boy with the guiltless face who was asking why, even as the death hatch opened. And without an answer, dropped to oblivion.

They would not let Moran bury him in the family grave. The boy's body was taken back inside the prison walls and flung into a pit of lime with the other two. A month later his mother died of grief and since that day the quiet butler lived only to avenge her. Now he worked for another master within Sir William's household. As ever, he stood silent and respectful in the hub of government activity where many confidences were freely available and many secrets unguardedly revealed. Now he was the prime source of information for men who were not England's friends. He knew the risks he was expected to take on their behalf and the penalty of being discovered. But he was unfamiliar with the ways of a man long skilled in the black art and this was his undoing.

సౌ

Greville Martineau believed that the world surrounding him was so threatening, so evil, his Church could only be made safe by using the weapons of evil and the strategies of evil men. He believed that Church to be so precious that, like truth itself, it must be protected by a cordon of cunning, lies and deceit.

When Captain Shelley had left for Skibbereen with his wagons of food, Martineau sent one of his trusted spies with him, under the guise of a wagon master. In time the man reported back all the captain did and said. He made mention of the young man's distress, his anger at the land agents for demanding rent from paupers, at the corn merchants for profiting from the rise in wheat prices. Shelley was seen shouting at the dockers loading the sailing ships with Irish wheat and oats, bound for England. The spy reported that the captain had since sold the Commission's wagons and horses, had bought food with the money and was giving it out free. Hundreds of families were flocking to him.

Dr Martineau sat reading the report in his dressing room. He was not alarmed by it nor was he surprised. He realised it was too late to have the captain arrested. Shelley had already thrown off his uniform and retreated to the hinterland with men not of his own kind, men jubilant they had recruited such a prize, an English army officer, a young gallant, now a rebel himself. The doctor decided that Shelley must go the way of all desperate men and he must go soon. It would not be enough simply to capture him.

He gazed into the hand mirror on his dressing table, daubed a touch of powder on his cheeks and a little more rouge to his lips. He caressed the heavy gold crucifix that rested in the cleft of his neck, saw his reflection in the shimmering candlelight and felt a surge of pleasure. He knew now what he must do and the prospect excited him. He snuffed out the candle and left the darkened room smiling.

∞

'She is not sick, Sir William, simply bored, and an empty mind is a dangerous vessel. It has been a long winter and Cork is not a place for young souls denied their hunting and prancing. It is not a doctor she needs but a little employment.'

Dr Martineau sat with Sir William Macaulay in the room of beechwood, drinking his mid-morning coffee. He continued.

'Your daughter is not herself. She is listless and depressed but I really do not believe she is suffering from anything more serious than boredom. We must find her something to do.'

'Like what?' asked Sir William. 'What is there do in this cursed country except what we are doing? I promised her lively company, people of her own sort, parties and the like and she has had none of these things. And she's changing. She is not the Kathryn I brought with me from England. She says the oddest things in the oddest way. Sometimes I close my eyes when she is speaking and wonder if it is her. Reminds me of someone I knew a long time ago. Indeed she does.'

For some minutes he said nothing. Martineau waited. Sir William poured himself more coffee. 'Damn it, Martineau, I'd send her back home if I could but Trevelyan insists that she stay, though for the life of me I can't understand why. She's hardly the flower of society and that's why he wanted her here.'

Martineau was soothing. 'You must not blame yourself. Ireland is presently the most upsetting country on God's earth.'

'It's cursed!' Sir William rose from his chair, angry. 'I tell you, it's cursed. That's why God cut it off from the rest of us and dumped it out here in the Atlantic. Ireland is damned.'

'I do not believe in curses.'

'Then maybe you should. Explain it any other way.'

'It's God's will.'

'And God's will be done. Well, he's certainly doing it here with a vengeance.'

'With respect sir, we must not blaspheme.'

Sir William settled himself in his chair again, his anger gone. 'You talked of Kathryn.'

'We must make her busy. Here in the Commission. I think it will lift her spirits and yours too, perhaps.'

'It wasn't so long ago that you told me she ought not to be privy to our work.'

'I did, and with good reason. But I think her temper has subsided. She has quietened decidedly. Now she needs employment.'

Sir William nodded. 'Perhaps you are right, Martineau. As you always are. Maybe she might work for me as my personal assistant, looking after all the trivia that flies back and forth from Trevelyan. He's a monster for detail and I'm finding it harder and harder to keep up with him. One minute he's complaining there is not enough activity here and the next he's protesting we are spending too much of his money. How can we be active if he's reined in our budget? He's now threatening to end this entire thing next year, close us up and have us go home. We've hardly arrived and they're still hungry out there. The man has no heart. He should come and see for himself.'

'And of Kathryn, sir?' Martineau asked.

'What? Yes! Do it. She'll help soothe me.'

Martineau bowed his head. 'Just one small thing, Sir William. It might be best if you make no mention of my part in this. She may consider it too patronising and young people are so sensitive. I suggest the initiative is entirely yours.'

Sir William did not think it important but he nodded. 'Of course. But before you go, Martineau, tell me, what news of Captain Shelley? Has he been seen again?'

'No, sir. Not since that report from Killarney. But we will find him. He cannot hide for long and he is no use to himself or others unless he is making mischief in the open.'

'God knows what we'll do when we catch him. I'd shoot him myself. Damn the man, his treachery and his double-dealing. A British officer and supposedly a gentleman. And eating at my table!'

'Be patient, Sir William. Just a while longer. Then you'll see. We will draw him out.'

'The man's a fool, Martineau. They say he burnt his uniform but kept his army boots. What do you make of that?'

'Let us not underestimate him. Remember it is a wise caution to fear the man who has nothing to lose.' He bowed once more and left the room, closing the door gently behind him.

ೋ

There was no one moment when Kate and Moran declared themselves allies. No formal pact, no secret signals. He would hear of things happening as far north as Sligo and Monaghan or as far west as Tralee and she would know that Shelley was still alive. For a month now she had been working with her father, copying and filing instructions to his agents, redrafting his hastily written letters, correcting his grammar. She found it no more and no less interesting than reading Trollope in the library, but she was now intimate with confidential information and there was little that happened within the Commission she was not aware of. Shelley had asked her to be his conspirator and now she was perfectly placed. She would be careful not to appear too interested, too diligent, and remember to heed his warning, that not all around her was quite what it seemed.

Dr Martineau had finally decided on a way to rid himself of Shelley without the risk of incriminating himself. He had chosen the place and the method of his execution. Droplets of information would be fed to Kate and she would, he knew, pass these on to Shelley. Early in March, he set his trap and waited.

A mixed cargo of flour sent by the Quakers and barrels of ship's biscuits, sent from the Royal Naval Dockyard in Portsmouth, had recently arrived in Cork and was due to be sent south to Skibbereen. Martineau ordered it instead to be trans-shipped to the small port of Kinvara in Galway Bay. There it would be stored in the Commission's newly built depot for later distribution. A platoon of well-armed Fusiliers would be aboard the ship en route and once the cargo was unloaded and their officer was satisfied it was safely stored in the depot under lock and key, they were to return to their barracks.

Some members of the Commission questioned whether it was prudent to leave so many tons of food unguarded, but Martineau reminded them that the military were better employed elsewhere. It was wiser, he said, to have them in their garrison ready for any emergency than to have them grow fat and lazy guarding food stocks. He assured them that the depot was secure, built of brick, well roofed and with strong doors. Few ever questioned his judgement. They

knew him to be profoundly efficient, a man who planned everything to the very last detail. So they agreed that the troops should do
as Martineau had recommended and he was pleased.

తు

It was the first day of spring. There was warmth in the sun.
Primulas and primroses, wild anemones and celandine rose up to
carpet the grass. The curling woodbine was in new leaf, entwin-
ing its tentacles through the hedges and there was a cuckoo in the
woods. As each day passed, the land became brighter and greener
and with spring came the resurgence, once again, of hope.

It was now that men thought of their potatoes. It was time once
again for the annual ritual of praying for a long, generous summer
of warm westerlies and a full harvest. Sick, weak and hungry men
found strength to work their plots, turning back the turf, cutting away the gorse and bramble. Across all of Ireland there was a
frenzy of planting. Everything was sold to the gombeen man – the
last chair, a hair comb, a marriage ring – for a handful of pennies
to buy the seed potatoes. It was the last desperate stake.

Kate felt the surge that spring gives and began taking her mare
out again beyond the walls of the city. She saw families spread across
the fields, men, women and their children on their knees. Those
without shovels were turning over the earth with sticks and bare
hands, breaking up the clods. Others followed with a dibber and
dropped the cut and dressed seed potatoes into the neat drills, nursing them into soft cradles, crossing themselves for God's blessing.
Every inch of the plots was patted into place, the line of the trenches
as straight and neat as a shovel could work them. Never had the
symmetry been so perfect, never had expectations been so great.
From Bantry to Lough Swilly, from Cape Clear to Malin Head, they
prayed more for their potatoes than they did for their own souls.

తు

John Shelley, former captain in the 49th, had spent many fretful days and nights planning for this night and this raid. It could not fail. He would not let it. Too much was at stake. Too many starving people were depending on him. To return with nothing would condemn them to die as surely as if they were struck by the plague. What would save them was the food, less than a mile away in the Commission's depot, right under the shadow of Dunguaire Castle.

Shelley had made a long and tortuous journey since the day he turned away from the England he had loved, burnt his regimental uniform and buried his sword and pistol. He kept only his boots. Soon afterwards he was recruited by a band of rebels who called themselves the Ribbonmen. But in time they proved too violent for him, dedicated as they were to murder and mayhem, torching the landlords' estates, terrorising those who laboured on them, burning crops and cutting the hamstrings of cattle. So he formed a following of his own. They had no name, no banner to fight under, no brutal intimidation and they carried no weapons. They were few but they did what others did not. They stole from the well fed to feed the hungry poor.

He was at Ennis in Clare when he received the message from Kate. It told him of the shipment of food arriving in Kinvara and where it would be stored. It told him of the escort of Fusiliers and of their orders to return to barracks once the food had been securely stored. As he read her note, the risks and doubts that, as a military man, should have made him cautious and suspicious were overwhelmed by the prospect of such a bounty so easily taken.

He had checked every last detail of his plan. The break-in would be easy. Emptying the depot would take time and labour but time was with them. The nearest army garrison was over twenty miles away in Galway town. And behind them, sheltering by Kinvara's harbour wall, was the labour: over a hundred families, willing and desperate men, women and their children, waiting for the signal to come and carry away what they believed was theirs to take.

೧೪

'This is not right, Mr Shelley. All this food and nobody here. Where are the guards?'

'Stop your worrying, Declan. The soldiers have long gone. People here saw them go and nobody has seen them return. They swear to it. The place is quiet.'

'But it makes no sense. Tons of it there, just waiting for us. Something is wrong, something's up, I can sense it and I don't like it.'

'Declan. Steady yourself. We've come a long way and we'll not be hasty. We will wait as long as we have to. We made a promise, remember, and lives depend on it.'

'Just as soon as this mist lifts and we can see a bit of light, send a man ahead to scour the place. Tell him not to hide himself, be open, just pass it by and back again. Tell him to do a circle of it, let him be seen. If there's military there he'll draw them out of their hiding place.'

'Better I send my son Ronan. If they are there, they may not harm a boy but they'll take a man for sure and keep him.'

'Can you depend on him?'

'With my life.'

'Then let him go. And mind what I said. Let him be seen.'

'And if he doesn't come back?'

'Then we must be away.'

'I must leave my son here?'

'We will have no choice.'

'Then I will stay.'

'I understand.'

They sat in a circle, the ten of them, Shelley cross-legged at their centre, all shrouded by the early morning mist drifting off the sea. They did not speak. They had nothing to say. They had walked five days to be here and were weary and hungry like those they had come to save, and hungrier still, knowing the feast that was stored so close. So they sat in silence, waiting for the young boy to return.

'Mr Shelley, he's been gone now an hour or more and the depot is only a half a mile off. How much longer do we wait?'

'You said you trusted him'.

'I do.'

'Then you must trust him a little longer.'

'What if they've taken him?'

'We would have heard the commotion. Soldiers do nothing quietly.'

'Should I go myself?'

'Sit still, Declan. And all of you be patient. We've come too far to be reckless now.'

The first touch of warmth of the sun was on their backs when they saw the boy again. He came running but he was smiling too.

'There's no one there, Mr Shelley,' he said, panting. 'I went round and around and …'

'Easy, Ronan.' Shelley held him by the shoulder. 'Get your breath, boy, and tell us what you saw or didn't see.'

'That's it, sir. I saw nothing and no one. I went up and down, making out I was searching for something I'd lost, stopping and looking at the ground but all the time I had my eye on the big barn. Then I went around the back of it and banged on the doors but nothing happened.'

'I can't believe it,' Declan said. 'Leaving it like that. Why should they do that, Mr Shelley?'

'This is a long way from the troubles. Maybe that's why they've stored it here. Whatever the reason, it's ours now. Come, let's go and get it.'

The depot was just as Martineau had described: a large barn, windowless, built of brick with strong oak double doors, coupled together by a single chain and padlock. The deep ruts made by the wagons that had brought the food from the harbour were still visible in the soft earth. For some minutes they stood by the doors waiting, as if they were unable or unwilling to believe that all they had prayed for had come about. How many times had they risked their lives to bring food to those who had none? How many times had they fought with their bare hands against men with knives who had tried to take it from them? How many times had they come close to utter despair, without hope, not knowing what to do next?

Shelley gave the nod and Declan's crowbar wrenched the lock away with one single pull. The doors were pulled open and they were inside. Ten men and a boy stood silent in the half light, stunned by the sight of so much food, the rows of barrels and sacks stacked so neatly and suddenly all theirs to take. Shelley beckoned to Ronan and almost in a whisper said, 'Go, boy, go fast to the harbour and tell them to come as quick as they can. If they have carts, bring them too. Tell them there's plenty for all.'

The bullet of the first rifle shot pierced a sack and flour came trickling out onto the floor. The second cracked open a barrel stave.

'Stay where you are, boy, or my third shot will be yours.'

The officer was behind them in the half light. He came forward, a pistol in his hand, flanked by six of his men, their rifles at their shoulders.

'Welcome, Mr Shelley. We have been camped here for ten very long days and nights waiting for you and your gang. It has not been a pleasant stay. This is the most rotten place to be but you are, at last, our reward. I must admit I had my doubts you would come. But they said you would, they were certain. They said you'd not be able to resist.' He waved his pistol towards the stacks of food.

'They said this was the bait to catch you and catch you we have. It has been cleverly done, you must grant them that. Twenty-two of us came but only sixteen of us left. And your little watchdogs out there didn't notice. You must admit it was very well planned.'

'What now?' asked Shelley. 'Will you take me and let these men go?'

'Oh! No. It's not like that at all. There is no deal, Mr Shelley. I have my orders and I think you know what they might be.'

'I expect a trial. I am a former English officer.'

'You are a traitor, Mr Shelley. Once you wore this uniform and when you threw it off you must have known the penalty.'

'I demand you arrest me and me alone. What I have done I have done for my reasons. Let me face the tribunal and I'll accept the punishment.'

'Not so, Mr Shelley. Not so.'

'I demand to be heard.'

'Too late, Mr Shelley. Too, too late. You have already been judged and condemned.'

He turned to his squad, their rifles still at their shoulders.

'Sergeant, close the doors. We have business to finish here.'

ನಿಚ

Kate was out that day to meet Edward Ogilvie at Kinsale, some twenty miles south of Cork. The rendezvous was not of her choosing. The more she met him the more repulsive she found him. It was election time and this was polling day. Ogilvie, confident he was about to become a Member in the Parliament of Westminster, was cantering about his constituency to ensure his tenants put their crosses to his name. Few dared to disappoint him.

The town was like a fair on market day, massed with people drawn out by the sun and the prospect of a spectacle. Even the pauper mothers and their ragged children seemed blushed with excitement. Kate had never been so enveloped by a swarm of so many people. The scent of burning peat from the tinkers' fires, the sweat of the horses, the pungent smell of their oiled harnesses, the sweet wisps of tobacco smoke, was both suffocating and comforting. A man on a stool was blowing a tin whistle and men came and danced around him, then staggered their way drunken back to the shebeens for another mug of whiskey.

Another man, wearing a scarlet jacket and a jester's cap with bells on its tips, held up a sack, shouting, 'A ha'penny a guess. A ha'penny to guess how many chickens I have inside my sack. And if you guess right you can have the pair of them.'

In the corner of the square a man stood alone with a pig in a cart. He beckoned to her. 'Look at the lovely lard on him,' he said. 'Look at his grand skull.'

He stuck his broad finger into the belly of the little pale-eyed pig, took hold of its tail and pulled it out of its bed of straw. 'Aye! There's nine weeks of fattening in him.'

At the bend of the square was a cow, old and thin; its udders had not given milk for years. Two men were arguing and Kate stepped closer to listen. They spat on their hands and whacked them together. 'I'll give you three pounds,' said the buyer.

'I'll not take it,' replied the seller.

Then a third man introduced himself, for it always takes more than two to make a bargain in an Irish fair. 'Divide the pound,' he said, to begin the haggle.

'Will ye split the pound?' demanded the buyer.

'I will not.'

'Will ye give him to me then?'

'I told you three pounds.'

The buyer walked off.

'You'll be back,' the seller shouted as men around him berated him for his obstinacy. The third man then ran after the buyer, seized his hand, pulled him back and smacked the buyer's hand against the seller's. They split the pound, the sale was made. The buyer took out his scissors and clipped his mark on the cow's rump and the three men went off to celebrate the sale at one of the steaming, crowded pubs.

Kate heard the sound of a hunting horn and at the far end of the market she saw Ogilvie. He was elegantly dressed with a black top hat, a pink hunting jacket and riding breeches of white broadcloth above his polished black knee boots. Blue ribbons were tied to his mare's tail and neck. He rode at the head of a long line of men who walked hesitantly, awkward and morose as if they were being led to a funeral. Behind them she saw his own bully-boys, broad and heavy men, with a blunderbuss over their shoulders and a shillelagh in their belts.

He was pleased to see her. He clapped his hands above the top hat and shouted above the din. 'Kathryn, my dearest girl. What an exceptional honour. Your father promised me you would come but I didn't dare expect to see you.'

'I've never been to an election before,' she shouted back. 'Like your tumbling gangs, I suppose it's something I ought not to miss.'

He was grinning. 'Kathryn, don't be sour with me, not on a day like this. You might regret it. Tomorrow I will be a parliamentarian and I could have you transported to the other side of the world for insolence.'

'Tell me what is happening, Edward. Who are these men behind you?'

'My tenants. Freeholders who've come to vote for me. Not that they are very free, nor do they have much of a holding. But they are beholden and that's what matters. Remember the hanging gale? They do and I don't let them forget it.'

He turned and stood in his saddle. He looked down and laughed at them. They did not look up.

He said, 'They're not over fond of me but they'll give me their cross or they'll be out on their backsides. No vote, no tenancy. It's a simple electoral choice.'

'It's blackmail.'

He stood in his stirrups and spoke loudly, as if he wanted to hear himself speak, to listen to his own words, knowing that they could sound one way in the mind and yet sound quite different spoken aloud.

'It's nothing of the sort, Kathryn. Remember you're in Ireland. Who do you think they would vote for if they weren't obliged to vote for me? They'd go for one of their own and then what would we have? A Parliament of papists. Don't call it blackmail. If the English want to keep this country, you must accept that what is happening here today is democratic and nothing less.'

Kate said, 'This is their country, Edward. It's their future.'

He laughed and raised his hat as he passed the paupers' tents, mocking them. 'The poor do not worry about the future. They worry only about today. Tomorrow is far too far away. And it is not their country. How often have I told you that land belongs to those who own it and my father owns this?'

As the procession of tenants passed through the market square, the crowd jeered and threw mud at them, ridiculing them for their subservience, shouting that they were following their Protestant master like sheep to the slaughter. Some of the mud hit their targets and a tenant voter broke line and began fighting. Ogilvie turned his horse. There was a crack of his whip over their heads. The crowds fell back, cowed, and the line of tenants shuffled on.

Kate was too ashamed to look at them. She felt their eyes on her. Honest, hardworking men, forced to march and vote for a man who held them captive. Ogilvie was talking to her again.

'Don't fret, Kathryn. The land is bright again. Given a good summer, we shall have wheat and some good profit. Prices are high and, given another blight, they will go higher.'

'You want another blight?

'Yes, of course. It will do a lot of good, believe me. The famine will be a great help, a calamity to some but with a purpose for others. It puts these people out. Gets rid of them off good land. It allows us to bring it together and make some really profitable farms. There's talk of bringing Scottish shepherds over and putting the land to sheep. You just see. Once this is all over, this country will be peaceful and profitable and who denies the common sense in that? If it wasn't all for the good then why did God make it happen?'

She did not answer. There was no answer to give. She vowed never to see him again. She had known him to be a braggart. She had seen his ways with her father and knew he was a self-seeking sycophant. She had seen such young men in England yet none had been as callously cruel as Edward Ogilvie.

Ahead of them she saw a crowd gathered around a man dressed like a scarecrow. He had a pole down the back of his tattered coat and another that went through both arms. He had stuffed straw into the front of his vest and more came out from his sleeves. His face was smeared with chalk so that his eyes were bright and his lips protruded fleshy red. He moved with the jerky action of a clockwork doll, stiff, his limbs unbending, imitating a scarecrow buffeted by the wind. Then he stopped as still as a stone and the crowd marvelled at his cleverness. Somebody dropped a penny into his hand. He bowed and they clapped.

She saw a small boy standing in her way, quite still, captivated by the scarecrow. He was no higher than her stirrups. She did not hear Ogilvie shout to the boy to move aside. He did not shout a second time. He brought the bullwhip high above his head and lashed the boy, the tiny bags of grapeshot cutting his shirt apart and tearing open the skin on his back. The whip cracked again like the snapping of a dead branch and blood spurted from the boy's legs. He cried out and fell. He did not move.

Kate jumped from her horse and ran to him. She held him in her arms, his blood staining her skirt. She looked for help. No one moved.

'Someone help me,' she shouted. 'Help me carry him to my horse ... Help me!' No one came forward.

'Curse you for your cowardice,' she screamed at them. 'All of you. Curse you for this!'

She turned. The end of Olgilvie's whip with its leather pouches lay only a foot away from her. She grabbed and pulled it quick and hard. The whip handle was attached to a loop on his wrist and he was jerked off his saddle and hit the ground hard. He was a heavy man and the breath was knocked out of him. She ran towards him, took hold of the whip end again and hit him across the face. Blood ran down his neck as his men pulled her away.

She turned back. The boy was unconscious in the arms of a man.

'Bring him here,' she shouted to him. 'Put him on the saddle and I will take him to a doctor.'

The man said. 'There is no doctor here, miss. If there was, the gentleman would have him first.'

Ogilvie was helped away, limp and barely conscious. Bloodied rags covered his face.

'Where can we take this boy?' she asked the man. 'Who will look after him? Where is his family?'

'He has none,' he replied. 'But I know him. I will care for him.'

'Then take my horse.'

'It is not far, miss. I can manage.'

'Please.' She held the boy's hand. The man nodded.

'I am a schoolmaster. My name is Keegan and my school-house is only a little way beyond the market. If you should come, I will ask the women to rinse your clothes. You cannot go to your home like that.'

The crowd was sullen and silent as they left. She had called them cowards and they knew that well enough themselves. But she had injured their landlord, made him look ridiculous in front of them and that was worse. Whatever he intended for her would be nothing to what he was certain to do to them. They knew his bullwhip would return to Kinsale and God help man, women or child that had its attention.

It was not a long walk to Keegan's schoolhouse. It was squat and thatched and the stone had been freshly whitewashed. By the side of it was a semicircle of small cottages bordering a patch of grass. Beyond that, a grand view of the sea.

Keegan said, 'I'll put the kettle on. You would like tea?'

Kate nodded. Together they undressed the boy, washed his wounds in warm soapy water and laid him in a mattress of straw.

The whip had cut deep but the wounds were clean and Keegan said the warm air would dry them and heal them.

'He'll have awful scars,' he said. 'They will last him all his life. He will not forget Mr Ogilvie.'

Keegan was a neat man in himself and all things around him. He had dark-brown hair, long sideburns and grey eyes that were never still, set deep in his ruddy face. He was small but with powerful shoulders and strong arms and might have been a stonemason or a woodcutter. He looked at odds with his schoolroom. There was a small square window on its southern wall. Nailed above the door was a piece of wood engraved with the words, 'Céad míle fáilte'.

'It means a hundred thousand welcomes,' he said. 'And never in my life have I been happier to offer one of them to someone than I am now to you. You have honoured me by your visit here.'

'May I come back tomorrow?' she asked him. 'I could bring some balm and new dressings. Maybe a little fruit.'

'Would that be wise, miss?'

'My name is Kathryn, Mr Keegan. I prefer to be called Kate.'

They shook hands.

'Why should it matter whether it's wise or not?' she asked. 'I would like to help.'

'I'm not sure that coming back will help him more,' he answered.

'I don't understand.'

'Ogilvie is a vicious man, Miss Kate. We know his cruelty here.'

She sipped her tea. 'I'm not afraid of him. He cannot hurt me.'

'Forgive me,' he said. 'I am not afraid for you. You are of his people. But he can harm us and he will. He will be back and I fear some of us might not see the end of summer.'

'Then I must come back here again. Don't you see? As long as I keep coming, he cannot hurt you. He can do nothing to me. I am your protection.'

Keegan studied her face as she helped herself to more tea from the pot. He asked himself why she was doing this. Why should she whip one of her own? It made no sense. Who was she, dressed in such finery? An English girl riding a horse that was worth more than most could earn in a lifetime. The saddle alone would keep his school in books for the rest of his teaching life and another teacher's beyond that. Such a fine young lady sitting here on a stool, drinking his tea.

She looked to him. 'Perhaps, one day, I will tell you why this is so important to me.'

This startled him. 'You must read my mind,' he said.

'I surprise myself. It is all happening very suddenly. But you must not think it sinister. I simply want to help and this is the first chance I've had. Let me come back.'

He said nothing for a while. He looked at the boy asleep in the cot. A draught whistled softly through a crack in the window frame. It was late afternoon, the sun had left the room. Soon it would be dusk.

He held out his hands to her. 'Miss Kate, this is a strange day. Some might say it was a day meant to happen. But whatever comes out of it can only be good for us all. That I know. Of that I'm certain.'

She took his hands and held them tight in hers. She looked at the boy. 'What is his name?'

'Eugene. A fine boy. He had a yearning to learn. But it's dead in him now that he has lost his family.'

'They are dead?'

'Dead or gone.'

'I will bring him a picture book. And the fruit.'

She ducked beneath the low door into the early orange evening. Keegan's neighbours had watered her mare and let her graze on the slopes. As she mounted, a woman came with a knitted shawl. She spoke in Irish.

'She wants you to have it,' Keegan said. 'To cover the blood.'

Kate wrapped it across her knees. 'I will bring it back tomorrow. Tell her I am very grateful.'

'And we are too, Miss Kate. If we seem shy, forgive us. We are strangers to kindness of this sort.'

She waved them goodbye and cantered away to join the road to Cork. When she was above Kinsale she stopped and looked down. She could see the schoolhouse shining in the last of the sun. Around it, like a litter of suckling piglets, the semicircle of cottages. How wonderfully safe it all looked, as if nothing that had happened this past year had touched it, as if all the suffering and dying had bypassed it, leaving it clean and tidy. Then she thought of the little boy Eugene in her arms, his blood trickling through her fingers, a child who had lost all and she knew that Keegan and his hamlet had not escaped that winter's sorrow.

∞

It was almost dark. On the rise she could see the lights of Cork. She had left the road and cut cross-country, following a route she knew well. At the Owenboy River at Fivemilebridge she quickly reined in her mare. Three horsemen were waiting on the far side. She was about to turn when one of them came trotting towards her.

'Mistress Kathryn.'

She knew the voice.

'Moran. Is that you?'

He stopped beside her and took hold of her bridle. 'Thank God we found you first, Miss Kathryn.'

'Moran. Why are you here? I am almost home. Did father send you?'

'No! But he has many men out searching. He knows what happened in Kinsale. He is not pleased but Mr Ogilvie says there will be no charges against you.'

'It was a terrible thing I did, Moran.'

'No man deserved it more. But that is not why I'm here. I must tell you ...'

He hesitated. Kate tugged at his sleeve.

'Go on, Moran. Tell me what?'

'Captain Shelley is dead.'

It was as if she already knew, as if this was simply confirmation. She had not heard from him for over a month and his smuggled letters had been so constant, so regular. This was expected. She did not feel shock.

'How did he die?' she asked.

'He and the others broke into a depot in Kinvara. It was full of food, over five tons of it, enough to feed all Galway. But it was a trap. They were waiting for them, waiting inside. There was nothing they could do.'

'Who was waiting? Tell me, Moran, who were they?'

'The military. Fusiliers. They shot them, every single one of them, a boy and all. They didn't have to. None of them was armed. But they shot them as they stood and dragged the bodies into the sea. It was planned. They were meant to die.'

She said nothing. Moran touched her arm.

'He is dead, Miss Kathryn. And we did it. We killed them just as sure as if we had pulled the triggers ourselves.'

There was a splash of fish downstream and the call of a coot.

'I don't understand,' she said.

'I sent them news of that food convoy. At first Shelley said they could do nothing, it would be too well guarded. But then you told me that the military would leave once the food was in place, that Martineau had not wanted soldiers there. I sent your note to him, telling him that, just as you asked.'

'Yes! Just as I asked. Oh! Moran, how could we have known?'

'It was Martineau, Miss Kate. It was his doing. He planned it. He let us know deliberately. The English could never arrest the captain. They could never have let him stand trial. He had too much to say, too much to tell.'

'He had to be silenced.'

'Yes, Miss Kate. They have silenced him. And all who were with him.'

From the far side of the river a man called out, 'Come, Moran. We must go. We have a long night ahead.'

Kate looked towards the horsemen. They were bareheaded. The collars of their coats were pulled high, covering their faces.

'Who are these men?' she asked. 'Where are you going?'

'They are friends. And I am going with them. I will be hung if the Redcoats take me. Your father knows my part in this. Martineau will have told him. I am a wanted man, Miss Kathryn. I am a criminal.'

'Moran, I must help you. I must do something.'

The two horsemen crossed the bridge and one edged closer. 'You can do nothing, Miss Macaulay, but go to your father and stay out of this business of ours. The road is safe for you from here to the city. I'll vouch for that. Say your goodbye to Moran for you'll not see him again.'

Moran held out his hand and dropped something into hers. It was a pendant. 'It is silver, Miss Kathryn. It belonged to my sister. Have it to remember me by. Others know me by it. Show it and you will not be hurt. We have been friends, you and I, and I do not believe that will ever change, whatever is ahead of us. Goodbye and may God always be with you.'

Kate watched the three canter away and soon they were lost in the half light. She listened until she could hear the pounding hooves no more. Then she too followed their path and left the river behind.

That night she cried herself to sleep. In her dreams he came to her once again, the ragged orphan in the flames, the boy with the despairing eyes. But this time she did not burn her hands trying to save him. He was reaching out for her instead.

CHAPTER FIVE

Sir William was shaken by Moran's sudden departure and Martineau's evidence that the quiet and respectful butler had been an agent of the Queen's enemies. More shocking still was the sudden capture and killing of Captain Shelley. Sir William had not expected it to end that way. It had not been his wish. He knew the man to be a traitor and he would most certainly have been executed for his treachery, but whatever a man's crime, he was deserving of a fair trial. That was British justice.

He had asked Martineau to find out why the outlaws had not been taken prisoner and who it was who had given the order to fire on the unarmed gang. Martineau assured him he would enquire and report his findings, but as time passed, he made no mention of it again and if Sir William had his own suspicions he did not pursue them. It was eventually agreed that, as Shelley's desertion and the killings had only a muted response from Whitehall, it was in everyone's interests to let the matter rest.

೧೧

It had been a bright and perky April. A warm, still May followed. With their seed potatoes in the ground, women guarded them as jealously as a miser guards his pennies. In the daylight hours they stood like sentinels on their plots to scare away the crows that dared to snatch at a juicy leaf. Their children patrolled the ridges, pulling up the weeds, throwing away the stones and crumbling the soft earth between their fingers so that not a single clod might delay a shoot's rise. Along the coastline, boys scoured the beaches and brought back baskets of seaweed and worked its goodness into the ground. Their sisters carried handfuls of soot, scraped from the hearths and chimneys of their razed cottages and spread it around the plants to ward off the beetles and worms. There was much labour earnestly given.

In better times it was the tradition to give the priest a fat chicken or a basket of duck eggs that he might bless the fields and sprinkle them with holy water. At planting time they were overly respectful towards him and never failed to attend Mass, crossing themselves a dozen times as they stumbled through the Act of Contrition. Special homage was paid to St Bridget so that she too might bless the little seeds snug in their holes.

April heralded the beginning of the season of mean and hungry months. Now Ireland would again swarm with armies of roaming men searching for food or work, begging, stealing, resting wherever there was a space, crowding into towns and cities, dirty, ragged and hungry, each looking out for himself. And they would all share the same longing for the day when their tubers were big and round in the earth and they could go home again.

In their mind's eye they could see them ripening, the stout green stems pushing their way up towards the sunlight, the fields glorious in the first blossoming, the dimpled ridges covered in delicate, shallow forests of yellow and white flowers. As they tightened their belts yet another notch, they would tell each other how, come early autumn, they would rip open the ground and gorge themselves.

It was their belief, sacrosanct and taught by their fathers and their fathers before them, that plenty always followed scarcity, that God first punished and then blessed. They had somehow survived a terrible blight and a fearful winter but surely there would now follow a glorious summer and a bumper crop.

In those wandering, hungry months of spring and summer, men were certain of only one thing. This time they must harvest well. They and their families had come through one famished winter. They could not expect to survive a second.

∽

Kate no longer pined for England, not even when she was most depressed. In those first months after arriving in Ireland, her father's promise that she would go home within a year had been her one salvation, an ever-present consolation and comfort. But now Lincolnshire seemed far away and as foreign as any distant land could be. She was becoming part of the life around her and the more she became engrossed in it, the more she demanded of it. She was content and yet there lingered in her mind a dread of the future, a contradiction that frightened her. She could not explain it, not to herself, not to Keegan.

She visited him now as often as she could. She had promised him that Edward Ogilvie would not take revenge on the village for what she had done. She had said that her visits would keep him and his bullwhip away and this had proved true. The bare little schoolroom had now become more a home for her than her father's house in Cork and the boys and girls who came every day so quietly and shyly to sit on the stone floor were her new friends.

Eugene's wounds had healed but the scars rose from his skin in hard white ridges and so they would always remain. He was small, clean and neat in his ways and Keegan had taught him simple words in English. After many days of gentle coaxing and with Keegan's help translating, Kate persuaded him to talk to her.

He said he did not know how old he was; he thought perhaps eleven. He had thirteen brothers and sisters and he was somewhere in the middle. His mother had died that January. The cottage had been tumbled and with his father away on the road, there was no one strong enough to build a shelter. A stranger had taken the two older girls away and had given him sixpence for each of them. His brothers had gone to an uncle in Galway and he did not expect to ever see them again.

'Why didn't you go with them?' Kate asked.

'I sat with mother.'

'But you said she was dead.'

'No one to bury her.'

'You stayed with her? By her body?'

'Yes.' He began to speak in Irish and looked to Keegan to translate. 'I sat four days with my mother to keep the dogs and rats away. I went back and gathered as much straw from the thatch as I could carry and covered her. I set it on fire and when it was cool I collected her bones from the ash, put them in a sack and buried them in a hole in the churchyard under the roots of the big tree. There is no cross but I know the place. I go to speak to her every Sunday. She knows I am there.'

Kate listened and wept. But it was all past for him. There was no longer any sorrow in remembering. He put his arm around her. She was no longer a stranger.

On every journey to the school she brought something from Cork. Fruit, pies, slates and crayons, picture books and always the Bible. She brought a Hessian rug to give warmth to the school-room floor, pinned cloth to the single window to counter the draught and set a brass oil lamp on the floor, taken from her own bedroom. It was now so welcoming and cosy that Keegan protested that his problem was not persuading the children to come to class but getting them to leave.

Except for Eugene, none of the children spoke English and it was Keegan's suggestion that Kate should teach them. He said it would not be a problem and it was not. She had seldom to repeat a lesson or speak an English word more than twice for them to repeat it correctly. They, in turn, would stand at Keegan's beckoning and recite in Irish, telling stories of the great feats of courage and sacrifice in Ireland's history. Kate did not understand a word but she clapped her applause and kissed their cheeks.

Whenever she spoke to them individually, the girls bent their knees in a curtsy and the boys stared resolutely at the floor. Keegan lifted the head of one.

'This is Declan. He walks three miles here every morning and three miles back every night. And you see that he is barefoot. That's how keen he is. He never misses a day, whatever the weather.'

He touched the head of the next in line, taller and older than the rest.

'Young Kevin here has a limp. He wasn't born with it. Show Miss Kate your legs, Kevin. Don't be shy now.'

The boy slowly and neatly rolled up his tattered trousers. The calf of his left leg was badly scarred. The right leg had been broken and had not set properly. It was twisted and a knot of bone pushed out the skin just below the knee.

'The tumbling gangs came into his village a year ago. It's a ruin now. The agent must have been expecting trouble because he rode in with armed men. So there were no protests, not even when they began taking away the few cows and pigs. The villagers went down on their knees imploring the agent to leave them their animals. But they went, the women weeping and the men mute. What could they do? How could they fight men with guns at their shoulders? So they watched as everything they owned was taken from them. But Kevin here followed the gang and ran among the cows and pigs, shouting and screaming and waving his arms, like an army of banshees. With all the blather the animals turned and ran back the way they came, straight into the village, straight back into their pens. The agent, in his rage, rode his horse at Kevin, trampled him twice over. They thought he was dead. But he is a fighter and here he is and a good fellow too.'

'Did the villagers keep their stock?' Kate asked.

'No! The landlord himself came back a fortnight later with thirty soldiers and there wasn't a Kevin to oppose them. They took the lot and set fire to whatever was left.'

'So he was almost killed for nothing.'

'No, Kate. Not for nothing. He did what no man twice his age and size dared to do. He'll not be forgotten for that.'

Kate brought Eugene a present. She had searched for it in Cork and had found a handsome edition, bound in brown Morocco leather with its title, *The Children's Encyclopaedia*, embossed in gold leaf. It was three inches thick and one thousand eight hundred pages long, beginning with 'Abu Simbel' and ending with 'Zulu'. There were entries about strange happenings in Tibet, the life of a crab and many beautifully coloured lithographs, including Queen Victoria's coronation, each picture protected within a thin sheaf of tissue paper. Inside the cover Kate had written: '*From Kate. To my good and learned friend Eugene.*'

It was heavy and he took it carefully as if it was made of the most delicate porcelain. He sat down by the corner of the hearth stroking it gently, hesitantly, as if he expected it to disintegrate on touch, caressing it in his lap, the guardian of a precious jewel. Now he would know the source of knowledge, the beginning of all learning. Inside its cover was everything that made a boy a man and that man full of the world of wisdom. It was all his for the taking. He had only to open it.

૨૦૧

'Eugene has a surprise for you, Kate.'

A fortnight had passed since the boy's surprise present and Keegan had asked her to come early to the school.

'He's been working at it every hour God's given him. He even persuaded the priest to give him an altar candle so that he could read by it at night. He's been a pest and I've lost sleep myself but by heaven, he's done it.'

'Done what?' she asked.

'I should tell you but I cannot. Or do I mean I can tell you but I shouldn't? Anyway, you will know soon enough. It's his surprise for you, to thank you for his book. From the moment you gave it to him it hasn't left his hands. I'll wager that if you asked him what was on page one thousand and one, he'd reel it off word-perfect. He's told me more about Tibetan monks than I've room for!'

The big black kettle over the peat fire began to boil. Kate pulled the rug closer to the hearth and waited. Every day here now was happier than the last and for the first time in her life she thanked God for it.

Keegan handed her a mug. 'I will call him. He's waiting not far off and nervous too. But for such a little lad I think he's brave with it.'

Kate held Keegan's hand. 'Tell me what to expect?'

'It's a poem, yet another Irish poem. But this one is special and a dangerous one too, although you'll find that hard to believe. It's been banned by the English, forbidden because they think its rebellious. You might think it is but it's really more a lament about Ireland's anguish and yearning and we're famous enough for that, are we not? But the English think it's a call to arms and if you're caught with a copy of it or even reciting it, you can reckon the worst will happen.'

'For reading a poem?'

'Yes! For a poem. Such are the times, Kate. Such is the canker of fear.'

'Then he mustn't do it, not for me. I won't have him do it … I won't listen. You mustn't let him.'

'It's not my choice, Kate. Nor is it in me to stop him. He's doing it for you and for all of us. It's just because it is forbidden that makes it so valuable and his little contribution so precious. Do you not understand?'

She nodded and said nothing. Keegan went to the door and called out his name.

He came in slowly, clasping the encyclopaedia to his chest. How thin he was, how pale. Again she wondered, as she had so often recently, whether he was the boy of her dreams, the boy in the fire. But it was not his face. They were not his eyes.

'A poem for you, Miss Kate.' He said it in a whisper, looking at his feet. 'It is Irish but Mr Keegan helped me put it in English. Not all of it because it is very long. It is called "My Dark Rosaleen".'

'Go on, Eugene,' she said. 'I'm proud that you have done this for me. It is a wonderful gift.'

He looked up, his face flushed with colour. Then he closed his eyes tight and began:

'I could scale the blue air
I could plough the high hills
I could kneel all night in prayer
To heal your many ills
And one beamy smile from you
Would float like light between
My toils and me, my own, my true,
My Dark Rosaleen

The Erne shall run with blood,
The earth will rock beneath our tread
And flames wrap hill and wood
And gun-peal and slogan-cry wake many a glen serene
Ere you shall fade, ere you shall die,
My Dark Rosaleen.'

§

Old Tom Keegan was long and thin, much taller than his son. When he was not crouched with the rheumatism that had tormented him all his life, he would, in the presence of strangers, and despite the pain, make the effort to square his shoulders and stand straight. He had a full head of white hair and a lovely dignity. He was self-taught, a teacher since he was sixteen, and almost blind now from a lifetime of reading forbidden tracts in the half light.

On bright days he could see clearly enough to tend his few roods of potatoes and the small patch of flowering herbs that sat prettily either side of the front door of his cottage. All his life he had worked longer hours than the sun itself, never allowing it to rise before him and waiting for it sink out of sight before he considered his day to be over.

He had built his cottage on land he rented at thirty-five shillings a quarter. He was known as a lifer and as long as he paid his rent, his landlord could not remove him. The cottage was low and squat with thick walls and a thatched roof and, unlike any other nearby, it had a small window with a single pane of glass, a prized possession given to him by his father on his wedding day.

On the day Tom Keegan married his Mary, they vowed that they would build their house of stone. They were strong and young with no fear of the future and wanted their first home to be their last, sturdy like them and destined to live a long life like them. For a full year, they gathered stones from the mountain and when they began building it, they dug two feet deep to give it a firm foundation.

For all that year they lived in a hole in the ground, roofed with turf, washing in the stream, and making love hidden in the heather. When they were not building, they were breaking the ground around them until they had a plot soft and tame enough to plant their first potatoes.

But young Mary Keegan died three months after she had moved into her new home, the morning her only son was born. Thereafter Tom lived a lonely, loveless life, unable to watch his infant son grow without the agony of knowing the sacrifice that had given him life. At first he wanted to move from the valley, away from the house whose every stone, so carefully laid, was a reminder of a day with her. Yet to leave would be to abandon her in her shallow grave beyond the potato patch. The cottage was her shrine and as long as he remained, so then would she. And the son she died for would be raised in her image, kind and good and gentle.

It was the first day of June and old Keegan's eightieth birthday. His son had asked Kate to join them to celebrate the day and she had been overjoyed at the invitation. He closed the school and together they rode the ten miles cross-country to surprise him, carrying a cake and a jar of honey Kate had taken from the cook's pantry.

Since that day she visited him every week and brought rations in her saddlebags. Salted herrings from Cork market, packets of Twankey Tea, twists of tobacco, candles and cheese and a sweet-smelling oil for his lamp. He spent his days preparing for her, fretting whenever she was a few minutes late, not wanting to lose a minute of her company. He would grumble when it was time for her to leave, complaining that he was forced to live a hermit's life, when, until the moment she entered his life, that was what he had always preferred. When she left, he would stand at his doorway listening to the sound of her horse long after he had lost sight of it. Then he would sit by his hearth and recall every morsel of their day's conversation, savouring his favourite parts of it, repeating them out loud many times.

Much time was spent preparing for her arrival. He would press his only pair of tweed trousers under the mattress the night before. His only pair of shoes, brown brogues bought in Cork for his wedding, were brought out of their wrapping and polished with spit and candlewax, caressed in his lap like the old friends he considered them to be. And although it was now many sizes too large, he wore the stiff white paper collar that had sat untouched in its box since the day of his wife's burial.

Kate loved his cottage. It smelt fresh with herbs. The stone floor was smoothed and polished by half a century and more of human tramping and shone like marble. The chimney breast was made of woven chestnut staves, plastered with mud and whitewashed with lime. His rosary hung from a peg above the hearth and by it was an enamel locket containing a band of Mary's red hair. Beside the hearth was his rocking chair and on the opposite wall his cot, its joints bound together by strips of willow bark. On a three-legged stool by its side was his Bible, worn by hands and curled by age.

It was a warm day but a square of peat smouldered in the hearth. Tom's fire was never out. He and Kate sat facing each other either side of it. Sunlight edged in through the tiny window, highlighting the freckles on his face. He had an audience and was content.

As they talked, he would hold her hand firm in his and hold it long, squeezing it as he spoke, as if special words needed emphasis.

'Have you ever wondered, Miss Kathryn, why it is I keep a fire on a summer's day?' She sensed mischief in his voice.

'I have, Tom, and you are going to tell me why.'

'It's to keep the evil spirits away. They can smell a cold chimney even out there in the bogs where they hide and it takes a mighty powerful spell to get rid of them because once they're inside they can do dreadful harm.'

'And what kind of spell is that?' she asked, not knowing whether she was expected to share his humour, nor even certain there was humour to be shared.

'Have you never seen how mothers protect their newborns from the banshees? How they put an iron poker over the cot and sprinkle salt on the floor around it?'

'Must I believe this?'

'Believe it or not, it's what they believe and that's what they do. You see, sometimes a fairy child is born deformed ...'

'Tom!'

'Deformed, I say! The fairies give it to the banshees to sneak into the newborn's cot and swap it for a human child.'

'And what must you do with a poker and salt?' She said it with a smile.

'Miss Kathryn! You should know that a fairy cannot lift iron and will never cross salt. Salt and poker and the child is safe. They dare not touch it.'

'And tell me, Tom, where do the fairies come from? Or is that a secret?'

'From the black lake of Lough Gur, east of Limerick. Least, so I'm told. Mind you, Rí na Sideog, the king of the fairies, can be found anywhere you need him. Like God himself.'

Again she protested.

'Listen, Miss Kathryn. Listen and believe. To the people, the fairy king is just like God. It is their faith twice over, and it's only a thin line that divides the two. When one lets them down they turn to the other. I've talked to them both myself all my life. Mind you, I must have a faint voice because neither has shown the slightest interest in listening.'

He took the kettle from its hook over the fire and filled the teapot.

'My mother was of the Church and never missed a Mass until the day she died. But when she was troubled, she would go up the hillside by the side of us here, and talk for hours with Rí na Sideog until she was peaceful again inside. She would take him flowers and little presents of herbs. We all knew and nobody said but when she passed on, we went to the top, and by the small lake up there she had built a little shrine on a rock and there were all her bits and pieces, untouched, just as she'd left them all those years. So you see, it does no good to laugh at people who believe these things for it gives them much comfort and there's precious little of it to spare nowadays.'

Tom Keegan was a keen chronicler of Irish history and Irish affairs and he would talk of Brian Boru, king of all Ireland eight hundred years ago, as if he had been on familiar terms with him. He referred to past and present-day politicians by their Christian

names, giving the impression they too were old acquaint-
ances. He was steeped in history and although he might search
for hours for a lost pipe or a tray of seeds, events and names
from centuries ago were imprinted indelibly in his mind. He
could effortlessly repeat the names of every Irish hero and every
English blackguard and made sure that every child he taught
could do the same.

He had been schoolmaster for the children from the hills and
valleys all his working life and in the early days it had been a
dangerous profession. He knew of men who were no longer in
Ireland because they too had been teachers in the time when
the English had forbidden the schooling of Catholic children.
He had been forced to teach his flock in secret wherever he
could, sometimes even under cover of the hedgerows.

'We called ourselves hedgers, Miss Kathryn. It was a nasty
game and a dangerous one to play. If I'd been caught, I'd not be
here today. The magistrates sent the police to search for us but
we were always warned and we would scatter and wait for them
to pass. If you were caught you were liable to five years or transportation. Only the Protestant children got proper schooling. It
wasn't until the emancipation that we dared come out into the
open. The day it was declared, twenty-five years ago, I opened
my own school and here I've stayed.' He said nothing for a while,
gazing into the past within the hearth. Then, 'What is to become
of us, Miss Kathryn? You and me? The English and the Irish?
How is it to end? Will we always be at each other's throats, two
islands and only a fair day's sailing between them?'

'Perhaps it's because you are so close that we fear you.'

'Yes!' said the old man. 'I can understand that.'

Kate paused, not certain she should say more. Then, 'I have
always been taught to believe that Ireland is England's enemy
and that good fortune for one was bad for the other. My father
says that England's difficulties are Ireland's opportunities and
that in every crisis you have always helped our enemies.'

'And your father is right. But you English have since made friends of your enemies. So why not us? Why possess us all these centuries? Why all these years of vengeance?'

'Perhaps this famine will change things.'

'Maybe, Miss Kathryn. But for better or for worse?'

'I have seen and heard so much since I came to Ireland, so many terrible things, but I wonder if it is all England's fault. Is it to blame for the blight?'

The old man thumped the arm of his chair and took the pipe from his mouth. In his sudden anger, colour left his cheeks, droplets of water trickled from his eyes.

'Don't blame the English for that. They're rightly accused of many dreadful things but don't lay this on them. What has happened this year and all the years past has been the will of God and not even the English can deter God in His doing. The blight is His punishment for our waste and our indolence. I am old enough to remember those years of plenty ... Yes, I can ... when we had too many potatoes to eat. We would leave them in the ground to rot or if we had a handcart and the gumption to pull it, we carried them to the market. As a boy I could stand all day at the pitch and not even give them away. On the way home I'd empty the lot into a ditch, for they were not even worth the price of the sacks. Then when the next year's crop failed we knew it was God's retribution. A wilful waste makes a woeful want, that's what we would say and that's the reason for it. The blight and the hunger is His punishment and only He can right it. And in the meantime we must trust the English to keep us alive.'

The old man sank back in his chair, his temper fading. 'Mind you,' he said, 'if keeping us alive is the government's intention, it is being painfully slow. It sends soldiers and we need food instead of Fusiliers. But forgive me. This is not polite, nor is it fair to you, Miss Kathryn. We need not spoil our little party with Ireland's many problems. All my life I've lived with them. Mind you, when I was a young man I thought we could do something to change it.'

He poked the peat ashes with his walking stick.

'A handful of wet straw on a fire can set up such a cloud of smoke that it obliterates the stars and that's how it was with us then. So much smoke but no fire, so much talk of doing but nothing done. We had our chance once, Miss Kathryn,' he said it quietly. 'At Clontarf we had our chance and we lost it to good common sense. Least that was O'Connell's excuse.'

'He is a sick man,' Kate said. 'My father says he is finished.'

'Oh, yes! He is dying. We all are. And when he's gone there'll be no one to take his place. When his heart stops, so will Ireland's.'

She waited for him to speak again. The only sound was the hissing of the peat. She thought he was dozing but he was not. He was lost again in his past and, like O'Connell's, it had been a lifetime of trying and losing. The past was despair. He was O'Connell's age and had once shared in the man's fury and ambition, as every Irishman had. But now the fury was spent and the great ambition withered.

The sun travelled away from the window, the room darkened, and with it, the old man's mood. He seemed smaller, fragile and when he spoke again, his voice was faint.

'Forgive me, Miss Kathryn. I am an old man drifting backwards and O'Connell's name put me in another time and another place when we talked of defiance and rebellion. Yet here we are, all these years on and nothing has changed. The soldiers wear much the same uniforms, fire with better muskets and still we pay our rents to the same masters.'

'Tell me of O'Connell,' said Kate.

'We used to call him "Swaggering Dan" because of the way he walked and talked. Such a figure of a man and with a voice that could charm the Devil into Paradise. It was said that he was the yeast in a mass of Irish dough. That was often used to describe him and it was right. When he spoke at his meetings, there was a hush. It was as if he could play tunes on the spines of people, like the great fiddler he was. He promised we would get our Parliament back, the one Pitt stole from us all those years ago. The English called it a union but it was nothing of the sort. They said it was marriage but it was more like a brutal rape. We were dragged to the altar. O'Connell spent his life working for a repeal, to break from the Union and get us back our Parliament and let us govern ourselves. Whenever he called a meeting, thousands – many, many thousands – came to listen. I went to one at Tara and there was such a crowd that the English surrounded us with what we thought was their entire army. But the only disturbance that day was somebody overturning the gingerbread stand. Not a fist was lifted. There was no drink, you see. Can you imagine all those thousands of Irishmen and no whiskey? He had his chance at Clontarf and that's where his legend ended.'

'What was Clontarf?' she asked.

'It was the test, his biggest ever meeting, a monster. I remember it was a Sunday. I thought it wrong to hold it on the Sabbath, but I went all the same. Clontarf was near Dublin, in a special field, the very place where eight hundred years ago our own King Boru defeated the Norsemen and drove them into the sea. Men knew the significance of that and thought O'Connell had chosen it because he had made his plan and the big day had come at last. He expected tens of thousands but they say there was nearly a million men there and every last one of them ready to march on Dublin Castle and pull down the Union flag. The English were prepared for it but it didn't matter. It was our hour. We needed only a nod from Swaggering Dan. But he failed us. He was always the man of lovely words, always preaching that the power of talk did more than a charge of gunpowder. But at that moment, the very moment it mattered, he couldn't bring himself to do the dirty deed. He said there were British warships in the harbour and that their cannons would blow every man among us to smithereens. Ireland, he said, would be a field of blood. So he told us all to go home and wait until another day. And go home we did.'

'Why?' asked Kate. 'A million men could easily have beaten the soldiers.'

The old man shook his head, the glimmer of a flame in the hearth dancing on his face. 'Because Swaggering Dan said he didn't want a drop of Irish blood spilt. As if a man's liberty has ever been won for less. So go home, he said, and we did, like sheep to their pens. And the English laughed.'

Tom Keegan raised himself forward in his chair and held out both hands to the fire as if in prayer. 'And to think we flocked after him like dogs in heat. We should have kept him in the Derry bogs where he was spawned. O'Connell is dying now and soon he'll be in heaven. But the saints will mock him there, yes, they will. He lived a hero's life but Clontarf branded him a coward.'

CHAPTER SIX

June was as hot a month as anyone could remember. In January, people had frozen to death. Now people fainted with the heat. What mattered most was that the potato plants were healthy and strong, their stems thick and heavy with leaf. There had never been such a crop and they thanked God.

He had put their faith to the test. They had endured the winter's hunger and not a day had passed without them crossing themselves and praising Him. The green fields were their redemption. To make doubly sure, they used their scarce pennies to buy salt and walked the boundaries of their plots, sprinkling it over the long beds to keep evil spirits away.

Kate had risen early. It was a sparkling morning and she had promised the schoolchildren a drawing lesson. Her saddlebag was filled with rolls of paper, coloured crayons and gum. She would stick their pictures on the schoolhouse wall and there would be prizes for every one of them.

It was too soon to ride directly to Kinsale. The children did not come before nine each morning, so she decided instead to go the long way, past Blackrock Castle, to Monkstown and on to the coastal tracks beyond Minane Bridge. She halted at Shanbally to watch the busy traffic of cargo ships passing in and out of Cork Harbour. She saw a single track, worn through the turf. She was curious and followed it until it widened and dropped away to a clearing. A horse was tethered by the edge of a deep pit, its sides covered in mauve heather and sprawls of clinging ferns. She rounded it and saw within its shadows a small cottage, almost hidden at the bottom. The sunlight barely touched it, its walls were green with mould and there was a dank smell of rotting vegetation. She shivered with the sudden chill and its desolation.

She reined her horse back to leave when she heard a woman's scream and the cry of a baby. A young man came out of the cottage door and looked up at her. He smiled.

'Would you perhaps have a clean piece of cloth to spare?' he asked.

He was in his shirt, his sleeves rolled up to his elbows. There was blood on his hands.

'I have a handkerchief,' Kate replied.

'Too small. Even for this baby. And I've seldom seen them smaller.'

'You have a baby in there?'

'Certainly I have. Arrived this very moment. Come down and see.'

Kate tied the mare's reins to a boulder and, slowly treading the steps cut into the steep wall of the pit, followed him inside the cottage. A peat fire smouldered in the middle of the dirt floor. The smoke stung her eyes.

The woman was lying on a pallet of straw, penned in a cot of staves.

The young man pulled back the rags that covered the mother and huddled around her like a litter of puppies were three small, naked children. She held her baby in her arms, still wet and yellow with wax. She was a big woman with wide hips, her breasts large with milk, her face glistening with sweat.

'You've done well today, Mary,' the young man said. 'I was hoping this young lady might have had something decent to wrap him in.'

He turned to Kate. 'I thought he deserved something nice and clean for the first few moments of his new life. After all, he's been waiting long enough to join us. By the way, I'm Robin. A doctor, as you might suppose. And this is Mary McMahon.'

'How do you do? I'm Kate.' She turned away, lifted up her riding skirt, tore out her white linen petticoat and gave it to him.

Dr Robin Fitzgerald was accustomed to surprises. He knew well enough who she was. Since the whipping of Ogilvie in Kinsale, her name and fame had spread well beyond the boundaries of County Cork.

'Thank you, Miss Kate,' he said, tearing the linen apart. 'It is a privilege to meet you although I might have preferred a pleasanter place for it.'

He wiped the baby clean, wrapped him tight in its swaddling cloth and put him in his mother's arms.

'I'll be back, Mary, the day after tomorrow. Now keep him clean and away from the fire smoke. It's no good for him or you and I've told you so many times.'

They washed their hands in the spring water that trickled from the rock face and climbed back up to the light. The sun was high. It was still some hours to midday but the cottage was already in dark shadow.

'Why do they live in such squalor?' Kate asked. 'Surely you can be poor and clean?'

He shook his head. 'Kate, it only takes a tub of water, a bar of soap and some scrubbing to keep yourself and your home tidy. But she will have sold her tub long ago. She has no pennies to spare for soap and she has lost the will to scrub. It really is as simple as that. She only has a little strength left and her baby will soon take that away.'

'She must have been a handsome women once. Perhaps even beautiful. Such lovely long brown hair and those blue eyes.'

'Yes! I understand she was something to be proud of. Her father was a weaver. But she's had a year or more of making do on her own.'

'How does she cope?'

'As they all do. Or they die. There is no other way. I have nothing to judge their lives by. You and I are strangers to them, aliens. We visit them, administer, give them orders, punish. We smell of brilliantine and perfumes, our hair shines, our faces are powdered, our shoes are well heeled. They see our belts loose about our fat bodies and they wonder at the mystery of us, alone in their miserable lives. As Mary is now, waiting for her husband Patch to come back to her.'

'Is he on the road, looking for work?'

'Who knows? This is the first time he's been away and he's been gone six months now. They lived well enough down there in that pit on his whiskey-making. Then the excise men came and smashed his still. They would have broken Patch too if they'd caught him. But he scampered away just in time and he hasn't been heard of since.'

'When he comes back, he will have a fine boy waiting for him, thanks to you.'

'She could have managed on her own. You saw three in the bed but she's had more.'

'Where are they?'

'Dead. Born healthy but disease took them. Things doctors can't cure.'

'You must despair. Seeing so much.'

'Yes! Despair is the word. I wonder, I really do wonder, what massive crime they must have committed to be treated so badly. There was a time when I would hold a newborn in my hands, straight from God's own cradle, and I would think what spirit there must be in these people to want another child when there is such a world to greet it.'

'Why then?' she asked.

'I think the poorer they are, the more precious their children. When you have nothing, to be able to create a child must be like discovering a jewel in a turnip field.'

'And they're always living with the dread of being hungry.'

'Yes! Always. It never leaves them. They say that hunger never sleeps. They seem to accept it as second nature, just as Mary does, as if it is hereditary. But she has her dream to keep her going. She tells me that one day Patch will take them all to America. She talks about the sea and the big ship that will take them to the other side of the world and all the things they will do there. It's her dream. It's all she has left. It's what keeps her alive.'

They rode side by side for nearly an hour and Dr Robin talked the whole way without stop. He spoke of the famine and his fear of the fever epidemic that so often follows the blight. Where would they find doctors and nurses if it came? Where would they find the medicines? Why was nobody preparing for the worst when that was what they must expect? He spoke as if all Ireland would soon be bare of people.

'I have read a report by a man called Tuke, an Englishman and a Quaker, who has come here to help with relief. He is compiling his own journal of the famine. He writes that he has been to America and has seen the wasted remnants of the great Indian tribes there living like prisoners on their reservations and how badly the Negro slaves are treated in the southern states. But he says he has never seen anything so degrading or so much misery and suffering as he has in the bog holes of Ireland.'

'Why are the people so patient?' she asked.

'Patient and without protest,' he answered. 'Can you understand that? Because I cannot. There can't be a country anywhere in the world where oppression has ruled and the oppressed have protested so little. I've never heard them complain about God or man, even though their misery is of man's making. We must be content, they say, with what the Almighty has put before us. They wait in their blind, patient hope until death relieves them. And they die, like the faithful they are, with a prayer of thanks upon their lips.'

'Don't we call it Providence?'

Robin shook his head. 'And don't the priests call it divine intervention? God's punishment for sins past and present?'

'And it's not?'

'Of course not, Kate. And you don't believe it either. We may never know what causes the blight but we know who's responsible for the suffering that's followed it. It's man-made, landlord-made. Do you think people would be dying if they still had their homes to live in? Would they be starving if the landlords had let them eat their own oats and barley instead of handing it over as rent? The blame sits squarely on the landlord's doorstep. Do you know, Kate, there are days when I come from such sights of misery I feel disposed to take a gun and shoot the first one I see?'

They came to a village. They stopped and he turned to her. 'I'm breathless, Kate. I cannot remember ever talking so much for so long. You must think me a prig and a bore. But you are inspiring.'

She laughed. 'I am just a very obedient listener.'

'No. You're more than that. I seldom ever declare myself so readily. You are good for the spirit, Kate, you really are. Will you come and meet my family? Will you do that? Come to my home? We're at Youghal, less than half a day's ride from Cork. Father will be delighted and my sister Una will be thrilled to meet you. We are twins. Do say you'll come.'

Kate nodded. She would go. It was ordained. Father and son. The Keegans and now the Fitzgeralds. How perfectly matched. How patterned her life was becoming.

'I will come. Of course I will. But you must send me an invitation. My father will be most impressed. He insists I've turned my back on what he calls civilised society.'

'Then it's done. I will send you a splendid invite in the largest envelope, embossed with the family crest. Your father will not be able to refuse.'

They laughed. They shook hands.

'The day ends well,' he said. 'It's wonderful we can laugh.'

'It's a sad time for laughter.'

'But there's great hope in it, great hope. Goodbye, Kate, and remember your promise to come and see us.'

As they rode off their separate ways, the crayons rattled in Kate's saddlebag and she thought again of the children waiting in Keegan's schoolroom.

∞

The glorious summer and the blossoming potato fields did nothing to lift Sir William Macaulay's depression. His gloom brought everybody down. There was no laughter now from the clerks and couriers in the outer offices and no welcoming dinner for Friday guests. Trevelyan had promised him that the Commission would have completed its tasks by the autumn but Sir William knew it would not. Week by week, he was sinking deeper into the calamity. Ireland was defeating him as it had defeated centuries of Englishmen before him. There was more than blight on this land. It was arrogance, indifference and greed. It was rank and corrupting.

All this he knew to be true. Yet he was obliged to say nothing. He had to pretend he could save Ireland when he knew he could not. The country's salvation was now in the hands of bankers, corn merchants and landlords, further encouraged in their profiteering by the dictates of his own government. He had asked for extra money to buy more grain, yet that morning he had received a prompt and terse reply from the Chancellor of the Exchequer, Sir Charles Wood:

May I remind you yet again that England's coffers will not be emptied to fill Irish stomachs. If they cannot buy their food they must stint themselves. They do nothing but sit and howl for English money. Rents must be paid. Landlords cannot be denied their dues. If they cannot collect their rents they cannot provide relief. So arrest, do what you must. Send horse and dragoons and the whole world will applaud you. I repeat, I shall not be squeamish about how close you come to the verge of the law. You may even need to go a little beyond it.

The landlords needed no spur from Whitehall. The Earl of Lucan had already evicted six thousand tenants from his estate in Ballinrobe. On his orders, as chairman of the Castlebar Union workhouse, he had turned the inmates out onto the streets and over one hundred died within a week. No mercy tempered his ruthlessness and from that day he was known by the name 'The Terminator'.

The Marquis of Sligo and his friend and neighbour Lord Palmerston, son of an Irish peer and a future British Prime Minister, were just as ruthless. Lord Lorton had razed the villages of Ballinamuck and Drumlish on his estate in Longford, condemning a thousand families to a slow death.

Sir William was obliged to write a daily communiqué to London reporting all these happenings. Trevelyan did not condemn but defended the landlords in the language of the moralist.

Concerning the landlords, I do not despair seeing them taking the lead which their position demands of them. A deep root of social evil remains and the cure has been applied by the direct strike of an all-wise Providence. God grant we can rightly perform our part in what is intended as a blessing. I think I see a bright light shining through the dark cloud that hangs over Ireland.

Sir William held Trevelyan's letter in his hand. 'I tell you, Martineau. I would resign this hour, this very moment, if I was not afraid of being branded a coward.'

'We need stricter control, sir. More soldiers.'

'Damn it! It's not more soldiers we need but more food. We need to open the depots and give out the grain. Why do we store it when they're starving? Have you heard the song they are singing out there? D'you know what they're saying? Look at it man … Look at it. I have it here.'

He shuffled through papers on his desk and handed Martineau a pamphlet. It had been scattered in the streets for everyone to read and recite out loud if they dared.

There's a proud array of soldiers.
What do they at your door?
Why, they guard our master's granaries
From the thin hands of the poor.

Martineau slowly crumpled the sheet of paper into a ball, rolled it tighter between the palms of his hands and threw it into the fire. He stood and watched it burn.

'With respect, Sir William, you make too much of trivia. People are too weakened by the winter famine to be a threat to anyone but themselves. When the summer ends, men you consider a danger now will be hurrying back to their hovels to grub out their potatoes and looking to sire more children. They are no threat to us, nor can they ever be.'

But the ever-calculating Dr Martineau was wrong. The calendar should have warned him. There were still three months to September when the potatoes would be lifted. Three more months of hunger. In the spring, men had been promised employment. It was now late June. Week on week they had searched for work and there was none. They had been promised food from the Commission's depots yet these remained closed. Reports of the continued suffering got little attention or sympathy in London. Instead, they were received with incredulity, exasperation and some ridicule. The Duke of Norfolk, in a letter to *The London Times*, suggested that as there was an apparent shortage of potatoes, the Irish poor should be encouraged to eat curry powder mixed with water.

Sir Charles Trevelyan had a more practical alternative. Ireland should be made to pay its own way out of its calamity.

A memorandum meant only to be circulated within his own department was published in *The Times*. It was Treveylan at his most emphatic and uncompromising.

Enough English money has been spent on the Irish. The Exchequer will not be pillaged further. It cannot cure the blight. It has not stemmed the hunger. It is possible to have heard the tale of sorrow too often. Let us be clear. The property of Ireland must support the poverty of Ireland. If the Irish once discover they can get free government money, they will lie such as the world has never known. That said, let it be done.

At the outset of the blight, Prime Minister Peel, as part of his emergency plan to stave off the famine, had repealed the Corn Laws which enabled American grain to be freely imported to Ireland. Associations were formed there to raise charitable money to pay for it and a Board of Works was established to create employment so that the destitute could earn enough to feed themselves.

Grand projects were announced. New roads would be built. New canals dug. New agriculture would be introduced to end the Irish dependence on their potato. Government money would be lent to finance the schemes, repayable at an interest of three per cent.

But it was Peel's undoing. Unpopular in the country, he was soon forced to resign by enemies of Ireland from within his own party. He was succeeded by Lord John Russell, who considered all his predecessor's measures expensive blunders and immediately instructed Trevelyan to dismantle what Peel had put together. He gave Trevelyan carte blanche to do as he pleased and as director of famine relief he became its dictator overnight. Trevelyan's power was now absolute. Life and death hung on his lips.

He immediately published a Treasury report which pleased both Parliament and landlords alike. He demanded that those employed on public works should be paid the minimum that would keep them alive. He considered ten pence a day too much. If bad weather prevented men from working they should only be given a half day's pay. If those who applied for relief owned even a quarter of an acre of land, they must sell it or forfeit their claim for assistance.

Corruption became rife. Tickets, necessary for a labourer to work, were bought by profiteers. Landlords bribed officials to allocate the cheap labour to their estates. Those paid to supervise the schemes were not qualified to do so. Work could not start because there were no surveyors and without surveys the engineers stood idle. Where there was work, men were not paid because the pay clerks had run off with the money. The destitute were being promised a fair wage for a fair day's work but among the hundreds of thousands who queued were women, widows and their children, unfit for manual labour. One magistrate in County Sligo reported:

It was melancholy in the extreme to see women and girls labouring in the gangs. They were employed not only in digging with spade and pick but also in carrying loads of earth and turf on their backs and breaking stones like men. Their poor neglected children crouched in groups in the sheltered corners of the line.

Works that began did not finish and hordes of sullen, emaciated men marched from one site to the next only to find that too was abandoned. Some carried guns and knives and violence was widespread. Desperate men fought each other, man against man, gang against gang. In Waterford they broke into the supervisor's house, carried him to the site and threatened to kill him if work did not begin. They beat him until he was dead. It changed nothing.

When the employment list was closed abruptly on work at Clare Abbey in Clare, the supervisor was shot and wounded. The site was closed and a thousand men with empty pockets were out on the road again.

The agricultural scheme to end Irish dependence on the potato collapsed just as miserably. Men were offered their ten pennies a day to harvest wheat, oats and barley on the landlords' estates. Thousands queued with their hoes and scythes in hand. But there was no work because there was no money to pay them and the grain, ripe and ready to harvest, was falling wasted to the ground. Trevelyan had decreed that Ireland would pay its own way of out its tragedy. By his hand, it could not.

The tumbling continued apace. The estates were now being cleared ever more ruthlessly. In five days, one hundred and forty cottages were razed to the ground in Moyarta. Another hundred in Carrigaholt. In two months, over one thousand cottages from Mayo to Wicklow, from Donegal to Kerry, were destroyed by the tumbling gangs and over fifteen thousand people sent into the wild to find protection in the ditches and woods and make-shift *scalpeens*, primitive shelters of branches and leaves. Drawings depicting their misery now regularly appeared in English news-papers and weekly magazines, even though their editorials expressed little or no sympathy. The calamity was presented as a simple economic equation, devoid of all humanity.

The surplus, unwanted population must be disposed of, swept from the soil. If a million people were to die in the famine it could only ben-efit Ireland. It is doing it far more thoroughly than any government legislation.

It was an opinion many of their readers found persuasive and morally digestible. Ireland was too small an island to accommo-date the Irish. It was dangerously overburdened by the weight of human stock. *Ipso facto*, the Irish must be reduced in numbers.

CHAPTER SEVEN

Like most Irishmen, Sir Robert Fitzgerald assumed that the dual calamities of blight and hunger were as natural as Ireland's long seasons of rain. Throughout his long life they had come and then departed, leaving Ireland unchanged, each new generation attempting to repair the damage done by the old. He was famous for his generosity, which took many by surprise, because he was both a landlord and a Protestant. He was a distant relation of the Duke of Leinster, Ireland's premier nobleman, and he had inherited a large estate which bordered both banks of the river Blackwater to Cappoquin.

Unlike most Irishmen of his standing, he helped the poor whenever he could, providing work when additional labour was not needed, cancelling the debts of those he knew could never pay. He milled his own wheat and during the months of hunger had provided a daily ration of soup from his own kitchen to the many who had nothing. What he had he shared and whenever angry men cursed the cruelty and greed of the landowners, they would touch their caps and say, 'The Lord excepting the good Sir Robert.'

He was standing in front of a large boiling cauldron, stirring his soup, dressed in a long leather apron and almost hidden in clouds of steam. He was a broad, well-built man with a head of curly grey hair, a red face and a moustache that hung either side of his mouth.

'They say that soup can nourish a man. But I doubt it does as well as a bowl of lumpers. That's what makes Irishmen strong. D'you know, Kate, we are taller than most of the English, and a damn sight stronger. Braver too, I shouldn't wonder. Why, half the British Army is made up of us. And who was it who beat Napoleon? Another Irishman, Wellington himself, born over there in County Meath.'

Sir Robert was short on introductions. Kate had been given a warm, wet handshake and told to sit between the twins, Robin and Una. Sir Robert threw handfuls of meat and vegetables into the cauldron that hung over an open fire in the centre of his cobbled courtyard. Ireland's politics was Sir Robert's obsession. When he was young, his heart had been full of reform and good intent but he had long since grown accustomed to the perpetual suffering of the poor and the indifference and cynicism that smothered them.

'Look at this,' he shouted at them through the steam. 'They've sent me a recipe for soup. It's from your father's office, Kate. I see that it's printed in London and concocted by a fellow called Alexis Soyer. They've sent a French soup-maker and savoury inventor who's never set foot in Ireland so that for a trifling sum he can feed Paddy. They say he cooks for a London club but God knows he must have been hallucinating when he devised this one. Read it – go on, read it!'

Before Kate could take the piece of paper from him, he read it out himself.

'A handful of beef cuts, some dripping, two onions ... Two, mind you ... Not two dozen ... A handful of flour and some pearl barley. Then – and here's the rub – you mix it with a hundred gallons of water. One bloody hundred! I thought they'd added too many noughts, but they haven't. Christ almighty! I don't know what size our Monsieur Soyer is but he could pass comfortably between the bars of my front gates after a month of that rubbish. It's not so much soup for the poor as poor soup. The government's even sending the stupid fellow to Dublin to build a kitchen to serve the stuff. It's a damned disgrace! Tell your father that, Kate, a disgrace. It'll run through them like water, which is all it is.'

'Isn't something better than nothing, Father?' Robin ventured.

'Nonsense, boy. You should know that filling famine-bloated bodies with water soup will do more harm than good. Must I tell you that? He might just as well serve them up river sand.'

'What are we to believe, Father? Who are we to believe?' Una asked him.

'There's nothing and no one we can believe, not if it is coming from London. They're all lying and fussing about and doing nothing that matters, and the few people who are trying are hitting their heads against a tree. Look at the Quakers. They have more charity and sense than fat-bellied landowners but they're mistrusted because they're not the Pope's people. The priests are telling their flocks that to take anything from a Protestant is to take from the Devil. They're even putting it about that the Quakers deliberately serve meat in their soups on a Friday so the Catholics can't eat it.'

'They're also saying that Catholics must renounce their faith to get any food at all,' Una said.

Sir Robert thumped the side of the cauldron with his ladle. 'What rubbish! Have them leave their Church for soup? Never! It'll take more mischief than that to make a souper out of an O'Sullivan. Can you believe it? The stupidity of blind bigots who think that men can be bought with a bowlful of broth. Mind you, if the government thought they could get away with it they'd try it. Such is their conceit. I'll wager that Monsieur Soyer will soon be back to his London kitchen with his dripping pans and sauce pots and good riddance to him.'

తన

Kate sat between Robin and Una on the terrace. Beyond them was the Irish Sea. The flagstones were still warm to the touch

after the day's heat. Behind them the sun was about to sink into
the other hemisphere. The sky was orange and its glow spread
across the shimmering surface of the sea like fire across oil.
Beyond the horizon was the Welsh coast and St David's Head
and behind the Welsh mountains were the lowlands of England.
It was not a day's sailing away, but it might just as well have
been on the other side of the world, so foreign did England
now seem to Kate. There were moments when she did not care
whether she ever saw it again, she who had so fiercely resisted
leaving.

She sipped a glass of Sir Robert's elderberry wine. It had been
a sparse but splendid dinner of roast hare. Sir Robert had shot
it that afternoon and cooked it himself. He thought it might be
the last.

'It took father four hours to find that one,' Robin said. 'In the
old days he'd have had him in minutes. There's nothing left out
there. Not a crow in the trees, not a fox in its hole. Every starling
and tom-tit has gone and I don't think I've seen a hedgehog or
a squirrel or even a frog for months. The hungry have finally
cleared this land of life.'

'That is why it's so quiet now,' Una said. 'Haven't you noticed
in the mornings? The only sound is the wind and the rustle in
the trees.'

Robin reached out and held his sister's hand. 'Even the nights
are silent now. Do you remember how terrified we were of the
owls as children? How we were told not to leave the window
open or they would come and tear our eyes out?'

Una laughed. 'And the bats would suck our blood until we
were dry and no bigger than a pumpkin.'

'And banshees were hiding behind the curtains to carry us
away and turn us into frogs.'

Robin and Una had come from the same womb at the same
time, but it was she who had been favoured in the making. She
was plump and round with full cheeks, her skin the complexion

of honey. Her hair was a tangle of chestnut curls, her eyes the colour of amber. She did not use face powder or rouge, nor did she wear a bodice, so her breasts stood full and firm against her blouse.

Her brother was slender, almost frail, and even now, in his mid-twenties, he had the look of a man who was already growing weary. Una told Kate how his health and strength had been taken from him as a little boy. She said that when he was a child he had decided that when he grew up he would become a bishop. He had turned their playroom into a chapel, with a tiny altar and a cross and every morning and evening he made her kneel and they said their prayers together. He was a determined little boy and his future as a man of the cloth seemed assured. Until the day of his conversion.

Una remembered it vividly.

'May I tell it, Robin?' she asked. 'Tell Kate the story?'

Robin nodded. Una began.

'He was ten years old and we were climbing a tree on the estate when he fell and broke his ribs. One pierced his lung and he could not breathe. He was screaming. He was in such pain but I sat helpless, not daring to move him, afraid the rib would dig deeper and tear his heart. Father had ridden off for a doctor and left the priest to pray for him. But it was father's fast horse and the doctor who saved him.'

'I remember the priest crossing himself and praying for my soul,' Robin said. 'But he could not ease my pain, he could not mend my broken bones. All he could offer was a prayer and a promise.'

'And so', Una continued, 'he said he would not become a bishop when he grew up. He would become a doctor instead and our playroom, which had once been a make-believe chapel, became a hospital ward.'

For the first time in her life Kate glimpsed family life, watching, listening to their banter, joining in their laughter. She had

never known what it meant, nor had she ever expected to discover it. Now she had been enveloped by two families, both so
different, and she knew she could love them both just as comfortably. She arranged to stay the night and as she lay in bed, she
wondered how she might join the two together.

She was woken by the sound of gunfire. She opened the
window wider. She counted twenty shots and then the boom of
a distant cannon. She heard Sir Robert shouting in the kitchen
below. She put on her dressing gown and went down. Robin
and Una were there. Sir Robert was still in his nightshirt and
sleeping cap.

'That's forty shots at least,' he said. 'What on earth is
happening?'

'I thought I heard a cannon,' Kate said.

Sir Robert nodded. 'So did we all. And I wish we hadn't.'

'The firing is coming from the harbour,' said Robin.

'From the harbour it is,' said Sir Robert. 'And by God, I think
I can guess what it's all about.'

Within an hour, his agent arrived at the door. Sir Robert had
guessed correctly. Crowds in Youghal had plundered the shops
and marched on the ships anchored in the harbour, ships about
to sail with their cargoes of Irish wheat and oats, bound for
Liverpool. The magistrate had sent troops to stop them crossing the River Bride at Youghal Bridge, but they had pushed past,
shouting that it was a sin for Irish food to be sent abroad to
England. Women had held their babies to the soldiers and bared
their breasts to show they had no milk.

'But the shots?' Sir Robert asked. 'The cannons?'

'It's Dungarvan, sir,' said the agent. 'Things are worse there.
They say that a thousand or more have marched on the town.
They charged through the line of soldiers and crossed the bridge
to the quayside. The first volley of grapeshot killed a dozen but it
didn't stop them. Before the ship's crews could cut the mooring
lines, the leaders were aboard, pulling off the sacks of grain and

heaving them ashore. Then the soldiers let go their second volley and there was nowhere to hide. Many fell overboard and were taken by the tide out to sea. When it was all over, the dead were thrown on the carts and taken to the lime pits.'

'It was long happening,' Sir Robert said. 'But I knew it had to. Youghal, Dungarvan. What next? You mark my words. There'll not be a ship that's safe. The government will have to send warships to escort them out and put a Redcoat in every field that's being harvested. The people won't put up with this any longer and who can blame them?'

Sir Robert was as close to his tenants as any landlord could be. He knew their grievances and the limit of their patience.

'The government was so sure that people would sit tamely by until the potato was ready again and maybe they would have done if there had been some work and a little money. But there's been precious little of either and when you grow thinner and hungrier and see the ships taking food away, what is a man expected to do?'

He rose and brought the heavy kettle from the cooking range and refilled the teapot.

'Is it any wonder the English consider the Irish so stupid? And is it surprising these poor people should need to do such desperate things to prove they are not?'

'I was told of something yesterday by one of the Quakers,' Una said. 'Something so desperate it made me cry. It was in a village at Tallow just below Lismore. They visited a young lady who was said to be alone and desolate. They say she could not have been older than twenty and very pretty. She came from Dublin, from a family of business people, but they had all broken up and deserted her. She was living in a small cottage on her own and when she knew the Quakers were visiting she had hurriedly made it trim and proper. She put on such a show of genteel respectability and laid out her table with little items of crockery and ornaments she had brought with her from Dublin.

She did her best to hide her worn dress with an apron and a silk scarf. They brought her a little bread but she refused it, saying it should go to the poor and yet she was herself starving. Such pride. Such sad, helpless, gentle pride.'

Robin nodded. 'It is the same with them all, Una, young and old. I heard of a fisherman's widow who walked twenty miles to the coast, pushing a hand cart with two planks of wood in it so she could give her dead husband a decent burial. He had drowned in a storm and was washed ashore at Curragh. She eventually found what was left of him, carried his body to higher ground and dug a grave with her bare hands. She put his body between the two planks and bound them together with rope. That was his coffin, the best she could do. But she would have been satisfied he'd had a proper Christian burial. Pride by another name. And proper.'

ೲ

For the first time in over two months, clouds covered the sky. Thin long fingers of sunlight poked their way through but then quickly disappeared as if God had clenched His fist. A chill sea breeze rushed in and shook the trees that had been still for so long. Kate tasted salt on her lips and waited for rain. But the clouds burst a long way out and thunder was only a soft rumble. Then came a perfect rainbow, a thick arc spanning half the horizon, each of its seven colours pure and vivid. Its beauty mocked the drama of the day.

Sir Robert and Robin had gone to Dungarvan to discover if any of their tenants were among the dead and wounded. Una had instructions to keep the gates locked and leave the loaded shotgun ready on the kitchen table.

The girls sat side by side on a bench in the garden beneath one of the old oaks. There had not been a gardener in the grounds for over ten years and much of it had now returned to nature's own indiscipline. The grass around them was long with scattered clusters of cornflowers, rosebay willowherbs and daisies and, beyond the lawns, creeping carpets of nettles. There was a mass of scarlet poppies where once there had been peonies, creeping ivy where there had been rose beds and a great sprawl of pink and white rhododendrons bending under the weight of a thickening canopy of bramble. Only the stone statues of the Connemara Bacchus and his sprawling maidens at the front of the house reminded a visitor of how splendid the house had once been.

'Why is the house called "Salvation"?' Kate asked. 'Was your father's family religious?'

'They bowed their head and paid their dues and kept the clergy in liquor. At least that's how father describes them. He has no time for either Church. He thinks the Catholics are servile worshippers and their priests dreadful bullies. I've heard terrible stories about them, especially what they do to …'

'I don't want to hear,' Kate interrupted. 'Not on a beautiful day like this. Tell me about the house. Why Salvation?'

'It was built by an Englishman, about a hundred years ago, we think. He meant to settle here and breed horses but it was the Irish weather that defeated him. Some scoundrel selling him the land must have told him our summers were always dry and warm. But when the winds turned in autumn and it rained until the next March, he packed his bags, went straight back home to England and never returned. The house stood empty for another twenty years and became the home of bats and crows and a succession of tinkers who tore the place apart. But then came the wonderful part. A sailing ship on its way to Cork was caught in a storm, blown inshore and floundered on Clonard Rock. All forty crew aboard were drowned except for one man. He was washed up on the beach and his name was Sir Walter Fitzgerald, a wealthy landowner from Country Antrim. The story goes that as he lay on the sand and raised his eyes to heaven to thank

God for his salvation, he saw this house beyond the cliffs. At that moment, he vowed he would settle on this parcel of land that had saved his life.'

'And so he did?' asked Kate.

'And so he did. With his wealth and energy he restored the house and named it Salvation and every morning, whatever the season, he would go from his bed to the balcony and bow respectfully to the sea that had so very nearly taken him.'

'It's a wonderful story, Una.'

'But that's not the end of it. When Sir Walter, my great-grand-father, died content in his old age, he left the estate to his eldest son. But he was a wastrel and cared nothing for the house or his father's love of it. Soon he mortgaged it to pay for his gambling debts and his drinking and whoring. The house went to ruin, and the parkland returned to a jungle. He died on his thirty-fifth birthday from a liver destroyed by gin and a variety of other ailments given to him by those he chose to live with. Then my grandfather inherited it and began its restoration all over again, all the time struggling to pay off the debts. Now my father carries on that same struggle. But every year he grows more weary and poorer. Like Ireland itself.'

'It must have been so beautiful,' Kate said. Una plucked a blade of grass and chewed its juicy stem.

'When I was a little girl,' Una said, 'one tiny stray weed would have caused a commotion and given the head gardener a fit. But it is not easy to worry about weed-free gravel, topiary and the symmetry of the lawns when people are so wretched beyond the hedges. I don't think a pretty garden would ever occupy my time again. If I ever had one, and I doubt that very much, I should let it grow like this, free and full of itself. Only the English seem to care so much for gardens.'

'Perhaps we have nothing more important to worry about,' Kate said.

Una laughed, in her loud, unaffected way.

'No,' she said, 'you mustn't ridicule your own people that way. The English have done many fine and wonderful things in this world. But father says the moment the name 'Ireland' is mentioned, they bid goodbye to their humanity and common sense. He says they act like tyrants towards the Irish.'

'I've heard my father say that whatever's good for England is bad for Ireland and vice-versa,' Kate said.

'But I remember my father once saying that if more of the world was English, it would be a better place.'

'I don't suppose he believes that now,' Kate said.

'I think he still half believes it. We are still a part of the Empire, even if we are forgotten.'

'How odd you should say that,' Kate said. 'Somebody once said that to me— ' She stopped and looked away.

'Go on, Kate,' said Una, laughing. 'Who was he? Your lover. Tell me he was your lover.'

Kate took Una's hand. 'No!' she said. 'Not my lover. He was someone I was very fond of. I didn't love him, not as you might expect. Had he lived he would have been more like a brother.'

'Tell me.'

'To tell you a little of it would not be enough and to tell you more might be unwise.'

'You make it sound very serious, Kate.'

'It is. Or rather, it was.'

'Kate, we are friends,' said Una, 'You can trust me. Do trust me. Share it with me. We can become allies.'

They had been Shelley's same words on the day he left Cork, the last time Kate saw him. Her reservations about confiding in Una faded with those words.

They sat in the shade of the oak on that hot summer morning and Kate told of her conspiracy with a young English captain who had become a traitor in Ireland's cause, of Edward Ogilvie and his bullwhip, of Eugene and his encyclopaedia and finally of Keegan's little schoolroom. When Kate had finished her telling, she and Una hugged each other and it was agreed: they would ride to Kinsale together and there Kate would introduce Keegan and his class to her new friend and ally.

CHAPTER EIGHT

The first spikes of the morning sun caught every colour of the convoy: the riders' uniforms of green and blue, yellow and scarlet, their helmets and the swords in their scabbards, the flashing polished brass of the horses' harnesses, the rifles of the infantry.

The line of wagons was the longest yet to leave Cork Harbour, thirty of them piled high with grain, the pulling teams pounding at the ground, the crack of whips over their heads and the shouts of the wagon masters urging them on. People lined the roads to watch them pass but no one cheered. Who could applaud such a precious cargo that was on its way to somewhere else? How could they believe there were others hungrier than themselves?

Kate saddled her mare and watched the column until it was out of sight. As she left the stable yard, Dr Martineau came from the house and stood in her way.

'These are dangerous times, Miss Kathryn,' he said in his soft and silky way. 'Is it wise to leave Cork?'

'I have left it too often to wonder now whether it is wise or not,' she replied coldly.

'Indeed you have,' he said coming closer. He held the bridle as she mounted.

'And I know the road so well, Dr Martineau, that I shall not need your escort to follow me today.'

'Dear me, Miss Kathryn! I'm surprised that you should take offence at what is only my concern for your safety …'

'An escort with a spyglass?' she interrupted him.

'Indeed. With a spyglass and a pistol too, which he has orders to use without hesitation should there be any risk to your safety. I wonder that you protest so much.'

'I shall tell my father you have me followed.'

'As you wish.' He ran his hand along the mare's neck. 'I can only hope he will not press me for details of your little excursions, innocent though they may be. It might worry him nevertheless.'

She wanted to bring her whip across his smiling face. Angrily, she pulled hard on the reins and, with a kick of her heels, she cantered away out of the yard and onto the track that led up the road to Kinsale. A minute later the cobbles echoed again as a rider in a black cloak followed, a spyglass and a pistol in his pockets.

The rendezvous had been arranged. She was to meet Una Fitzgerald by the ferry at Glanmire and from there they would ride together the twenty miles to Kinsale and meet with Keegan and the children.

The sun was already warm and at Ballygarvan they stopped to water their horses. Una had brought a basket of her father's oat-cakes and a small flagon of his homemade ginger beer. They sat by a stream and ate breakfast.

'Una, I've asked this of so many others but let me ask you too. Why have the Irish always been so dependent on the potato? Why don't they grow wheat? Why don't they bake bread?'

Una reached out, touched the tips of Kate's fingers and began the rhyme: 'Tinker, tailor, soldier, sailor, rich man … Kate, I'm running out of fingers. You'll marry a beggar man.'

'Una, don't play. Answer me.'

Una rolled on her back. 'Kate, you'll not see bread baked any-where from Valencia to Malin Head. An oven is unheard of in any village in the whole of Ireland. There's scarcely a woman among them who knows how to cook anything but a boiled potato.'

'But they could be taught.'

'And what would they bake?'

'Bread, of course.'

'And you bake bread with …?'

'With flour, of course. What else?'

'And where would they get their flour?'

'Una, you're teasing me.'

'No, Kate! It's just that you assume too much. How can they afford to buy flour when they can barely find the money for their seed potatoes? If they have enough land to sow wheat or barley or oats, it is to sell to pay their rents. They can't afford to eat them. They call the potato the lazy crop but what else can a poor man grow to keep his family alive? All he needs is a quarter acre, a spade and a pocketful of faith.'

'I'm sorry, Una. You must think me stupid but I know so little of the Irish. When I was in England I thought of you all as foreign. Now I am the foreigner and I'm struggling to understand. Why are there so many extremes here? Kindness and hatred all in the same mix.'

Kate waited for her to answer. Una ate the last of her cake and blew away the crumbs. A small bird, yellow and blue, hovered and dropped into the long grass in search of them. Una turned and lay on her stomach.

'I was born among these people, Kate. All I can ever remember is their fun. They were famous for it. They would help build each other's cottages, all coming together, the women and children too, gathering the wood and the stones and the thatch. The tenant brought the food and there was always a lot of drink. If he could afford it, he'd have music and as long as it was light they would work to the fiddler's tunes. There was always a song then, always singing, whatever the reason. A child was born, a girl was married, an old man buried. There was a fiddler at every wake and sometimes even a piper. They would have poteen and whiskey and tobacco for the men, talk for the women. There was such kindness. They would never close a door on a stranger. There'd be a plate of potatoes for him, a jug of buttermilk and a stool for conversation. But it's all gone and how I miss it! I wonder if it will ever come back.'

Una stood and brushed off the grass. 'Come, Kate. It is time to meet your lovely schoolteacher. Let's be off. We'll go the pretty way.'

The wicker basket, hidden in the long grass, was forgotten. Who would stumble on it? Who would find the few oatcakes and a little of the ginger beer inside and thank the Lord for His many miracles?

ာ၁

'As sure as God made them, He matched them.' They were Tom Keegan's words and Kate would always remember them. The old man had come to the schoolroom that morning because his son was afraid he could not cope on his own with Una's arrival. He would instead rely on his father, with his flow of easy words and warm ways, to charm her. Old Tom would take the awkward stiffness out of it all.

Young Keegan had woken early and had fussed every minute thereafter. He was on his hands and knees, scrubbing the school-room floor a second time even before the sun rose. He had tramped the hillside, picking the tallest fern fronds which he had placed in stone jugs in the four corners of the room. The fire was burning in the hearth, water for tea was simmering in the kettle that hung from the hook above it and peat was neatly stacked by the door. The children's slates and sticks of chalk were placed in a row along the bench, in line and exactly spaced, like toy soldiers on parade.

Keegan was worrying that there was still more to be done when he heard the sound of the riders arriving. Old Tom was first out the door to greet them. He grabbed hold of Una's bridle.

'*Céad fáilte romhat. Go mbeannaí Dia thú agus fáilte romhat. Is mór an onóir domsa agus do na leanaí tú a theacht inár láthair. Cuireann sé áthas an domhain orainn.*'

'Father, father!' Keegan shouted above the old man's greetings. 'Have you forgotten? When Kate is here we speak English?'

'Oh! Dearie dear. A hundred apologies!' The old man repeated it twice over. 'Forgive me, Kate. We are a little flustered at the sight of you both. It's the expecting that's done it. But you're welcome. You are so welcome.'

He helped Una from her saddle, bowed and shook her hand. 'I am the father of this young schoolmaster you've come to meet. We are honoured to have you here. We have tea brewing and we shall have some talk. The children will be coming soon and there'll be little time for chat when they do.'

Keegan had barely slept all week, worrying about the words he must find and the ways of saying them to the daughter of Sir Robert Fitzgerald. Would she be as Kate had been to him at their first meeting? He thought not. Then Eugene and his wounds had been the bridge between them. The drama of that day had been the reason for them coming together and it had held them as friends since. The prospect of meeting Una had unsettled a normally confident Keegan. It had occupied him and irritated him. But that morning, to his surprise, he and Una did not meet as strangers meet.

The children arrived together. Eight of them had brought a penny. They paid it to Keegan once a week for their schooling. There were times when some did not, and they brought sods of peat instead. Eugene was first at the schoolroom door. Kate introduced him to Una. He shook her hand and showed her his book of Irish poems, translated and carefully written in English with a quill and blackberry ink. The other children followed and those who had shoes took them off and left them outside.

Keegan, in his worrisome planning for this special day, had given their mothers fifteen pence to search the market for food to cook for him. At ten o'clock, they left the steaming covered pots by the door. It was time for breakfast.

Old Tom arranged the seating. The four sat in a circle on the floor, surrounded by the children. The children closed their eyes and clasped their hands as the old man said prayers. The potatoes were hot and they danced them from hand to hand as they skinned them. Then Tom mashed them in a bowl filled with buttermilk and nuggets of coarse salt.

'Now, ladies, gentlemen and little folk,' he said as if he was addressing an association dinner. 'We have an Irish speciality known only to those who can afford nothing else. It's our boxy: mashed-up turnips with fern leaves and dandelion. I see the mothers have done us a favour and added a sprig of mint so we'll have a banquet! Now God bless us, every one of us.' The children crossed themselves and mouthed their amens.

Keegan had indeed been wise to have his father attend. He could never have managed the morning on his own. The old man turned breakfast into a party with his talk and tales of Jack-o'-Lantern, the banshees and the mysteries deep within the fields of fairies. The children sat and listened to him, entranced and as still as statues.

'Father,' Keegan said, laughing, 'enough of your banshees and Jack-o'-Lanterns. It's all nonsense, you're dumping rubbish into this classroom of mine. This is a place of learning.'

'Nonsense, is it?' the old man replied, attempting a scowl. 'Are you asking for a *pishogue*?'

'What is that?' Kate asked.

'It's a curse and the worst one,' the old man said. 'You can be cursed by a fairy or a saint. The Irish saints are forever putting curses on people and no county is more cursed by them than Cork, though Limerick might compete. We're full of our silly stories and Irish bellies would be emptier still if we didn't have them.'

'Do we have time for one of them?' asked Kate.

The old man laughed. 'If I tell you one, I'll tell you a dozen.'

'Start with one, then.'

'Well, let me think and, son, you will put it into Irish for the children?' He scratched his head and winked at Kate. He loved an audience and none had ever been as lovely as this. The children quietly pushed their way closer. The old man was going to tell them a story. No one had ever sat with them like this and they had never known such a thing as a story.

The old man began and his son, sitting beside him, whispered the translation.

'There was once a poor man who worked hard all day. But he couldn't sleep at night because he had no bed. He had to sleep on the cold stones and that made his bones ache. He couldn't even afford to buy straw to sleep on because he had to give it all to his donkey. You see, if his donkey couldn't sleep, it wouldn't work. And if it did not work and pull the cart then the man would starve. But his bones ached so much that one day he built himself a cot. Then he put legs on it to raise himself off the cold ground. That night he was warm and he slept well. But when he woke he found his donkey dead. He reckoned the saints had put a curse on him for impudently raising himself above his station. So he buried his donkey and burnt the cot.'

'Poor donkey,' Una said and wiped her eyes in mock sorrow.

'Poor donkey,' the children shouted in a chorus, repeating it in English.

'I bet you haven't heard of the headless horseman of Limerick?' the old man said.

'Is it right for the children?' Keegan asked.

'They'll have seen worse themselves,' Tom replied.

Una put her arms around the children either side of her. Kate did the same. Keegan poured more tea. Tom began: 'There was once a coachman on his way to Limerick. The city was under siege by the Dutch and the coachman gave them information about where the Irish defenders were hidden for a reward. All but one of them were killed and when the survivor reached the city he told them of the treachery. When they caught the coachman, they cut off his head and stuck it on a pike on Thomond Gate. Then, on Halloween night, the feast of the dead, they threw the head into the Shannon and cursed his spirit, so it would ride around the city forever. But then the good people of Limerick asked the fairy king, Rí na Sideog, to be lenient. If the coachman ever found his head as he rode his rounds, he would be forgiven.'

'And did he find it?' Kate asked.

'No one knows,' the old man answered. 'Nobody's ever dared to look because if you see him, you are cursed to ride with him too.'

The children were not frightened by it. They laughed as old Tom moaned like a ghost and held his head in his hands. He looked about him for applause. He saw his son was at ease and he was pleased. He waited for the moment.

'Young Keegan,' he said. 'The horses will be needing some water and grass. Be a good man and look to them.'

Keegan rose and went to the door.

'And maybe,' his father continued. 'Miss Una might like to see a little of the valley. You have the time.'

When they had gone, Kate took the old man's hand.

'Are you the cunning matchmaker, Tom?' she asked.

'Just a little bit of mischief,' he said, smiling. 'My boy's a shy one but I've been looking at him. Did you see his face? The way he looks at her? All he needs is a bit of a shove.'

They rode from the village a little after midday and Kate knew Una would soon be returning to it. Old Tom's last words echoed – the ones he had whispered to her as they left: 'As sure as God made them, He matched them.'

Kate stopped on the ridge overlooking the village, so that Una could see the view for herself.

The air was suddenly still. There was no rustle of a breeze as it turned the grass. No leaf moved. No birds sang. It was a strange silence.

'What is it, Una?' Kate asked.

'I don't know. Maybe summer's on the turn early.'

'Keegan said we mustn't have rain before September.'

જ

They were a half an hour's ride from Cork when they saw them in the distance. They could not count how many because they were spread so wide, like a battalion of infantrymen. But they were not soldiers. Una halted.

'We should go another way,' she said.

'Is something wrong?'

'I don't think it's wise to get too close to them. I've seen men on the march like this before. They're looking for food and work and it's best not to confront them. They can be frightening.'

They turned and cantered away until they came to a narrow gorge. Kate knew it well. It would lead them across country in a wide semicircle beyond Ballinaboy and back onto the Cork road. They would be well away from the threat of the men.

The gorge that split two hills and they were only halfway through it when they were suddenly surrounded by gangs of men running down the steep slopes either side. Rough hands caught their bridles.

'Get off your horses and empty your purses,' the leader shouted. 'Now, before we do it our way.'

He was a large man, tall and big-boned, but the skin around his neck hung in loose folds and his eyes were sunk in shadow. He held his fist to Kate's face and she saw the bare wrist was covered in sores and scabs.

'Do as we say!' he shouted again. 'And we might let you walk home, the way we have walked all the way from Skibbereen and Baltimore. Now give us what we want and if we cannot sell your horses, by God, we'll eat them.'

The men roared their approval but none moved to pull the girls down. The leader coughed and spat and Kate saw blood in his spittle.

'If I give you money,' Kate said, 'will you promise to let us through?'

She saw the hatred in his eyes. 'I don't have to promise you a damned thing, missy. We have been promised food from the depots and work on the roads and we are still looking for it.'

He grabbed her stirrup and as she lashed out with her whip, he shouted, 'At them, boys, and do what you bloody well like. But for Christ's sake don't let the horses go!'

Then the rock above his head exploded and tiny splinters hit him in the neck and head. Blood trickled into his eyes and he fell to his knees. They heard a voice above him.

'Fall away, Gleeson. Your men, too. I'll aim better the second time.'

Three horsemen side-stepped their way down the hill. The leading man held a pistol. Cloths covered half their faces but Kate knew the man who had fired the shot. He was the same rider who had come with Moran on Fivemilebridge, the day he had brought the news that Shelley had been killed. There was no mistaking his eyes. He looked at her and nodded. He might have been smiling, mocking.

'Perhaps you didn't expect your day to turn out to be so dangerous, Miss Macaulay,' he said. 'But haven't I already warned you to stay out of our affairs and keep yourself safe in Cork?'

She pulled on her reins. 'Riding from Kinsale to Cork is no affair of yours and God forbid it ever will be. We shall ride where we like and when we like.'

'Which is obviously not true, not when there are men like Gleeson in your way. And I warn you that he has a more gentle nature than some you are liable to meet. Ireland has become a land of hungry men and hunger makes them a different sort. So take heed of what I say and stay in your father's house. You too, Miss Fitzgerald. I know of your father and your brother and I've much respect for them both but I wouldn't be doing them any favours letting you gallivant around the countryside in times like this.'

He kicked his horse and came closer to Kate.

'We've come from Cork and we have seen the ships there full to the gunwales with food. Your father is pleased with himself, least so I'm told. But he's a fool if he thinks any of it will find its way into Gleeson's belly or any man here, because they haven't the money to buy it. Ships are leaving full of Irish grain and meat, off to feed foreigners while Irishmen here starve. You ask your father the justice of that. These men have followed the shoreline all the way here, eating seaweed to stay alive. The beaches are bare from here to Cape Clear. Isn't that right, Gleeson?'

The big man struggled to his feet and nodded, holding his head. Blood trickled through his fingers.

The masked rider continued. 'You tell your father, Miss Macaulay, that there's worse to come, much worse, and it's not far off, not a day's ride away. Tell him that.'

'Now may we pass?' Kate said defiantly, as if she had not listened to a word. She saw him stiffen.

He backed his horse away. 'Yes. Go! But I cannot promise to rescue you a second time.'

'I cannot say I want you to,' she replied.

'You are a very cocky young woman!'

'And you are a very impudent young man.'

His eyes were fixed on her, unblinking, grey-green, almost translucent. He paused and said nothing. Then, 'Let them pass. And I'll blow the hand off any man who touches them.'

The men parted, leaving a narrow corridor for them to ride through. Kate turned in her saddle and looked down at Gleeson. She took the silk scarf from around her neck and gave it to him. 'Wrap it tight and it will stop the bleeding.' She took her purse from the saddle bag and dropped it into his bloodied hands. He clasped it tight but he did not look up.

They rode off and put five miles between themselves and the gorge before they stopped. Kate waited for her pulse to slacken and the throbbing in her head to stop.

'Who are they, Una? How can they ride about the country masked and armed like that?'

Una shook her head. 'He said it was none of your business and he is right. It is not.'

'It is my business,' Kate said. 'I'm certain he is the man who was with Moran when he told me Shelley was killed. He knows who's to blame. You must tell me.'

Una hesitated. 'He's known as 'the Rebel' but he has another name.'

'What is it then?'

'Coburn, Daniel Coburn. He is the leader of the Young Irelanders. Once they followed O'Connell but they left him because they thought he was too old, too sick, too patient. Coburn is different, full of talk about freeing Ireland from the English, full of threats. He has many supporters and there are rumours that they are arming themselves. My father says it's only talk and maybe that's all it will ever be.'

'What will happen if the government catches him?'

'They will hang him. Which is a shame.'

Kate thought of the soft voice behind the mask and the grey-green eyes and said nothing.

They cantered on following the river's bends as far as the crossroads near Sligga Bridge. Then they climbed the shallow rise of a hill until they came to its brow. Here again the air was cold and still, as if all of nature's sounds had been silenced. The horses kicked the ground. The entire valley below was covered in a thick white mist and, as they watched, it rose before them until even the sky was hidden. And from it came a smell, the evil, sickly stench of corruption.

'Dear God,' Una whispered. 'Oh! God save us.'

'What is it, Una? What's happening? What is it?'

'Listen,' she said. 'Can't you hear them crying? Women and men too, down there, inside it. Smell it. Smell it, Kate. It's what

Coburn meant. He said there was worse to come. He must have seen it already.'

'What, Una? What did he see? Tell me.'

Out of the blanket of white came an old woman, her apron covering her head, wandering blindly and wailing. Una turned to Kate and there was fear in her eyes.

'It's the blight, Kate. It has come back. God help us! The potatoes are dead.'

CHAPTER NINE

Dr Martineau was an obsessively punctual man. For any agreed appointment he would neither be early nor late and it was his fashion to quicken his pace or dawdle in order to arrive exactly on time. For him, punctuality was next to godliness and cleanliness in the neat and disciplined order of his day's routine. Which was why, that morning, Sir William was puzzled by his lateness. It was past eight o'clock. Precisely on the stroke of the hour, he would have expected to hear the soft knock on his door that had so regularly announced the doctor's arrival.

By nine o'clock Sir William was anxious. By ten o'clock he was in a state of mild panic, such was his dependence on the cleric to lend order to his day. Messengers were sent to the doctor's house and they returned without him. They said his housekeeper had not seen him since the previous evening. Sir William alerted the constabulary and waited, expecting the worst.

It came shortly after midday. Dr Martineau had been found in the woods at Glanmire, some distance from Sir William's house, hanging from an oak by Sunday's Well. His clothes had been stripped from him, his naked body was still warm and green ribbons hung from his feet. Pinned to his chest was a piece of paper and on it the scrawled name, 'Shelley'.

∞

Storms wracked Ireland from coast to coast. It was as if Nature herself had joined Ireland's enemies. The wind froze the rain that hit the ground as sleet. It grazed the hands and bit the face.

It ripped up the stalks and shredded the plants that lay rotting on the long beds. The people watched and wept, drenched in despair.

The potato fields were as black as if they had been covered in tar. Families were deep in mud, pulling the mounds apart on their knees. They found nothing but stinking pulp. Women clawed their breasts and wept. Their men roared curses at the sky, threw themselves down and beat the ground with their fists.

What did it matter? Soon they would feel nothing. Not the wind, not the lash of rain, not the salt in their tears. What was there now to care about? Their sacred plots were lakes of decay, their hidden store of food diseased. Soon it would be the winter of dying. Habit and hope. Hope and habit. They fingered the beads of their rosaries and mouthed their Hail Marys.

The summer of great promise had given way to the autumn of dread. There was not a green potato field to be seen and in no man's memory, nor in any of the stories that spanned grandfather to grandson, had there been such devastation and disbelief. And why? Had they not danced to the piper on the Eve of St John, confident of the coming harvest and the promise of a bursting crop? Had they not, as custom bid, lit their bonfires and carried hot coals along the boundaries of their fields to frighten off the evil spirits that would poison the ground? Yet the death spot was now spread across the leaves, brown and shrivelled, the last of their goodness sucked out.

'It is God's hand that is painting them dead,' they wailed, 'a biblical pestilence.' 'No!' said the others. 'It is the Devil's finger-marks!' Did it matter who was to blame? It was done and no miracle would undo it. For a second winter, the hungry would beg for charity and there would be precious little of that.

Soon a great silence, like the plague itself, spread across the country. Women stopped their complaining and men their cursing and children played no more. No dogs barked, no cocks crowed to start the day and no crows signalled its end. Hungry days became hungry weeks and they became months of famine. The lanes were black with silent funerals but no crooners followed the carts to recite lullabies for the dead. They were dropped into their graves without inquests or coffins, their deaths unrecorded, their stories untold. Hunger denied death its sorrow.

Panic travelled faster than the blight. People took to the roads as rumours spread. Was it true the government had opened its depot in Wexford and was giving away food? Was the Board of Works paying a shilling a day for labour on a new road in Kilkenny? Was there talk of a soup kitchen in Tralee serving free broth? Who could risk being left behind?

So many were on the roads. The whole country was in motion, the hungry following their noses on a journey that led them nowhere. There was no work or food in any direction and the doors of hope, like doors everywhere, had shut tight for the poor.

Five thousand beggars roamed the streets of Cork. They squatted by the workhouse gates waiting for the death cart to leave, ready to fight for the vacancy. They crouched by the bakers' shops where the walls, warmed by the ovens, kept them from freezing to death. Such was the stench of death that fires were lit to purify the air. Dublin gentlemen went about their business in their curtained liveried coaches, turning their heads away from the beggar's bowl and the misery congesting the streets. Yet there was not a tree-lined square, not a sweep of terraces, not an alley or gutter that was not massed with the helpless hungry. They stood by the railings of the great houses, waiting like starlings for the cook to throw scraps to them. They peered at the windows of the prosperous, saw the roaring fires in their hearths and the bright chandeliers in their splendid drawing rooms and they knew what they had always suspected. God belonged to the rich.

The fierce winds from the east had turned the season around. The grey skies dropped low and heavy and in that first week of December, the snow blizzards put an end to people's wanderings. With a bellyful of potato mash and a sup of warm buttermilk a man could trot off to the North Pole and come back smiling. But when the buckle of his belt is scraping his spine and frost has cracked his lips, he can only reflect on his own absurdity, look for a space to settle and await his time.

The horrors were now being reported by those who could no longer turn their heads away from them. Crown servants, magistrates, priests, land agents, sea captains and even the Relief Commission's own inspectors.

At a farm near Michelstown, County Cork, a land agent found a woman and her two children dead from starvation and half eaten by dogs. At Kenmare in Kerry, the priest had kicked open a door and found a man barely alive, lying on the bed with his dead wife and five children, rats eating an infant.

In Mayo, a man named John Connelly had been charged with theft. He pleaded with the magistrates for mercy. He said he had stolen bread to keep his family alive. They had been so hungry, he had cut off the flesh from the leg of his dead son to feed them. The plea seemed so outrageous that the magistrates ordered the boy's body to be exhumed. And Connelly had been telling no lie.

Commander Caffyn of Her Majesty's steamship sloop *Scourge* had sailed to the port of Schull to discharge a cargo of meal, a gift from the Quakers. He wrote in his log that in the town of eighteen thousand inhabitants, more than three quarters of them were walking skeletons and they had once been prosperous people. He wrote that a mass of bodies had been buried without coffins and lay only inches below the soil as the ground was too hard to dig and the people too weak to try. Bodies were being eaten by roaming dogs. He had shot two dogs. He ended:

There were more dogs than I had ammunition and so I was forced to leave them to their meals. I have been to many corners of this earth and seen much suffering and wretchedness among its many peoples. But never in my whole life have I seen such wholesale misery as this nor, God help me, may I ever be obliged to witness it again.

In the Killeries at Westport, County Mayo, a Revenue cutter, having just loaded sacks of corn, nearly capsized in port with the weight of the starving people who clambered aboard, scratching the decks in search of loose grain. The captain was forced to order his crew to throw them overboard – men, women and children – for fear his boat would turn turtle and be lost. He wrote:

Some of the starving wretches were strong enough to reach the shore but some, still alive, were too weak and drifted out to sea. What was I to do? Tell me, how do I face my Maker when my time comes?

Nicholas Cummins, a respected magistrate in Cork, sent a letter to the Duke of Wellington and to *The Times of London*, pleading for help.

I write this as an example of what is happening along the entire line of this southern coast. I went to Skibbereen and being aware that I should have to witness scenes of frightful hunger, I provided myself with as much bread as five men could carry. I entered hovels. In the first, six famished and ghastly skeletons, to all appearances dead. I approached with horror and found they were alive, four children, a woman and what had once been a man. Within a few minutes I was surrounded by hundreds of such phantoms, such frightful spectres as no words can describe. No man should be obliged to witness this. What man who sanctions it can face his Maker?

All these reports, one by one, found their way to the desk of Sir William Macaulay, representing a catalogue of horrors that Ireland, in all its centuries of suffering, had never known before. He sat fingering two letters he had just received, one from Whitehall, the other from Captain Wynne, one of the Commission's own officers at Ennis in County Clare.

He placed the letters side by side and, after a long pause and for the first time since his arrival in Ireland, there were tears in his eyes, tears of pity, tears of anger, tears of shame and disgust. Captain Wynne had written:

Sir, the people are starving here, as yet peaceably. The snow is deep, the roads, such as they are, are blocked and no one has seen food for a month and more, not a single shred. I do not know how they survive. I do not know how much longer they will.

Today I went through the parish and although I consider myself not a man easily moved, I am not a match for this. Women and children are in the turnip fields, crowds of them, scattered like a flock of crows, clawing at the frozen ground with their bare hands, fighting each other, even each other's children, so as to feed their own. And in silence, such silence as to make a man believe he is watching phantoms in a dream. Sir, they are too exhausted even to make a noise. That terrible, terrible silence, I shall never forget. No pen of mine can adequately describe it. For pity's sake, help them.

Then Sir William picked up that morning's communiqué from Sir Charles Trevelyan and read it out loud as he had a dozen times already:

The tide of Irish distress seems now to have overflowed the barriers we opposed to it. You may ask what more we can do. I suggest we cannot do more. The rest we must leave to God. The lamentable loss of life among the Irish lower classes and the impotent poor is to be regretted but we must not forget there are principles to be kept in view. If food is scarce, then a smaller quantity must be made to last longer. Harsh as it may seem to some, I must insist that their misery and distress run their course.

Sir William wiped his eyes with a handkerchief. That week he had buried Martineau and, with him gone, impotence and despair were coursing through him. He left his desk and did what he was now in the habit of doing often. He went to the drinks cabinet and poured himself a large tumbler of whiskey and then another and swallowed them both in one gulp. He would have another one or two at lunchtime and another two or three at dinner before his claret and his port. How else, he asked himself out loud, was he expected to cope?

He felt betrayed, degraded. What was it he had been promised two years ago standing in Trevelyan's Whitehall office? A short stay in Ireland, home by late summer, a brief excursion to this foreign land to sort out and settle an aggravating problem, the shortage of potatoes. How very minor it had seemed to him then, how trivial, how temporary, such a lesser thing in a lifetime spent witnessing great events. Was he not the senior commissariat officer at Waterloo, personally commended by Wellington himself? Had he not fought the Boers with Baden-Powell and, against all the odds, helped keep Mafeking alive? Had he not knelt before Queen Victoria and felt her sword on his shoulder as he was knighted for his services to her Empire?

He felt heavy with the exhaustion that comes with defeat, for he knew he was close to losing. His drinking provided hours of respite, long evenings of drunken oblivion. But with the dawn, he woke to utter despair. Without Martineau's punctuality and discipline, he now slept longer in his bed. One morning he summoned his clerk to his bedroom and dictated a short letter to Trevelyan.

Sir, I am exhausted. I feel there is a fever upon me. I cannot write more as I am an invalid today and intend to remain quiet for some time yet to regain my health.

Within a week, Sir William received his master's curt reply:

I am somewhat alarmed, indeed aggravated, to have received your note. I hope to hear tomorrow that you have got rid of your indisposition. We have no time to be ill nowadays.

The following month, August 1847, Trevelyan, citing tiredness from overwork, went on holiday with his wife and son, to France.

∾

Tom Keegan was saddened and disappointed with himself. He had always been a faithful Catholic and in all his eighty-four years he had never once forgotten his prayers at the start and end of each day. He had always tried to think good thoughts and on occasions when he failed, every bad thought was followed by a brief Hail Mary and every curse by a solemn Novena. He had never questioned his faith, not even on the day God took away his wife and gave him a son in her place. God had been his companion as well as his master in an otherwise lonely life and if He had chosen to ignore the old man's requests, as He did more often than not, then that was the Almighty's prerogative. He was comforted by the Holy Pledge, that when a good man dies there is a place for him in heaven. He would reflect that if life with God had not always been easy, how much more dreadful might it have been without Him?

He held his hands over his eyes to shield them from the rain. He could see only a yard or so in front of him as he stumbled in the mud, feeling for the path with his toes, touching familiar corners of rock, which served to guide him.

'God is salvation!' He shouted it to the wind and again to the black sky as the sharp rods of rain stung his eyes. 'God is salvation!' He shouted it again and again as he struggled up the mountain's slippery slope.

That morning, while he was working in his garden, talking to his plants as if they were a class of schoolchildren, a stranger had come by. He could not see who it was and he did not recognise the voice, for it was no one local. But the man told him that the blight was coming from over the hills and that some fields in Cork and Kerry were already black. 'Get your praties out of the ground,' he had said. 'Get them out while the air is still fresh, for tomorrow you will smell it coming and the next day it will be too late.'

Although Tom Keegan did not know the voice, he believed its warning, for if a stranger brings bad news, it is seldom wrong. So he left his herb patch, brought a basket from the kitchen and went down on his knees to dig away the soft earth with his hands and pull the little tubers from their mother stems. He would then wash them clean and place them on straw in the dark dry loft over his bed, beyond the blight's reach.

He had not been on the ground for more than a few minutes when it began to rain, gently at first so that he welcomed it, washing away the sweat on his brow and cooling his aching muscles. But then the sky broke open and, through the middle of it, the rain came down in spiteful, painful bolts. He bent lower, feeling for his crop, pushing the earth aside. He knew every inch and ounce of it. He had spent a lifetime nurturing, feeding, turning, hoeing, weeding, every grain sifted through his loving fingers, earth so familiar it was part of him. Now suddenly it was a bog, alien and hostile, and he was frightened. He tried to stand but the cold knocked him to his knees again. He fell sideways and there was mud in his mouth. He spat it out and, cursing the sky and every living thing, he crawled back to the cottage door and lay exhausted on the floor by the hearth.

It was an hour or more before he felt strong enough to kneel. He reached up, took the rosary from its peg on the chimney breast and, resting his elbows on the stool, began to pray. When he had finished, he waited and listened. He heard only the storm, so he whispered another prayer and waited again. But the thunder was even nearer and louder and the white flashes of lightning only grew brighter and more terrifying.

He ended his prayers, pulled himself up and rested against the chimney breast. He nodded. It was as he had always feared, something he had secretly suspected ever since he was a child. No one was listening.

At that moment Tom Keegan realised he had spent his long life paying homage to someone who was not there. Painfully, slowly, he straightened himself and unhooked the tiny locket of Mary's hair from its peg, kissed it, wrapped it in his hand-kerchief and put it into his waistcoat pocket. Then, without bothering to put on his coat or cap, he went out into the storm and to the mountain path. He needed only his memory to guide him.

He climbed slowly, edging himself forward, until at last he came to a hollow where the mountain spring fed into a clear shallow pond. Here the wind seemed to him barely a whisper and the rain no more than a soft, warm and gentle drizzle. At the pond's edge was an old twisted hawthorn covered in a mass of mistletoe and to its right a rock so smooth and straight it might have been hewn by a mason. By its side was the Cairn Beag, a small mound of stones he had built many years before as atone-ment to his Fairy King. He pulled the locket from his pocket and placed it on top of the mound. Then he turned slowly in a circle and then half a circle again so that when he stopped he was facing the pond.

He saw a mist, a delicate shimmering gauze caught in soft white light spread across its centre, changing its contours as the breeze caught it. With his hand on the rock to steady himself, the old man went down on one knee and spoke to the Fairy King.

'*Sláinte leat* and forgive me, Rí na Sideog. My bones are crippled with the cold and the pain of old age, as if you didn't already know. I have a gift for you here, the most precious thing I have left, taken from the most precious person I ever knew. It is yours to take, or for her if she is with you.

'You will have seen what is happening down there, so you'll know why I have come. There is no one else I can turn to for help. Maybe it is too late. I think it is. Do you think it is?'

Still kneeling, he waited for an answer. The breeze dipped into the hollow, rippling the pond. The mist stretched out a finger beyond the edge of it, curled itself around the hawthorn tree and enveloped the nests of mistletoe.

The old man knew what the Fairy King was telling him.

'It will cover everything then? Not a field spared? Not one of us saved? No one? Tell me, Rí na Sideog. No one?'

There was a sound, like the puff of distant bellows. The mist flowed out and spread itself, completely enveloping the water beneath it. The old man nodded again, understanding. He waited until he was sure his audience was over, cupped his face in his hands and began to weep. When the tears stopped he rested his shoulder against the rock and stood again. He kissed the locket for the last time, bowed to the mist and the Fairy King that sat forever within it and began his journey back down the mountainside.

෨෨

Not a mile away, on a lane that led to the sea, a hundred people stood silently by the church of St Patrick. For two hours they had waited in the rain for the priest but what else were they to do? He arrived, without apology, just as the storm was directly overhead, so close there was no counting between the lightning and the claps of thunder. They thought it an omen.

The village was famous for a well that had been visited by St Patrick when he had stopped and refreshed himself, one of the many wells he made holy on his long walk through Ireland. The young priest led the villagers in a wide circle around it, stopping every few yards or so to recant each of the Stations of the Cross. They bowed their heads and bent their knees and walked on, reciting out loud the ten decades of their rosary, along with the five sorrows of Christ's death.

The cold numbed their fingers so that they barely felt the beads and the wind chilled their lips so the sacred words tumbled incoherently from their mouths. Their feet bled. They were barefoot and the stones cut, them but the more it hurt, the more their blood mixed with the rain, the more certain they were that God was witness to their penance and would hear their pleas and cover their fields in some holy cloak.

Then the priest stopped and they followed him into the church to receive the holy Host. Cold and desolate, they watched as he put on the robes of Benediction and lit a single candle. Then, kneeling before the bare wooden table of an altar, he prayed for them and for himself, for he too had potatoes. None could see his anxious face and the rain drummed so loudly on the roof that few could hear his words. The icons of painted wood and plaster, the pious celebrities of prayer, heard nothing. Even Christ, limp in the lap of Mary, now seemed truly dead and she uncaring.

The priest ended his pleading, quickly de-robed and walked back down the aisle past his flock, careful not to look at any one of them. They followed, hurriedly pushing their way out, afraid

to be there without him. As they crossed the churchyard, lightning lit up the gravestones and in one bright, single flash, the
Celtic crosses and the names of the dead were suddenly magnified and leapt out at them. The women screamed and pulled
their aprons over their heads. The men walked on, knowing it
was just another of the Devil's tricks.

⚮

Tom Keegan had almost reached the bottom of the mountain slope when his son and Kate saw him. His clothes were
sodden and heavy with mud, his face white with cold and
splattered with dirt. The rain lashed unseeing, unblinking
eyes, for he was now completely blind. Keegan ran to him,
lifted him over his shoulders and carried him to the cottage,
shouting.

'Father, you fool. You stupid old fool. You will die. What are
you doing on the mountain on a night like this? For God's sake,
get inside and stay inside and get warm. Kate is with me to get
your praties out.'

But the old man seemed not to hear and when he spoke he
was talking only to himself. 'I can hear water,' he said.

'Of course you can, father, we all can and a lot of it is inside
you, I shouldn't reckon. Great God! I've never seen a storm like
this in all my life.'

But the old man could now see things that men with eyes
could not.

'There's water coming,' he whispered. 'The river's rising, it's
coming and flooding and it'll drown my praties. I have to get
down to them.'

He struggled to free himself from his son's grip but Keegan
held him tight and, once inside, they undressed and dried him,
wrapped him in a blanket and sat him as close to the fire as they
dared. Then he was silent.

The garden was now under water so that only the heaped potato mounds showed where they should dig.

'Throw them up to the ledge, Kate!' Keegan shouted to her. 'There on the rock. They'll be safe until morning.'

The water was like ice and Kate's hands and feet throbbed with the pain. The spade slipped from her fingers and she splashed around, searching for it beneath the muddied water. Soon she was crying with the cold.

They moved to the second row, Kate at one end, Keegan the other, where water was now gushing in like a frantic stream that had lost its course. Kate dug deeper but her spade felt nothing. She dug again but pulled up only mud.

'There's nothing here,' she shouted, but already Keegan was on his knees, pushing his hands deep into the mire, his powerful arms breaking the mounds apart, as frenzied as the storm around him. Then he stopped and straightened his back and held out his cupped hands to her. She waded towards him but she knew even before she saw it. She knew the smell. A mass of pulp, brown and glue-like, oozed from between his fingers. They had come too late. The potatoes were lost.

Kate fell on her knees beside him, exhausted, and rested her head on his shoulders. There was no pain now. No throbbing. She was sitting in mud and water but she could not feel them. It was as if her body had been pulled apart and the stinking, corrupting, fetid odour belonged elsewhere. Then, as the sky was bright with lightning, she saw the old man.

He was behind them, white and naked in the rain, standing as straight as a ramrod in the wretched swamp that had been his life's garden. The smell had brought him out, the stench of miserable defeat. He was looking at the sky and talking, asking questions she could not hear above the storm, talking to the sky or something above it. He held up his arms, beckoning as if he was calling someone to him, the way a gentle shepherd does to a lamb. Then he dropped his arms to his side and walked slowly back to the open door. As his son ran after him, Kate sank back into the mud and was sick.

The old man lay on his mattress of straw, dirtying the sheets he had always been so careful to keep white and pressed. He held his ankles tightly together and his arms were crossed over his chest. His son pulled the blanket over him and knelt by him, knowing what he was about to do and knowing he could do nothing to stop him. He sat that way, watching his father's face for nearly an hour, not moving his gaze even when Kate came and sat behind him.

The old man stirred, opened his eyes to the son he could not see and whispered for him to come closer.

'I cannot do more, my boy. All these long years I have fought and fought and finally I have lost. I think I've known that for a long time, but no matter now. We might have had better days together, you and me, a better life, but it was not to be. I had always believed that when things come to their worst they must mend but now I know that to be false. I will not struggle more. I cannot. It is time to leave.'

'Yes, father, I understand. May God bless you.'

'And you too, son of mine. And speed you to a better fortune, for it must be out here somewhere for someone. I'm away at last to meet my Mary. She has waited so long. Bless you, son, and bless you again and remember only what was good in me.'

He closed his eyes and lay still. Keegan whispered his prayers and crossed the old man's forehead.

Then he bent over and kissed his dead father's lips.

მოთ

Keegan wanted his father put into the ground without fuss but the women would not let him. For more than half a century he had taught two generations of their children and there were grandmothers who still remembered the quiet young man with a stammer who had risked going to an English prison ship so that their sons and daughters might count to a hundred and recite the alphabet. Merchants and farmers in Cork and Kerry, and even as far away as Clare, owed much of their good fortune to the schoolmaster who had taught them the mysteries of division and multiplication, which had propelled them on the road to profit.

So Keegan could do nothing. The women did it all with rites that had prospered long before the first monk had ever stamped the first holy cross on Ireland's shores.

The old man was laid out on his table, washed from head to toe, his hair neatly brushed and a white and newly pressed sheet was tucked around him, tight and decent. The little mirror over the hearth was covered with a cloth and the clock was stopped, its hands turned back to the hour and the minute he had taken his last breath. Copper pennies were laid on each closed eyelid and his Bible was placed under his chin.

Then the keeners began their wailing and crooning, hands on hips, rocking back and forth, their aprons over their heads as cold ashes from the fire were sprinkled over them and scattered around the front door to frighten away the evil spirits that might bar the old man's journey to heaven.

All that day of the wake, people filed past to look at his face for the last time and say their goodbyes. In better times, Tom Keegan might have expected a little jollity around him, some whiskey, some poteen and perhaps a fiddler too. But only talk was free now and there was little enthusiasm for that.

They carried him to the graveyard at St Nicholas. The grave was already open and the diggers had placed their spades across it in the shape of the cross so the evil spirits could not hide there. They sprinkled the coffin with water and as it was lowered the crooners began shouting, 'God is glory ... Open your gates.'

When they were gone at last, Keegan sat alone by the mound and pushed a lighted candle into the soft earth of his father's grave. Then he bent down and touched the earth with his lips.

'Goodbye, Father,' he whispered. 'You were a good man, noble and kind. I know how you grieved for your woman and I love and honour you for that. We shall meet no more on earth but whatever your doubts at the end, you are with God now. May he fit us both for a better world.'

He spoke no more and sat there weeping.

CHAPTER TEN

Kate had never thought of death as violent or bloody. She had imagined it to be peaceful, wreathed in its own private dignity. Now she was no longer a stranger to the faces of the dead and the agonies of their dying.

The Fitzgerald family had taken her as their own and seldom had a day passed when she was not in the company of one or other of the twins. But Una had begun to visit Keegan on her own and those journeys were becoming more and more frequent. The bond was forming just as Kate and Tom Keegan knew it would.

Robin was working all the hours that daylight gave him, tending the sick and the dying in the makeshift hospitals and the overcrowded workhouses. Kate offered to help. He did not hesitate and promptly recruited her as his own nursing orderly. It was then that she began her descent into the suffocating mire of death and despair. Every day she suffered the sight of bodies twisted in pain, mouths open in silent screams. Women were giving birth to babies so deformed from malnutrition that Robin needed the help of another man to pull them out of the wombs. It was the silence of the children that shocked her most. In the moment of their dying there was not a movement, not a cry, not a tear, just their unblinking eyes, condemning. They could not speak because starvation had weakened their bones and the slightest pressure on the jaw forced their tongue to the roof of their mouth. Hunger had silenced them.

Many did not look like children at all, bent and wrinkled, their skin taut and thin, like grey muslin. They had lost the hair on their heads and it grew instead on their foreheads and cheeks and even their chins. It was written that they resembled monkeys, which was how the cartoonists in the British newspapers depicted them. The ape-like Irish.

That morning, Kate saw a donkey carrying two dead children. They were stuffed into wicker baskets hanging either side of it, like a harvested crop off to market. A man, a walking skeleton, their father perhaps, led the donkey by its mane but there were no other mourners. No mother, no sisters, no brothers, no black cloth, no wailing keeners. Death was anonymous.

She watched until they reached the church. The man sat down. The donkey ate grass, and the two wicker coffins swung with the rhythm as it moved.

'He will bury them where he can,' Robin said. 'If he has the strength. If he does not, he will do what so many do now and leave them by the church gate and hope someone stronger will do it for him. Did you ever think, Kate, even in your worst nightmares, that it would come to this?'

'A year ago, I was hardly aware these people even existed,' she said, 'let alone have any sympathy for them.'

'You can't have sympathy for suffering you haven't seen.'

'You can be blamed for not knowing it exists.'

'Why are the righteous so severe with themselves?'

'Is that what I am, Robin? Righteous?'

'No, Kate, you are not. Not righteous, but you must forgive yourself the past. You have left it behind.'

'Have I?' she asked. 'Is it possible to become another person?'

'Is that what you are?'

'You wouldn't have recognised me when I first arrived in Ireland. You wouldn't have wanted to. I loathe what I was. I want to disown my past'.

'The calamity has changed us all, Kate.'

She paused. 'Do you suppose that underneath, deep down, I haven't changed at all? That I'm still a spoilt little English lady simply infatuated by it all?'

He leant forward and held her arm. 'That's a silly word, Kate, and a silly thing to say. Nobody could drain an ulcer or dress a septic wound as you have done and call it infatuation. You are real, Kate. Why do you doubt it?'

'It's what I want to believe,' she said.

'You must believe it. You have changed, you know you have.'

'But Robin, I don't feel I have, at least not yet. I don't feel I've crossed a boundary, like changing my religion or my country.'

'You have changed, Kate. I've seen it myself and it has nothing to do with being English or Irish, papist or Prod. It's about what's decent and whether you care. And you do. You've declared yourself and everything you are doing proves it. You'll not turn back now.'

Robin knew it to be true. For a month now she had been at his side, helping him, travelling with him, nursing his patients as best she could. Not once had she distanced herself from the suffering. Not once had she allowed herself to be overwhelmed by it. She could have retreated and he would have thought no less of her. But she had not. She had become more resolute every day, even as their work became more grotesque and unrelenting. How could she call it infatuation?

❦

A man can be as brave as a legend but the day will come when the snap of a twig will alarm him. A woman can endure a lifetime of abuse and then, in the space of a moment, turn on the torturer and end it. So it was that day with Kate.

She and Robin had ridden south to Skibbereen. He had received reports that the suffering there was worse than ever. They rode for three days. Five miles from the town they came

to a derelict tumbled village. It looked deserted but the sound
of their horses' hooves had woken someone. They heard a moan,
like the lowing of a cow. They dismounted and Robin gave his
reins to Kate.

'Stay here. I'll call out if I need help. Promise me you'll not
move unless I call.'

Kate nodded. He had been gone some minutes when she
heard a cry behind her. She tied the horses to the stump of a
tree and went to the nearest cottage. There was no roof, no door.
It was an igloo of mud. She saw bundles wrapped in sacking on
the floor. They were the small bodies of children. In the corner
a woman lay half naked. Rats scampered at her feet. She looked
at Kate, her lips moved but there was no sound. A bloated rat ran
across her stomach.

Kate ran to her horse and was sick down its flanks. She called
out to Robin but her voice was barely a whisper. As she held
on to the saddle to steady herself, arms suddenly clutched her
scarf, twisting it, choking her. She turned. A young woman was
screaming at her, pushing a baby against her lips. The child's
body was suffocating her. She could taste its filth. She struggled
but the woman's arms were tight around her like a clamp. She
could not turn one way or the other. Then her horse reared as
Robin wrenched the woman and her baby away and they fell to
the ground.

'Help her, Robin,' Kate pleaded. 'For God's sake, help her.'

He shook his head. 'There is nothing I can do for her. I cannot
save her. Nothing can save her now.'

The young woman pulled herself to her knees, picked up her
baby and wandered away from them, her strength exhausted.
They watched as she sat by the edge of a ditch, the child in
her lap, talking to it, caressing it. She cupped its tiny face in
the crook of her elbow and tried to feed it with a weed she
had squeezed and rolled into a soft ball. She put it into its
mouth and turned its chin with her fingers, trying to make

it chew. The baby stared back, puzzled. Then it swallowed the ball, convulsed and was still. For a moment she held it tight to her. Then she dropped it between her knees and with her feet buried him in the mud.

တလ

They rode south towards Baltimore. The Quakers had established a depot there to distribute food and clothing sent from America. Within weeks a thousand hungry people had besieged the port. They brought their diseases with them. There were no doctors, the small hospital had closed its doors and the workhouse was full.

Robin halted their horses to rest at the cliff top. To the south he pointed to Sherkin Island and beyond that the outline of Oileán Chléire.

'A simple bit of Irish for you, Kate. It means "Clear Island", which is a bit of a misnomer because there are very few days in the year when it shows itself quite as well as this.'

The wind was high and the spray from the waves carried forty feet up. They sat behind the natural shelter of rock and ate their oatcakes. Kate took Robin's hand and pointed.

'Robin. Over there by the gorse. Do you see? It's moving. What is it?'

He paused. 'It looks like …' He stood and went slowly towards the shrubs.

'What is it, Robin?'

'Don't come, Kate. Stay where you are.'

She would not. She came close. She saw a mound covering the body of a girl that had not been buried deep enough. The soil around her head had been swept away and the wind had picked up her long black hair so it flowed like silken strands above the grass of her shallow grave. Dr Robin took Kate in his arms and guided her away.

He looked to the sky. 'Dear God, hear me and do not blame us for what is happening here.'

✿

Mary McMahon sat in the gloom at the bottom of Patch's pit. Her baby suckled at her hanging breast but drew no milk from the bruised and sore nipple. Her three other children clung to her thighs under the filthy blanket on the bed of straw that smelled of urine and human waste. The baby boy, born only five months before, was no bigger than the day Robin Fitzgerald drew it from her womb.

'And how could you be?' she said out loud to him. 'You teasing my breasts and knowing there isn't milk there for you?'

At the sound of their mother's voice, the children whimpered, drew closer and hugged her tighter. Their emaciated bodies were streaked with dried blood and pus where sores had broken.

'There, there, my babies,' she cooed. 'Mother will find you something. I can only feed you with what God gives and what's a mother to do when He deserts me? I've sold everything I had, my dears, even your father's shoes and Sunday jacket, and I was so hoping to keep them for when he comes back to us.'

She had killed his dog and its meat had given them nearly a month's food. He had been fond of it but she knew he would understand when he returned. He had been gone for so long but she never doubted he would come back, good husband that he was. There would come the day when she would hear him whistling and calling … 'Mary, Mary, I've come to take you and the little ones on the big ship to America.'

There had been a time when she feared the peelers had killed him but someone brought her a message that he had been seen working on a road near to Enniskillen and that made her happy. It meant he was earning the money to buy the tickets for the big ship that would take them all away. Perhaps he would bring back some whiskey. She missed his liquor.

Her Patch had been a happy man, a good man and father. The children's stomachs were never empty and their faces were always full of fun. He had never done anyone any harm with his whiskey-making and it had given them all a good living. She remembered the times when men climbed down into the pit and sat by the still as it bubbled over the peat fire, talking of their debts and doubtful dealings, of how they had been wronged by this man or that woman – and it was mostly women. Listening to them and their moaning, you would think the world was a poor place and they the most unfortunate devils in it. But after a cup or two of Patch's brew, they would leave laughing and singing, different men altogether, full of spunk.

But then the shebeen owners in the county reckoned Patch was taking too much of their business away so they agreed that one of them would lead the excise men to Patch's secret little place and put an end to it. Big Jim O'Rourke brought them and as the excise men were chasing after Patch, it was he who broke up the still and smashed the full bottles hidden in the ferns by the stream. It was big Jim O'Rourke who had then her in front of her children even as Patch was running from bullets in the hills above.

Quietly and carefully, she pulled the sleeping infant away from her, got up from the bed, placed him into the nest of straw with the others and drew the blanket over them. Then she draped her shawl over her head and shoulders, closed the cottage door behind her and wedged a large stone against it.

The ground was white with frost, the tall ferns like stiff and delicate filigree. The night was stark and clear with stars and a full moon lit up the icicles on the aspen tree. The track up the steep slope was slippery so she crawled on her hands and knees to the top and stood there for a while, waiting for her heart to stop pounding. She looked around her, surprised at how beautiful it was and how quickly she had forgotten it. The long, smooth stretch of hills swept down so casually to the sand and the sea and the great walls of rock that changed colours with the seasons were now towering white with the scattering of snow. She could hear the rumble and swish of surf breaking and, as she had often done, she looked towards the horizon, searching for the ship that was not there.

'I must hurry.' She spoke the words out loud to herself. 'I must be back before Patch comes. He'll not take the babes without me. Oh! Love … Oh! Love … Come for us. Come for us quickly.'

She hurried off, her bare feet crunching the carpet of frost, half running whenever she had the breath. Her shawl fell to her shoulders and her long black hair streamed behind her like a mass of silk.

She had a plan. She had thought about it for a week and now she had decided. She knew where there was food and she knew how she would get it. Then her babies would eat and when their bellies were full they would play and chatter as they had before. She would not let them die of hunger. God had given them to her and she would not give them back. They would stay safe and well until Patch came to take them away on the big ship to America.

It took her an hour to reach the walls of Cork. She waited in the shadows on Lavitt's Quay. There were always people loitering long after the shops had closed, waiting patiently outside the butchers and bakers, hoping for a scrap to be thrown to them.

It was past eight o'clock. She had heard the bell on St Olave's church. She pulled the shawl over her head and around her face.

'Just as long as you're careful, Mary,' she whispered. 'Just as long as you're careful, no one will ever know.'

But another voice from an inner part of her mind whispered back, 'And if you're caught, Mary McMahon, they'll send you to a prison ship and who'll look after your babes then?'

She nodded to her other voice. 'Don't fret. Mary knows how to look after herself. Hasn't she been doing just that since Patch went on his way? And won't I still be doing it on the day he comes back for us?'

She watched as, one by one, the candles inside the shops were snuffed out, and the shopkeepers, content with their week's profits, pulled on their heavy greatcoats, wrapped woollen scarves around their chubby necks and pulled their hats down tight. They rattled the steel mesh that covered their shop windows, making sure that they were locked, then double-bolted their front doors and, tapping their shop signs with their walking sticks, walked along the river bank towards the comfort of their warm and welcoming homes.

Mary waited until the shadow of the last of them had gone. She looked across the street to number eighteen and the sign above the window:

J. O'ROURKE. CORN MERCHANT AND GROCER

She knew him to be a bully, a rapist, a cold and cunning man. The rapidly rising price of imported American corn had made him prosperous and his new money had given him new ambition. With it, he was buying the favours of every merchant in the town and he was now their favourite to be Cork's next mayor. She remembered the days when she was younger, when her hair was a shining raven-black, tied up with a strip of scarlet ribbon. O'Rourke would look long at her whenever his wife was not looking at him, his eyes wandering over her body, making her feel naked, and he would lick his lips as if he was feasting on her. She had been a handsome woman with a full bosom and full hips and she knew what men liked and she knew that they liked her. She could have had the pick of any of them but when she chose Patch she knew there would not be another man brave enough to take her from him. But still O'Rourke continued to eye her in his lecher's way, violating her as he sat on his sacks of flour.

'Yes!' she whispered. 'Tonight the dirty man will fill one of those sacks for me and my babes. He knows what he did to me, tearing me and making me bloody in front of my own. Now it's time for him to pay the bill, some flour and perhaps a little something special.'

She looked out once more from her hiding place. There was no light in O'Rourke's shop and slowly, step by step, she edged along the wall until she came to a narrow cobbled alley by the side of the shop. How bright it was, how close the moon was and how white. It might almost be day.

'Oh, dear God! What if my babes wake thinking it morning? Will they cry out for me and come wandering out on a night as cold as this? Holy Mary,' she pleaded, 'put the moon away.'

She knew where O'Rourke kept the spare key for the side door. He had told her of it many times when he had tried to convince her to change beds. She crossed herself and reached up to the loose stones above the lintel, feeling for the key. Carefully, she slid it into the lock, turned it quietly and let herself in.

She stood still and breathed in the smells, the perfumes of food, the coffee, the spices, the tang of oranges and the heavenly scent of soap. To be clean, to feel her skin white and fresh again, her hair soft as silk, a scalp without lice, a body without sores. The moon lit the room as she tiptoed from counter to counter, from shelf to shelf, lightly touching all these things, like a child on Christmas morning circling the laden tree. Then her fingers dipped into a barrel of flour.

She worked quickly, scooping it into a sack. But how much? How heavy could she make it if she was to carry all the way back to the pit? She looked around at all the lovely foods she might have taken if only she had been stronger. She tied the head of the sack in a knot and went back to the door. As she turned to take her last breath of the scented shop, she saw a jar of molasses on the shelf above the weighing scales. Yes! She would take it to sweeten the cakes she would bake, what a treat for her babes. She reached up. The jar was inches from her fingers. She stretched on the tips of her toes but her arm failed her and the jar came crashing down and exploded on the marble counter.

She stood still, barely able to breathe.

'Who's there?' She heard him coming down the stairs from the loft. She had thought he was at home in bed with his wife.

She waited. Should she run to the door? If she did he would chase her and catch her and beat her, bawling out for all of Cork to hear. Then he would give her to the peelers and then what of her babes?

The sack of flour was heavy but she dared not put it down. If she was quiet and still he would not see her and if he heard nothing more, he would think that he had been dreaming and sleep again.

But nowadays Jim O'Rourke seldom slept the night through. Like other merchants, he lived in fear of being burgled and having his shop set on fire by the mobs who crowded his door every day, ragged beggars banging on his window with their fists, demanding he gave them credit to buy his food when he knew there was not one among them who could ever pay him back. So he slept above his shop in a makeshift cot with a loaded shotgun on the floor beside it.

He came through the door holding it in one hand and a candle in the other.

'Jesus! It's you, Mary McMahon. All these years and in my shop alone at last. But thank God because I thought it was the mob come for me.'

He came closer and saw the broken jar and the molasses dripping from the counter. Then he saw the sack of flour in her hands.

'You're stealing from me. Is that it? That's my flour you have there and you've smashed my molasses. What else have you hidden up your skirt?'

'Nothing, O'Rourke. I've only a little flour for my babes. We have the hunger and I must feed them until Patch comes home.'

He laughed and then spat and wiped his mouth with the hem of his nightshirt. 'Patch comes home, is it?'

He was menacing, blocking her way to the door. She could smell the sweat and whiskey on him.

He snatched the sack from her. 'I'll tell you what Mr Patch will find if ever he dares to come back. He'll find his whore in prison and in irons.'

'Give me back the flour, O'Rourke,' she said defiantly. She came close and put her hand on his bare chest, the hair warm and wet. 'Do what you like with me. Do what you did before and do it any way you like. I'll not tell Patch. But give me back the flour. Don't call the peelers.'

He was a large man but she was no longer afraid. He pushed her away. 'Do what I like with you any way I like, is it? You bitch. If I rammed you now it would be with a marlin spike. You are a filthy woman inside and out and I wouldn't touch you with any part of mine. My God! How I've lusted after you all these years and now you offer me this'.

He spat phlegm into her face but she did not move. He took her arm, twisted it behind her back and pushed her towards the door. 'Come, you dirty hag. Get your filth out of my shop or I'll raise such a commotion we'll have the peelers here before a scream leaves those scabby lips of yours.'

She clawed at the counter but there was nothing to hold on to. She grabbed at the shelves. She clutched the weighing scales but they crashed to the floor. Furious, he hit her again and again.

Above her she saw a ham and by it, on the chopping block, a cleaver. She grabbed it and, closing her eyes, swung it in a wide arc until it stopped at his skull. He gasped and fell and she fell with him, still in his tight grip. There was a gurgling in his throat and she felt the warmth of his blood on her arms. He shivered, his body heaved and then with a sigh he was still. She unlocked his fingers, kicked his legs away and sat up. She had sliced off the back of his head and in the bright moonlight she saw the glistening white of his brain.

She stood by his body a few moments longer, then, slinging the sack over her shoulder and pulling her shawl over it, she left the shop and began her journey home.

∞

They should have been asleep in the ditch, huddled together for warmth, man, woman, friend and stranger, body by body. The ditch ran along the wall of the city's workhouse and the homeless and the hungry slept there, waiting for the gates to open at dawn. Then they would count the dead in the carts coming out and know, with some certainty, how much longer they would have to wait until it was their turn to be admitted. But tonight the moon kept them awake. Two women sat on the edge of the ditch, cuddling each other for warmth and a little conversation. In the bright light they saw a figure coming slowly down the road towards them.

'It's a cripple,' said the first woman. 'See how it walks.'

'But out on the roads at this time of the night?' said the other.

'Maybe she's come to join us.'

'Then tell her she'll be dead before she's head of the queue.'

'Look how bent she is. She'll not squeeze into this ditch.'

'She's got a hump. D'you see? She's a hunchback and that's queer. Did you ever see one hereabouts? I never did.'

'Have you ever seen half the bodies in this ditch?'

'No. But I'd remember a hunchback.'

Their talk roused the others who sat up, curious, and watched the bent figure come closer. The deformity on her shoulder seemed to make her weary. She was almost level with them and about to turn onto the track that led up the hills and the sea beyond, when someone shouted. 'Hunchback, is it? That's no cripple. That's Mary McMahon. And there's blood on her.'

It was just as she had feared. The moon had waited for this moment of treachery. How much brighter it suddenly seemed and she was too well known to hide herself under her shawl or disguise herself with the sack of flour beneath it. And O'Rourke's blood was still wet and glistening.

'Hey, Mary,' they shouted. 'What's that you have on your back? Is it another baby or a bag of gold? Or is it food you have? Christ alive! I do believe it's food she has there.'

They ran towards her, fifteen or more of them, baying like hounds. She stood upright and faced them. She had killed for her prize and she was ready to kill again to keep it.

She snarled at them. 'I've a knife and I'll cut him apart, the first who touches me. I've done O'Rourke already tonight. Try and harm me and I'll mix his blood with yours.'

But they did not stop. Mary McMahon was as brave as the bravest and as fierce as a fighting lion. They all said so afterwards.

It was quickly over. She was too weak to fight them off and she had no knife. When they had finished with her they took the sack of flour and fought among themselves for the biggest share. When they were full, they sank back into the chilled earth and slept.

It was an hour or more before Mary opened her eyes. She crawled a little way from them, her body torn and smeared with her own blood. She had fought and she had lost. She had killed and still her babes were waiting. Were they crying for her now? Was it them she could hear in the wind?

For an hour or more she crawled and stumbled her way along the track towards her pit, all the time listening for her children's cries. She would hear them better if only the sea would stop its noise, if only the pebbles on the beach would be still.

As she wandered she spoke out loud.

'I must walk faster to be home sooner, the poor dears, waiting for their supper. Haven't I left them snug and warm by the peat fire and wouldn't they be longing for their supper of potato broth and buttermilk?'

She pictured their little faces, playing their games among the ferns, splashing at the stream in the summer's sun as she sat and suckled her baby boy, her full breasts making him big and strong.

She walked many miles over the hills that night in the bright light of the treacherous moon but she was not walking home. How could she know which way to go?

Exhausted, she sat by the cliff's edge and watched the soft salmon glow of another dawn. She heard nothing now but the roar of the surf and the breaking of the waves on the rocks below. She did not hear the dogs. They circled around her like hyenas at their prey, snarling at each other, waiting for the first to leap on her. A hound took her by the neck and shook her until she was limp. Then they devoured her.

♘♞

Patch McMahon came carefully, a few steps at a time, stopping, listening, and then a few steps more. His feet crushed the wild mint, heather scratched his bare legs. How good the moon had been to him. There could be no tricks: no ambush with such a light, no man could hide, no peelers could spring a trap in it. He looked up and nodded his thanks to the bright moon. He stopped to listen. He heard only the sea breeze stirring the grass like the incessant whisper of hidden men. He waited, like a hare on alert.

He came closer. He whispered, 'Mary, Mary, it's me come home, do you hear? It's me, your Patch come to fetch you.'

Where was his dog? No one in the old days could come into Patch's pit without a warning from his scruffy mongrel sentinel.

He saw the cottage below and the white-feathered ferns and the black hole where he had kept his secret store of poteen. The stream was running as fast and clean as ever.

He called again. 'Mary! For Jesus' sake, wake up and get your-self ready. I've come for you and the babes.'

He came to the front door. He pushed aside the small boulder and opened it a little. It was too black for him to see but he knew the smell. He kicked the door wide open and stood back to let in the moonlight. It shone directly onto the bed. There was no movement under the blanket.

'Mary,' he whispered. 'Is that you? Are my babies here?'

He knelt and drew back the blanket and the dead eyes of his children stared back at him.

It did not take him long. He wrapped their little bodies in rags and pushed them into a wide crevice in the rock. Then he heaped stones into it until they were safely wedged together in their grave. No fox, no rats, nothing would ever touch them again. He sat down and rested his head against their gravestones. He took off his cap. Inside the rim were five yellow tickets with the name 'S.S. SARA JANE' printed in large letters. The sailing time was noon in ten days' time. He dropped them between his feet and ground them into the earth with his heels until they were gone. Then he looked up at the moon and howled, a long and tortured primaeval howl.

By his side were the scattered bits and pieces of his whiskey still and fragments of the bottles O'Rourke had smashed the night he brought the excise men. He leant forward and picked up a long, thin shard of green glass. He held it up, sharp and sparkling. How beautiful it was. A precious, lethal emerald.

The moon moved slowly across the pit and the last of its light shone bright and glistening on the blood oozing from the suicide's wrists.

CHAPTER ELEVEN

The old priest was drunk. He crossed himself a dozen times and swore by the name of his favourite saint. He had already sent a letter to his bishop, and would he do that if he was lying? Mr Hughes, the Inspecting Officer for the Relief Commission, had also seen it. He urged Dr Robin to go with him and verify it himself.

'The baby has stigmata, doctor. I would not believe it if I hadn't touched the child and seen the marks. It is the most extraordinary thing.'

Kate went with Robin to the church, which was two hours' ride away from Cork. But trifles of gossip and rumour travelled fast across the counties and they expected to find nothing.

The priest led them through the maze of derelict tumbled cottages to a small church on a rise. Where a crowd of thirty or more people were gathered in the graveyard. They held wooden crosses and fell on their knees as the priest approached. He ignored them and pushed his way past into the church. Kate and Robin followed.

Altar candles had been placed on the floor and they shone onto a makeshift crib tucked into the corner under a plaster cast of the Virgin Mary. A man and a woman were crouched by it.

'Bring him out, Maggie,' the priest ordered sharply. 'Be hasty, and show him to the gentle people here.'

The woman reached into the crib and brought out a baby boy, wrapped in a dirty, ragged shawl. She put him on her knee and pulled the cloth away so that he was naked. Robin looked closer. On the baby's hands and feet were small red marks where

the skin was broken and the blood had congealed. At the sight
of them, the man and woman crossed themselves twice over and
began a prayer.

'It is the divine favour, the marks of Jesus,' the old priest said.
He went down on his knees by the child's parents. 'It is a miracle,
a blessed sign from God that he has forgiven us. Now he will
save the potatoes.'

Robin turned the child to the candlelight. Its eyes were glazed
and its legs and arms hung limp. He snapped his fingers in its face.
The child did not flinch. He examined the stigmata, smoothing
the skin around the tiny wounds, gently touching the soft scabs
that were beginning to form over them. He leant closer, opened
the baby's mouth and sniffed its breath. Then he pinched its arm.
The baby did not move or cry.

'For God's sake!' said the priest, 'What are you doing? This is
a holy child.'

Robin stood up. 'This child feels nothing and it is certainly not
holy. It is unconscious and someone has been feeding it poteen.
Smell it. Go on, old priest, you'll recognise it if anyone can. This
poor thing has been drugged so that it won't cry. Drugged, so
they could burn it and make the marks. That's what they are,
priest. Burn marks.'

The woman pulled the child to her and covered it again with
her shawl. She began rocking on her knees, wailing and pleading to the effigy of Mary above her. Her husband ran from the
church. Robin held the priest with both hands and shook him
hard.

'This infant has been tortured. If you had anything to do with
the making of it, old man, then you too are damned.'

The priest did not reply. He stood up, slowly shaking his
head, gaping at the woman crying at his feet as she rocked the
drunken child in her arms. Robin pushed the priest aside and
left the church with Kate, walking past the hushed crowd waiting outside.

'The father put the marks on the baby with a burning ember and poured liquor down its throat to hide the pain and keep it from screaming.'

Robin sat with Kate in the front parlour of the Inspecting Officer's house.

'How could they do that to their own baby?' Kate asked.

'Hunger gives cruelty a different look,' Robin answered. 'It was a desperate act of survival, and hunger is the master. I suppose they thought they might get something from it – money, food, clothes – especially if the bishop had come.'

'Do you think the old priest knew?' she asked.

'Perhaps. Perhaps not,' he answered.

'Surely it wouldn't have fooled the bishop. He would have seen it for what it was?'

'Maybe. But like the priest, he would want to believe. Fakery is the core of all religions, and most especially theirs.'

'What will people do to them?'

'The old priest will probably say nothing. He'll keep it a secret and let them go on believing. Such is priest-craft.'

But Robin was wrong. The revelation shook the drink out of the priest. In his rage, he took the burning altar candle and beat the mother with it, then chased her out of the church, screaming his curses. The crowd joined in. They chased after her and when they caught her they beat her and her infant with their wooden crosses and left them to bleed. Then they searched for the husband who had held the stick of burning peat to the child and when they found him, hiding in a hole by his wrecked cottage, they punished him the same way they had punished the gombeen man who had sold them human flesh. The next day, the Inspecting Officer came again to Robin. He said the woman and her baby had died from the beatings and their bodies had been carried away by the dogs. He had searched for the husband and found him nailed to the gibbet on Maundy Hill.

When Robin and the Inspecting Officer arrived there, they saw that the killers had stripped the body of its clothes. Crows had already taken the eyes. It would remain nailed there until only the skeleton remained.

'His body has turned black, doctor. He wasn't like that yesterday.'

'Stay back, Hughes, stay well back. We must leave him where he is. We can't afford to touch him now.'

'What's happened to him, doctor?'

'The worst, Mr Hughes. For this village and for everyone who nailed him there. It's the fever, the black fever. It's come at last. God help us, Hughes, God help Ireland. For now the real dying will begin.'

Robin did not delay long. That afternoon he and Kate rode directly to Kinsale. The snow had drifted high in places, hiding the road and disguising the ditches, so the going was slow. They rode side by side and trod their horses carefully. Robin was anxious. He knew how rapidly the fever would travel.

'The children must be kept inside the schoolroom. They must sleep inside, eat inside, no one must touch them until we know which way it's moving.'

'You call it the black fever.'

'It's typhus. Black because the blood congeals and the skin colours. The body feels as if it's on fire, as if every part of it is being pricked by a million needles. It can be so intense I've known people throw themselves into the rivers to cool themselves and drown because they could not swim … I've seen many different ways of dying, Kate, but the black fever is the most terrible.'

'Is it because of the hunger?'

'If the potato fails, the fever is never far behind. When the hunger is on them, people sell everything they have to buy food, their clothes, their bedding and sometimes, God forgive them, even their children's bodies. When the pennies are gone, all they have left is the warmth of the peat fire. They stay in their hovels, getting hungrier and weaker by the day. It's then that the fever gets them.'

'I've heard that it's the rats that carry it,' Kate said.

'Yes! You can get rabies from a dog or a fox or a badger so it's possible a rat bite could give you the fever. But I'm not convinced.'

'Why, Robin?'

'I've seen hundreds die from the fever but I don't suppose I've seen more than a dozen or so rat bites on the bodies. Think of a tiny breadcrumb in the palm of your hand. You'd barely notice it on the body of a dying man, would you, such a crumb? Yet I've seen things no bigger than this on the dead and the dying.'

Kate nodded. 'They were on the dead at Skibbereen. Their hair was crawling with lice.'

'That's right. I would have seen a rat's bite on a fevered man. But I wouldn't see the bite of something so, small would I?'

'Could something so tiny kill a man?'

'Probably not. It would be a strange act of God, Kate, having made us in His image, to let us be destroyed by something so small and so vile.'

They rode into the valley shortly before midday and Robin they were already too late. The schoolroom windows had been painted over with a lime wash, the little board with the 'Hundred Thousand Welcomes' had been taken down from over the door. There was not a movement from the cluster of cottages.

The sound of the horses brought Keegan and Una out. Their eyes were red with weeping.

'Stay in your saddles, both of you!' Keegan shouted. 'We have the fever. Seven of the children are inside. We're waiting to bury them. Only the dead are left here now. Go! The pair of you. While you're still clean.'

Kate and Robin dismounted and went to them. Robin took Keegan's hand and held it tight against his own chest.

'I have known you and this house and all this valley in the happiest of times. I'm damned if I'll leave you now.'

Then he went to his sister and put his arms around her, his face next to hers.

'Why didn't you go?' he whispered. He felt her tears on his cheeks.

'I couldn't leave,' she sobbed. 'Not Keegan, not the children.'

'Who else is inside?' he asked.

'Only them. Their families left them where they died. How could they do that, Robin? Leave their own children unburied. How could they?' He stroked her hair to soothe her.

'The fever is a terrible thing, my sweetheart. They know how it kills. They've seen it before and there's nothing they can do. You mustn't blame them.' He turned to Keegan. 'We will bury the children together, and properly, like good little Christians.'

Kate came to Keegan and held his arm. 'Is he inside there too?' she asked. Tears swelled and dribbled down his face. It was his answer. She left him and walked to the open door.

The schoolroom was dark inside. She could see the seven little mounds laid side by side on the flagstones where once they had sat and listened to her stories. She rested her head on the doorframe and wept for them. And especially for him.

'Oh! My little warrior, my little learned friend. How well you were doing, so bright, so sure. How wonderful it would have been for you.' She whispered his own favourite lines from the poem he'd given her:

I could scale the blue air,
I could plough the high hills,
I could kneel all night in prayer
To cure your many ills,
My dark Rosaleen.

They brought the bodies to the graveyard in a handcart. In death they were thinner than she remembered them, their faces drawn inwards as the slow process of dying had sucked out all life. The last of the fleeing villagers stopped at the gate, dropped their bundles and came and stood in a circle around the shallow hole in the ground. It was yet another goodbye and there had been so many of them. They remembered the cycle of their existence, the years when they had plenty and the bad years when the earth gave nothing away. Through it all, their families had struggled and survived to carry the valley on into another generation, to live for another harvest. The potato had always put hope into their bellies. But not now, not here, not ever again. The village and the valley were silent and they knew they would never come back.

Soon the cottages would crumble and cover the bones of those who had died inside them. The winter winds would scatter the thatch and the floods of spring would help bury the stones. When a man came visiting in a hundred years' time, only the lines of the potato ridges would tell him that, once upon a time, there had been life here.

Una read out the children's names and Keegan recited the last prayer of contrition. As the men began shovelling the earth onto the bodies, Una began singing and one by one the others joined her. In that little graveyard on that cold December morning, their voices swelled into a glorious requiem.

∽

Major Euan Halliday, formerly of the Hussars and now a Poor Law inspector, had been ordered to visit the workhouse in Skibbereen. Magistrates in the city had received unfavourable reports of the conditions for the thousands of inmates there.

The major was recently retired from the army and new to his employment. This would be his first visit to a workhouse. The magistrate's instruction was an inconvenience. It was snowing and the ground was hard with frost.

The gates to the Union Workhouse were some distance from the main doors. The figure of a young girl was leaning against the gates, barely clothed and covered white with snow. The major spoke to her but she did not reply. He pulled the bell cord and waited. Then the snowdrifts around him began to move. Hands brushed away snow and uncovered faces. The waiting spectres crawled towards him. The sound of the ringing had woken them. It was their alert that more dead were about to be brought out on the death cart and spaces had become vacant inside the walls. The turnkey unlocked the gates and the young girl in white fell, frozen stiff and long dead.

Major Halliday entered the yard and the paupers settled back into their bed of rags under their blanket of snow.

The major was a Christian man. He had seen much misery in his long service life and was no stranger to people's suffering. He had spent many years in the primitive outposts of the Empire, and was familiar with the infinite capacity of man to inflict cruelty upon his fellows. He had come to accept it as a basic, degrading, unalterable fact of the human condition. But his thirty years of military service had not prepared him for the Skibbereen Workhouse.

He knew the fundamentals of the Poor Law regime as laid down by its director, Sir Charles Trevelyan. Successive communiqués to his inspectors had repeatedly emphasised that:

Relief for the poor must contain a penal and repulsive element and provide only the minimum necessities of life. The workhouses are places of last resort for the destitute. Bear in mind the principle that giving free food for doing nothing is demoralising for those who receive it.

Those who administered relief knew well enough the subtext of Trevelyan's words. They were to provide the poor with only enough food to avoid death by starvation. They were to make the workhouses as abhorrent as possible and some were so foul the starving would attempt any number of crimes, preferring the refuge of jails.

The workhouse had been built six years earlier to accommodate eight hundred paupers. Major Halliday asked the workhouse guardian to show him the current register of inmates. It listed the names of over two thousand adults, one thousand six hundred children under the age of twelve and nearly one thousand old and sick.

The guardian took him to each of the halls. They were bare, without windows, without beds, without heating. There was strict segregation by sex. Families were separated, husbands from their wives, boys from girls, all children from their parents. Many would never see each other again.

The floors of the halls were marked out in spaces two-feet square in which a single occupant could squat all day and crouch, foetus-like, in sleep at night. The major saw the living side by side with the dying and all within reach of the dead. In the corner of the men's hall, he counted fourteen bodies piled one on the other, like abandoned rotting rubbish. Rats scampered among them.

'How many dead this past week?' the major asked. The guardian replied that he had yet to make a tally, but thirty or more adults had died the previous night and fifteen children had been dumped outside the kitchen door that day. He assured the major they would all be buried just as soon as the snow eased and the ground thawed.

In the kitchen, the major saw four sacks of oats. It was the week's entire ration for the four thousand six hundred inmates. The guardian said he had not enough fuel for the fire to boil it so he would ration it out uncooked. He said the oats were given by the Quakers but he had heard that they were soon to leave Ireland and he had no idea where any further rations would come from.

At the far end of the building was a door marked in white paint with the letter 'M'. The guardian was reluctant to open it. He said it was for the other people, the idiots and the mad. The major insisted. The guardian turned his key on two locks and both men stood back, sickened by the stench. The floor was covered in the slime of human filth. Men and women, barely more than skeletons, hardly human, squatted motionless inside. Saying nothing, seeing nothing, they might already have been dead.

That night Major Halliday went to his desk and began the report he had intended to write much later:

Sir,

I have this day, upon the orders of the magistrates, attended the Union Workhouse at Skibbereen. I have witnessed such sights of suffering and wasted humanity that I will never ever be able to wash from my mind.

What I describe below is my honest and truthful account. My heart sickens at the recital. There is much I could add, but must not in my capacity as a servant of the Crown. Never in my life could I have imagined such distress could exist in a Christian country and that country mine. I do remind myself, with shame, that I report this from a corner of the world's greatest Empire. Death is indeed the Emperor here.

He wrote for over an hour. When he had finished, he dusted the ink and folded the papers neatly into an official envelope embossed with the crest of Her Majesty's Service. He rose from his chair as the clock in the corridor chimed twelve times. It was Christmas day.

જી

'Father! This morning, outside our house, I saw a dying man crawling in the snow towards the graveyard on St John's Street. He was like a skeleton. Cook took him bread but he didn't know what it was. It was as if he was blind. He was whispering to her that he didn't want to be dropped into a fever pit. He wanted to be buried with his family.'

Sir William seemed not to hear his daughter. He sat opposite her at the dinner table and carved more mutton. It was his second helping.

'And yesterday, Father, I watched a small boy push his dead mother past this house in a wheelbarrow. Our house again! I asked him where he was going and he said he was taking her to the lime pit by the workhouse. Do you know they have hinged coffins there? They pull a lever and the body drops through the bottom. It is like an abattoir. That's how they're burying them.'

Still Sir William did not answer. She watched him as he pushed more food into his mouth and poured more brandy from the decanter. Suddenly she stood and swept her plate off the table. Food and broken china littered the floor.

'Do you not care?' she shouted at him. 'Are you ignorant of what's happening outside your own front door?'

She ran to the dining-room window and flung it open. 'Smell it, Father, smell the death out there, hear how the dying are crying for help!' She collapsed onto the window seat and sobbed into her arms.

There would have been a time not so long ago when Sir William would have been outraged by such behaviour at his dinner table. He would have ordered his daughter to her room and she would have gone. But that was another age and they were now other people. He pushed his plate away and walked slowly to her. His shoes crunched on the broken crockery and his napkin dropped to the floor.

The evening fall of snow had pulled a thick, white curtain around the house and it made him feel more isolated than ever from the dreadful realities outside. Famine and now fever. What had these people done to deserve it? Their God was his God and he had always believed in a forgiving God. He reached down and touched Kate's hair.

'Is that what you think, my darling? That I do not mourn as well? I was commissioned to save them but I seem to have become their executioner. I don't know how to stop it. This disaster has simply become too great, too vast, too overwhelming. Ireland is already dying. Things have gone too far, and it was not meant to be. We came to rescue these people, but we came with too little humanity, too little concern. It is too late, my dear, to save them now.'

Kate raised her face to him. He cupped her chin in his hand. 'No, Father,' she said. 'It cannot be.'

'Oh yes, my dear, this country is dying. A metropolitan province of the richest kingdom on God's earth brought to its knees by the potato.'

'No, Father,' she said. 'By callous Englishmen who've never cared whether the Irish live or die.'

'No, Kate, not callous. That would mean we are cruel when we are not. This calamity has swamped us. We could never have prepared ourselves for anything so monstrous, so unimaginable.'

'Father, they wanted food, and you offered to sell it to them. They had no money, so you made them work for it.'

'Listen, my dear. You asked me how we've let it come this far and I've asked it myself again and again. I have stood at this window and seen the ships in the harbour deep in the water, heavy with grain, and then I look into the streets and I see an army of hungry beggars and I ask, who is to blame? All I know is, it is not in our character to behave as we are behaving here. I know how we are elsewhere. I have spent my life with the English abroad and I know we are capable of great generosity and tolerance to those under our care. Yet in Ireland we rule in opposites. Mention the name in Whitehall or Westminster and you can say farewell to kindness and common sense. I wonder if that is how we shall be judged, how history will condemn us. Will anyone forgive us? Are all of us guilty?'

He turned again to the window and was quiet. Kate stood and touched his shoulder, but he did not turn. 'I'm sorry, Father,' she said softly. 'You have never spoken this way before. I never knew you felt it too.'

He sighed. 'Be patient, my darling. Soon we will leave. I have failed here, and in the New Year I will demand to be brought home. If Trevelyan refuses then I shall appeal directly to the Prime Minister and, if he fails me, to the Palace. With the Queen's permission, we should be home early in the new year. Think of it, Kate – spring in Lincolnshire! How I long to leave. We English do not belong here.'

He turned and kissed her cheek. 'Do you know what they're calling her here, Kate, Queen Victoria? They've dubbed her 'The Famine Queen'. Soon she will have inherited the biggest grave-yard in Europe.'

He smiled at the description and, saying no more, kissed her again. Then he refilled his tumbler with brandy and left her for his bed.

She stood listening as he climbed the stairs, heard his bed-room door close and then his habitual soft nightly coughing. His words had come as a shock to her. Could she leave now? Could she go easily and leave Una and Keegan and Ireland behind her? Suddenly she was afraid. Her heart throbbed. Life was pull-ing her sideways again. Her father's voice swelled around her, echoes upon echoes, rebounding, distorted, magnified. 'Home … Spring … The Palace … Do not belong here …'

The floor moved and the room began to spin. Snow came in through the windows, clouding the room with a white flurry, snuffing out the candles. She felt she was in a children's game of blind man's bluff, spinning, not seeing, afraid to reach out. She held the edge of the table and, like a blind person feeling her way across a stranger's room, she guided herself to the door. She was in the hall, reaching for the banister rail and screamed as she saw herself in the hall mirror. Blood was trickling from her

nose, and tiny red droplets speckled her arm. From his bed, Sir
William heard the crash of glass as she fell.

ᖇᖇ

How well she would later remember that nightmare of journeys.
How perfect, how vivid the sequence of images. The clarity
of her fevered dreams, the smells, the sights and the emotions
would remain indelible.

She was walking across sweet-smelling heather and the
ground was as soft as a cushion, the rocks like pillows. She kicked
them into the sky and they soared, like puffed-up balloons. Then
she was crossing the tops of mountains in great bouncing, flying
steps with her toes barely touching, her nightdress billowing,
caught by the wind.

She soared higher and higher until she could stuff the white, puffy
clouds into her pockets like handfuls of gossamer. She pranced on
tiptoe from one peak to another and the days changed into nights
and back again in seconds. Then it was cold, she was naked and the
goose down turned to snow and melted in her hands.

She was plummeting to earth, tumbling and twisting in the
vapour clouds, the wind screaming in her head, the sky closing
fast around her, black and thunderous. Her heart pounded as she
fell faster and faster. She put out her hand and the earth opened
up and swallowed her and she was golden and warm again.

She saw a fire and someone standing by it, pouring liquid into
a glass. She tried to raise herself to speak, but in that instant he was
gone and a hand pushed her down. She saw Keegan by her side,
she felt his hand on her cheeks, a touch of ice on her burning skin,
and it was Una, stroking her hair, her voice calm and soothing.

Again she tried to rise and again hands pushed her down.
Above her she could hear the low, monotonous chanting of
monks, like a funeral chorus that came nearer and louder. She
screamed out for them to stop and her stomach came up

through her throat and a river of bile gushed from her mouth. She reached out to stoke a fire, but as the poker touched the embers they exploded and the room was ablaze. She was burning. Water was pouring off her and yet she was on fire. The torrent turned to steam and she felt herself being dragged down it into a furnace. She watched her body begin to melt, but there was no pain and no fear any more. Fire without either.

Then the gradual coming of a beautiful peace, without guilt, without anxiety. Free of her body, she began drifting away.

'Kate.' She heard voices singing her name together, like a choir. 'Kate,' they called again. 'Stay with us. Don't leave us. Stay, Kate.'

But they were faint appeals, becoming fainter. She was too far from them now and too content, travelling on that same cushion of soft, sweet heather. The voices were below her now, a long way below, down there with the fire. She turned to see them for the last time, but she saw him instead, the little boy standing in the flames, just as she remembered him on that night in Lincolnshire. His hands were stretching out to her, reaching for her, his eyes imploring, 'Reach for me. Touch my fingers. Catch hold, catch hold.'

She reached down with her hand and clasped his and held it tight. And the fever left her.

જ

'What colour am I?' she asked. Robin smiled at her and wiped the sweat from her brow. 'You have a colour, Kate, but it is not black. You've a tinge of yellow, a little jaundice, but you're here and as beautiful as ever. Welcome back.'

'Was it typhus?' she asked.

'No, Kate. Thank God it was not. It was relapsing fever, or five-day fever, as some call it. That's how long you've been away from us on that journey of yours.'

'You know about my journey?'

'Oh, yes. I reckon we all went on every part of it with you, Keegan, Una and myself. We took it in turns to be with you. Last night was the worst. We thought we'd lost you, we really did.'

She turned her head away. He saw her tears. 'Now, now, Kate, this is not the time for a weep. We have to put some business back into that body of yours. All that travelling has tired you.'

He wiped her eyes and packed the pillows around her. Cook brought soup and he took the spoon to her lips.

'It was such a journey, Robin,' she said, 'I was about to give in, I know I was. But he brought me back.'

'Yes, Kate. I think somebody must have done. Now rest. Let the soup work. Rest is all you need now.'

He got up to leave but she took his hand. 'Who is he, Robin? Why is he always there, watching? Why does he …?'

She closed her eyes to sleep. As he reached the door she said, 'I wasn't bitten by a rat, was I?'

'No, Kate, you were not.'

'Perhaps it was one of your breadcrumbs.'

And he nodded, certain of it.

ରଞ

Sir William was comforting. 'You have fine friends, Kathryn. I am proud of my daughter who has such friends. Day and night they watched you, swabbing all the time to keep you cool. Your Mr Keegan was even reciting poetry to you. I think it must have been in Irish.'

The week had passed. Kate was up and getting stronger by the day. The yellow had gone from her face and the dark shadows under her eyes were fading. She felt as if she had been reborn.

'They are my only friends, Father,' she said. 'The only ones I'll ever have. If I leave here I shall have none.'

'That's nonsense, Kathryn. Why, you have dozens in England. Your life there was full of them.'

She was sitting by the fire in his large, padded leather armchair. He had tucked a rug around her legs, draped a shawl over her shoulders and put a few drops of his best cognac into her lunch-time broth. It had been many years since he had had any reason to fuss over her this way.

She knew this was the moment. All week she had been pre-paring for it, hoping to judge it right.

'Father,' she said, 'I don't want to leave here.'

He drew up a stool and sat by her, a tumbler of whiskey nest-ling in his lap. 'Not leave here, Kathryn? You mean Cork?'

'No, Father. I do not want to leave Ireland, at least not yet. Not until I know how all this is going to end.'

Sir William hesitated. This was not the time to remonstrate with her. She was convalescing and still a little emotional.

'My dear, we must leave. I have already drafted my letter of resignation and I intend on sending it to Trevelyan very soon. I've intimated what I shall do if he refuses me.'

'Then I shall not come with you.' He recognised the spirit in her voice. He knew it well. Like her beauty, she had inherited it from her mother. He stood and warmed his back by the fire. He seemed very calm.

'Kathryn, you cannot stay here without me. I shan't permit it. You have nowhere to go.'

'I have the Fitzgeralds.'

She looked up at him. How old he was now, suddenly with-ered. It was as if some part of him had already left Ireland and was speeding its way home to England.

'Kathryn, I'll say this once, and only once. Even though you are a grown woman, I cannot, I will not, let you stay here without me. This country is no longer safe for us English. Fear hangs over this island like a thundercloud. When this hunger is done and the fever has taken its last, there will be a war. I know the signs, and these people have a good reason for it. There's a momentum gathering out there that will not be stopped except by our battalions. It will be '98 all over again, except this time we will not put it down so easily or so cleverly. There is an inheritance to this famine as there has been to no other, and it will be violent, believe me. It will last long and God only knows who will be the winner. I will not leave my only daughter, my only family, here among people who are preparing for such a thing. That is my last word on it, Kathryn. You will not mention it to me again.'

He leant down and kissed her forehead. He smelt the fragrance of her hair. He kissed her again, but she did not move. He waited, but she did not speak. He knew then that he was losing yet again. Ireland had taken from him his self-respect, the reputation he had once treasured, the chance to end a life's career with honour. Now Ireland was vying for his daughter.

CHAPTER TWELVE

The black fever travelled as fast as it took one man to touch another and the fool who doubted it was a dead fool. The rich died like the poor, the well-fed with the starving. Upstairs and downstairs, in Dublin's grand houses and in the hovels of Baltimore, among the fat landlords in their great estates and the inmates in the filthy workhouses, it did not discriminate. In all Ireland's history there had never been such an epidemic.

It spread like a summer fire across bracken and no one could tell where it sparked first. Was it Skibbereen? Did it jump from there to Schull and leap again to Killarney and Limerick? Within weeks it had taken a giant's stride, spanning Drogheda, Galway and Sligo. No part of Ireland was left untouched. In two days and nights it killed everyone in Castlebar Prison, including the governor, the matron, the chaplain and the turnkey. The twenty-eight hospitals in Ireland were so full they closed their doors, deciding it was more merciful that the diseased should die quickly and suffer less.

At Lurgan, there was nowhere to bury the dead except in a pit by the hospital walls, next to the well that supplied it with fresh water. In the workhouse at Castlerea over a hundred men, women and children died of fever in one night, and in Cork, eight hundred in less than a fortnight.

Some people lit fires to purify the air or locked themselves inside their cottages, afraid to breathe outside. But no locked door could bar its entry. The mist came to their eyes, their bodies burned with the fever, their skin went as black as the soot in their hearth and they screamed out for water that no one dared bring them.

Bodies littered the streets and when the graveyards were full, the stone quarries were consecrated as mass graves. They dragged the corpses along the coast to the beaches and left them on the sand for the sea to carry away. The fish ate their flesh, the surf broke the skeletons apart, and the returning tides scattered the bleached bones along the shores. Sometimes, a wave would lift a skull and it would grin at the living and they would know that they, too, were doomed.

The government announced it would pay for quarantined fever sheds to be built, but Robin would not wait. He erected a tent in a meadow on the outskirts of Cork, a mile beyond the city boundary, as close as the council elders would allow. It was an old marquee, bought for his father's wedding fifty years before. With Keegan's help, he had it staked and standing in two days and within the week the two of them had built primitive cots. Una helped sew together cloth mattresses and filled them with straw from her father's estate. On the seventh day, the hospital cart came with eighteen men and women and twelve children. Robin shook Keegan's hand, kissed his sister, then went inside and closed the flaps of the tent behind him.

Keegan dug a shallow trench in a five-yard perimeter around the tent and filled it with ash and Robin forbid them to come beyond it. The Quakers gave fifty pounds to buy rolls of cotton, which Una cut into sheets. Sir Robert brought buckets so that fresh water could be carried from the nearby stream.

Keegan and Una worked as many hours as the light of the short winter days allowed. They came at dawn and left at dusk, just as Robin was lighting his candles for the night's watch. There was never a moment inside the tent when Robin's shadow was still. They called out to him regularly, and he answered with his list of things to be done, medicines to be brought, messages to deliver. Not once did he come out, not once did he show himself.

He died from the fever on his father's birthday. In a month of continuous nursing care, he had not saved a single soul. Una and Keegan had arrived in the early morning as usual, just as the light was showing, but there was no candle, no moving shadow silhouetted against the canvas. They called out but there was no reply. They moved closer and shouted louder, but there was nothing to be heard inside. Una ran towards the moat of ash and screamed out Robin's name, over and over again, but no voice answered. She ran to the tent flap but Keegan caught her and held her tight until she was quiet. She and her brother had come into the world together. Now he had left it.

A police inspector came with an order from the magistrates signed and stamped for them to see. Twice he called out Robin's name, and went as close to the tent as he dared. But the only sound was the shuffle of the harness on his horse and the rooks cawing in the trees.

The canvas was brittle and dry with age and it needed only one torch. It exploded. The heat lifted it into the air like a balloon, twisting and snapping as the flames took it higher and through the smoke they saw the lines of the blackened dead, curling and twisting in the heat. Una and Keegan turned their backs and prayed as the brown, cremating smoke spiralled up behind them.

ഌ

As Kate grew stronger, so did her resolve. The life that was now ahead of her was her own and only she would decide its direction. During her convalescence, Una had written to her every day. Describing every detail of Robin's tent hospital and the work she and Keegan had been doing to help. She wrote of her growing affection for him and the plans they were now making.

They came to her on the day of Robin's death. She listened to them, the room shrouded in the faint light of that winter afternoon, three shadows at a proxy funeral. She did not cry. She had read somewhere that it is not a man's death that causes the greatest grief, but the manner of his dying and Robin had died nobly. There had been purpose to his living and a reason for his dying and he would want them to celebrate both equally.

Una sat on the rug by the hearth, holding her hands to the fire. Keegan stared out of the window.

'What else is there to tell me, Una?' Kate said. 'There is something, isn't there?' She waited for Una to speak.

'We didn't want to tell you today, Kate, not today.'

'I've heard the worst. What else is there?'

Una sat and took her hand.

'Keegan and I have decided to leave Ireland. We're going to America. There's a sailing soon from Limerick. Don't be angry with us, Kate. We are not running, we are not cowards. But there is nothing to hold us here. Ireland is dying, and we will not stay to be among the dead.'

'We have run out of hope,' Keegan said. 'We stay and we die. We could die in the coffin ships. Either way it is a risk.'

Una kissed Kate's hands. 'Come with us, Kate. It's a new world where there's no famine and no fever and no hatred. Come with us.'

'We'll not be alone, Kate,' Keegan said. 'The docks are crowded with people on their way. Ships are leaving almost every week.'

'There is another reason,' Una said. She turned to Keegan. 'Will you tell, or shall I?'

'He was your brother.'

She was trembling and spoke fast in her excitement.

'Kate, we have found something wonderful. It was tucked away with Robin's papers, along with his microscope and things. He must have been working on it all summer. He was so thorough and it is so detailed. It made no sense to us at first, just a jumble of dates and Latin names. It was his research, Kate. He's been researching the black fever.'

'I don't understand, Una,' Kate said. 'Why should this make you want to leave?'

'It's in his writing. On the last pages before he died. He even made drawings and there are jars full of them.'

'Una, drawings of what? Jars of what?'

'Lice,' said Keegan. 'Robin believed it is lice that cause the fever. Not hunger, not the rats. But the tiny lice.'

Kate leaned back in her chair. 'His little breadcrumbs.'

'We are taking his work to America with us,' Una said. 'Father says it is the only way. There are doctors there who can prove Robin right. Kate, do you understand how much this means to Father and me? To know that Robin died for something?'

'Yes, Una. I understand. He died nobly, the way he lived. But why America? Why not England?'

'We don't think Robin would have wanted that,' Keegan said. 'He never condemned anyone for the blight, but he did blame England for doing so little about it. Doctors in America are bound to be concerned. We will talk to the Irish there.'

'Say yes!' Una pleaded. 'Kate, say you will come with us.'

'I don't know,' she answered. 'I was beginning to hope that my home was here with you and Keegan and Robin. But without you, what is there for me here? I shall be alone again.'

'Then you will come,' said Keegan. 'I will buy three tickets tomorrow and we'll have a carriage to take us to Limerick.'

But Una already knew the answer. She saw it in Kate's eyes and felt it in the firm hold of her hand. She kissed Kate on her forehead, and again on her cheek and whispered to her, 'But you will come to see us go, won't you? You will wish us well as we sail to the New World?'

And Kate nodded.

Keegan did not have to pay to hire his carriage. Sir William Macaulay provided it himself. He was relieved to see them go, convinced that with their sailing, Kate would resign herself to returning to England with him. Sometimes he could not help but marvel at fate's happy coincidences.

෧෩

They came to Limerick in the early afternoon. The sun was warm. The walls of King John's Castle were reflected in the waters of the Shannon and on the far side of the bridge they could see St Mary's Cathedral. Every street in the town was blocked with people, a dense swarm moving slowly towards the piers. Men searched for lost wives, children ran in and out of legs, screaming for lost mothers. Some pushed their belongings in carts, others humped them on their backs, a bewildered, frightened, swirling current of people. English soldiers in their blue and red tunics were posted along the quayside, their rifles at the ready. More lined the gangplanks, guarding the dockers as they loaded the cargo ships bound for Liverpool.

'Irish bacon and Irish wheat,' said Keegan bitterly. 'Off to make English bellies even fatter.' He pointed to the ships on the far side of the harbour. 'And those over there are waiting to take our people to America. Do you know that second only to food, we Irish are the chief export from our own country?'

He left them to collect the tickets. They sat in the carriage and watched him go.

'Will you marry him?' Kate asked.

'He hasn't asked me yet,' she said. 'But he will. I wonder if he would have done if we'd stayed? He might have been frightened off.'

Kate nodded. 'Yes! He may well have been. How different we were once.'

'Father says America is a big melting pot,' Una said, 'filling up with people from everywhere in the world and all coming for the same reason. To get away from the old and begin again. He says we will all cling together. All be the same.'

'You will always be Irish, Una.'

'Then I'll be American-Irish. Or Irish-American. Do you think that will be allowed?'

Kate looked out of the carriage window at the commotion around her. Close by, a man in black top hat was standing on a box holding up tickets and shouting out the prices for the passage on all the ships moored there.

'We have just returned from the shores of North America and we leave again in ten days. So buy your ticket now and be sure of a good space aboard the *Alice of Galway* for we're off again soon to the flourishing city of New York where demand for labour is more than double hitherto. The *Alice* is the finest ship in the harbour, five hundred tons under its master John McKay. You will get a pound of meal or bread a day and as much water as you want. But only the sound and healthy can come aboard. Come along ... Come along. Five pounds on deck, two pounds below.'

'Una, I have one last thing to ask.'

'I think I know what it might be, Kate. And the answer is no.'

'You can guess?'

'You want to find the rebel. He's told you it is none of your business and he's right. You are English, and always will be, just as you said I will always be Irish. We cannot change what we are. You cannot change what is.'

'But you have, Una. You have changed what is.'

'But I have had to go away to do it.'

'And so have I. Don't you see? This is my America. It's here that I've discovered my freedom, just as you're off to find yours.'

'But not with them, Kate. Not the rebels. It can't be right to be with them.'

'Una, I don't know what is right or wrong. I only know I cannot go back to England with my father. I will not be able to resist him unless ...'

'Unless you leave him?'

'Unless I leave him.'

'Do you want to stay with my father?'

'That won't help me. They will come after me. My father will send men and take me back the same day, I know he will.'

'Then what can I do?'

'You must help me find Moran. He went with the rebels. He will find me somewhere I can hide until I know what I am supposed to do and who I am supposed to be. I know he will help me.'

'Then you must go to my father, Kate, you must. Tell him what you've told me. He knows somebody, a Protestant like us and a landowner too. He's a young man with a head full of dreams and I think he's a friend of Coburn. Father will help you.'

They had kissed and hugged and had dried their eyes by the time Keegan returned. He held up the tickets.

'We're on the largest ship in port and the master tells me it is the fastest and most reliable of all the ships here. Five pounds each, water is free. We can carry our own food or buy it on board at sixpence each sailing day. We leave in an hour's time, bound for Quebec.'

'Why Quebec?' asked Kate. 'Isn't that in Canada?'

'It is,' said Keegan. 'But there are no ships sailing to America this week. One has already left for Philadelphia and there's another in ten days but we can't wait that long. Quebec is where most of them are going now, to a river called the St Lawrence. We must wait there on an island before they will let us land. They say the border with America is less than a hundred miles from there. Most of the Irish are making for a place called Boston.'

'I was born only twenty miles from Boston in Lincolnshire,' Kate said.

Una squeezed her arm. 'Then that's a fine omen if ever I needed one.'

'Do you want to go to Boston?' Kate asked.

'We want to go to America,' Keegan answered. 'And wherever Boston is, I'm assured it is in America, and that will do us fine.'

'Do you know how long it will take?'

'The master said it could take six weeks or longer if the sea is bad. He said some ships have been, blown hundreds of miles south before the winds turned and brought them north again.'

They pushed their way through the crowds towards a tall ship with a black tarred hull and the figure of a stout lady on her bow. On both sides of her, the name SS *Sarah Jane* was painted in large gold letters. There was not a spare inch of space on deck. Some of the passengers were dressed in top hats and heavy coats, their wives in woollen shawls. The poor and the ragged were ushered below.

A bell rang and there was shouting.

'Aboard! All aboard the *Sarah Jane*. We're on the tide and have a wind. The last of you aboard now and be quick with it!'

Crew scurried up the rope ladders and stepped out onto the yardarms a hundred feet up to unfurl the great canvas sails. They loosened the lines to the pier and the gangplank. The master, high up by the wheel at the stern, shouted to Keegan, 'If you're coming aboard, young man, you'd better do it now, or find yourself some lodgings ashore!'

Kate hugged Una for the last time. Then she held Keegan tight.

'Thank you,' she whispered to him. 'Thank you for bringing me into your life. Thank you for sharing it and for giving me all the things I could never have had without you. Thank you for the children, and Eugene and your father and all the happy times we've had in the valley. You've lost hope here, but I've found it. God bless you.'

'Why did it have to happen this way, Kate? Promise me that one day you will write us a letter and tell us why Ireland is so badly treated. How did the world forget us? Are we like the ancient Jews, wandering the earth, looking for a place to rest?'

'No, Keegan,' she answered. 'You will stop your wandering soon. You will find your new home in America and you will marry Una and have fine children. One day we will meet again, always believe that. And on that day we will look back with no regrets, because then we shall know that this was just the beginning.'

He kissed her again and, without looking back, ran with Una up the gangplank. They dropped down onto the deck and out of sight behind the gunwales. Kate did not wait for the sails to fill. She could not watch them go. She ran to the waiting carriage and closed the curtains tight. She shouted an order to the coachman, heard the crack of his whip and his call to the team. Soon the bustle of Limerick was behind her.

Now she was abandoned. One by one they had all left her, all those who had been so precious. How soon would she forget their voices and their faces? How quickly would she have nothing to remember them by? Alive or dead, it did not matter. They were gone.

She had been in Ireland for such a short time but she had experienced more happiness, grief and misery than she could ever have dreamt existed in one world. She had faced it, braved it and suffered a little of it herself. She had survived because she had been among those she loved and who had loved her back, Irish people who knew well enough who she was, people who had cause enough to despise and reject her. Yet it had all been for a purpose, and now she must find out what it was. She could not span her two worlds any longer. She must choose which one to live in and, having chosen, become immersed and prosper in the middle of it. It was the day of her turning.

CHAPTER THIRTEEN

It cheered him as nothing had done since he had first stepped foot in Ireland. Was this a reprieve? Were the odds reversing themselves? Could he really believe this was the beginning of the end, the final chapter in a lengthy tale of horrors?

Sir William looked from his window towards Cork Harbour. Sailing ships were rafted there side by side, their hulls lined so tight together there was barely sight of water in between. How wonderful they looked in the sunset, like an armada, a fleet of hope and charity. He had spent the day watching them arrive as they manoeuvred their way up the river Lee to their moorings, their vast sails shivering as helmsmen brought their bows into the wind, the capstans spinning, the tangle of lines thrown from deck to deck, the running of the chains as the anchors dropped to steady them.

'Yes, indeed,' Sir William said to himself, tapping the window pane with his whiskey glass. It was indeed a splendid sight.

Thirty thousand tons of Indian corn were now waiting to be unloaded, ready to be stored in the warehouses, corn that would turn Ireland around, corn that would feed the destitute and put an end to their hunger. Had Trevelyan been right after all? He had insisted that the free market, his laissez-faire approach, would repair what the blight had undone. Imports of American maize, diverted from pigs in Cincinati to feed the Irish poor, would end the famine. Soon it would be for sale on the open market and at a price even the poor could afford.

What had Trevelyan so often reminded him in his terse communiqués?

Private enterprise is sacrosanct. There must be as little disturbance of private trade as possible. Indiscreet tampering with trade is dangerous. The laws of commerce are the laws of nature and are consequently God's laws. Interfering with them risked God's displeasure.

Sir William sat at his desk and drafted a letter of congratulations to his master confirming the ships' safe arrival and his assurance that at last the worst must surely be over. Soon he was to discover it was not. The tonnage of maize the government allowed to be imported into Ireland did not and would never match the tonnage of potatoes lost. The deficit was irretrievable. The maize would be sold by the corn merchants at such a profit that few would be able to afford it. It was also a foreign grain, a stranger to Ireland. How was it to be eaten?

The resourceful Trevelyan announced he had personally tested various recipes in his own kitchen and having decided on one he ordered pamphlets to be distributed with instructions on how it should be cooked.

The grain may be crushed between two good-size stones. Soaked all night in warm water, then boiled with a little fat, if at hand. It can then be eaten with milk, with salt, or plain. Ten pounds of the corn so prepared is ample food for a labouring man for seven days.

Very few among the hungry Irish had heat to boil water, or milk or salt. Fewer still could read English.

The maize was hard as flint and had to be crushed. In America, they knew it as 'hominy' and gave it to the steel mills to chop into tiny cookable fragments. No miller in Ireland could do that. So Trevelyan proposed that the poor should mill it themselves and promptly ordered the manufacture of hand-grinders. A few prototypes were made at a price of fifteen shillings each and a shilling was a stranger in the pockets of the poor. Losing patience, Trevelyan finally told the hungry to eat it unmilled and uncooked. But eaten raw, it could not be digested. It pierced the intestines of the hungry and weak and their stomachs twisted with convulsions. Eating it to stay alive, they died agonising deaths.

The starving thousands along the west coast, from Donegal through Connaught to Galway, knew nothing of this new foreign food because it never reached them. The Admiralty had sent two steamers from Cork loaded with the grain, only to discover there were no harbours big enough to take them.

Only the corn merchants of Cork did well from the ships moored in their harbour. All made great profit. One boasted a gain of over forty thousand pounds from rising prices in three months of trading.

If Kate knew any of this, she did not seem to care. Very little now seemed to matter at all. Her life had become a vacuum. It was already the third month of spring, the days were warming, some trees were already in bud. In the garden below her bedroom window, daffodils were sprouting a foot high and purple wild anemones were scattered below the oaks but it no longer thrilled her. She was in limbo, the place of the lost, the forgotten, the abandoned. When they had all left her she had felt resolute, preparing for the journey ahead, ready for that critical moment of decision. Now she felt sapped of ambition, lacking the courage to make a decision. It was Queen Victoria who made it for her.

∾

Buckingham Palace had announced that the Queen, still young and agreeable, would make her first visit to Ireland that summer. She would be accompanied by her consort, Prince Albert. They would sail to Cork and then journey by carriage and train to Dublin. There they would be feted with a banquet and ball in the castle.

Dublin, like every town and city in Ireland, had not escaped the ravages of the famine. Many of its grand terraces were derelict, abandoned by their owners, who had taken themselves and their savings to Liverpool and London or to the New World. The merchants' grand houses on Dame Street and Grafton Street were dilapidated wrecks, homes to squatters, without doors, their windows smashed and covered with brown paper, their wooden shutters hanging from their hinges. The fashionable shops along Queen Street had long been ransacked and boarded up.

Cholera had spread into every filthy court and alley. There was not a poor family in the city who had not lost someone. It had been carried into Phoenix Park and an English regiment garrisoned there was now living under strict quarantine.

This was the face of Ireland's capital and it could not be shown to Her Majesty. Dublin would need to be given an emergency facelift, but, given the lack of funds, it was to be confined only to those parts the royal carriage would travel through. Every effort would be made to conceal the decay behind and beyond them. The mayor, with an eye on a baronetcy, issued his memorandum:

It would be highly expedient that such houses that have deteriorated are cleaned as the short time allows and fully furnished with window curtains, muslin blinds and flower pots. We must have people properly dressed, parading themselves. They must be impressive. It must be arranged promptly.

The Queen's route from Cork would end by train at Kingsbridge railway station. The mayor had plans for that too.

The sundry back settlements in the purlieu will not fit with the magnificent carriages provided for her. There should be a screen of boards from the first flourishing suburb at Beggar's Bush all the way to the final platform.

A great lie was being arranged, false impressions created, and false conclusions would be drawn. There was much discontent, high and low. The *Dublin Evening Mail* wrote:

Is it possible that Her Majesty could be gratified by this wretched display of wealth when thousands upon thousands of her subjects are starving? She would see a truer picture of Ireland if she was shown humanity perishing on the dung heap. She need go only a further mile beyond the places prepared for her to witness the falsehoods. If we have funds to spare, let them be spent on her starving subjects. Why should we be called upon to rejoice when gaunt famine and cold poverty reign? She is Queen of the greatest empire in the world. She is also matron to the world's biggest workhouse.

In advance of the royal visit and as a rehearsal for it, Lord Clarendon, the Lord Lieutenant, sent out invitations for a gala ball. It would be held on the first day of summer in Dublin Castle's St Patrick's Hall. Among the first to receive the gold-embossed envelope was the Commissariat General, Sir William Macaulay. His daughter was expected to accompany him.

They travelled for three days to the capital, resting for a night in Kilkenny and then again in Carlow. On the evening of the third day, their carriage entered the castle gates to the salutes of mounted Hussars lining the drive to the front steps. St Patrick's Hall smelt of new paint and beeswax. Great tapestries, borrowed from churches and noblemen, lined the walls and portraits of the Queen were spaced in exact intervals between them. Union flags were festooned across windows and draped across damp patches on the walls that could not otherwise be disguised. Five enormous crystal chandeliers were a blaze of candlelight.

Sir William and Kate were announced as the orchestra, assembled from the regiments garrisoned in the castle, began a polka. Squads of young officers in their blue, green and scarlet dress uniforms pranced with their pretty partners in a revolving swirl of bodies. Sir William retreated quickly to an alcove to smoke his cigar and sip champagne. Kate was obliged to shake many hands and curtsy to those in high office who expected no less. She was asked to dance many times and as many times refused.

She sat alone, avoided conversation and watched the polite and impeccable formality of the early evening slowly transform as the young officers, full of food and fuller still of Lord Clarendon's wine, became rowdy. Within hours, they were dancing with extravagant flourishes, exchanging banter, loud and loutish, brushing aside older men who tried to restrain them. The ball began to resemble a drunken, brawling night in the young officers' mess.

They sprawled at the tables, pouring claret down their throats and stuffing their cheeks. One held up a leg of roast rabbit to Kate. 'Here's to your Irish, Missy Kate, for we know who you are. Your friends are rabbits. They live like them, breed like them and one shot from us and they run to their filthy burrows like a buck with a thistle up his crotch.' He banged the table. 'They sleep with their pigs and eat with their pigs. Rabbits and pigs. Rabbits and pigs …'

Like children reciting a nursery rhyme, his fellow officers followed his chant, shouting the words faster and faster. 'Rabbits and pigs, rabbits and pigs …'

A hand grabbed hers. 'Now come on, young Missy Kathryn. I'll not take no for an answer. Not even if I have to carry you over my shoulder to the floor.'

He came close to her, grinning, swaying, a glass in his hand, a cheroot in his mouth. He was tall, blond and drunk. She pulled her hand away. He laughed. Red wine dribbled down his chin. It was an ugly laugh.

He grabbed at her again pulling her onto the dance floor.

'So you are Sir William's black-haired beauty. Well, my luvvie, you may love your Irish piggies but tonight you are with me, an English officer. Come along, they're playing a polka, let's have some fun.'

She felt his body tight against her. She smelt the liquor on his breath. He held her by her wrists and swung her round wildly, once, twice, three times, to the cheers of the others watching. The music vibrated inside her, louder and louder as the drunk cavorted around her, high-stepping, twisting her arms, spinning her around. She was dizzy, ready to fall. Feeling her relax in his arms, the officer spat out his cheroot, guided her into an alcove and pushed her backwards against the wall. He forced his knee between her thighs and put his hand on her breast. His fingers fondled her nipple. Then he kissed her neck and licked her ear. She felt his hand moving up her thigh.

The shock stunned her. She felt limp. Then rage. She brought her knee up hard into his groin and felt her kneecap sink into the soft flesh of his scrotum. She pulled her nails across his face and spurts of blood dribbled onto his collar. With the howl of a child, he let go of her, spun backwards into the room holding his hands to his face and fell blindly into the orchestra. His fellow officers rushed forward but, too drunk, they tumbled among the scattered instruments.

Sir William, hidden away, settled and content with his cognac and cigars, heard nothing of it. It was Lord Clarendon, holding Kate by the wrists, her gown speckled red, who shocked him out of his reverie. Clarendon was white-faced and trembling.

'Macaulay!' He was only feet away but he was shouting. 'You will take this daughter of yours from my sight this instant. She has behaved wretchedly, abominably, despicably, more a market harridan than a lady of our society. She has attacked an officer on my staff, unprovoked, like an animal. She has abused my hospitality and disgraced you and your position. You will leave here immediately – immediately, I say – or I will evict you myself. Do you hear? Myself!'

∽

She sat in the dark. The fire had died. The house was silent. The clock in the hall had chimed three times but she would not sleep tonight. This was no time for sleep.

Three days had passed since they had arrived back from Dublin but she was still re-living the blood, the commotion, the screaming, the jostling and the anger. What had they shouted? 'Go back to the boglands. Go to your traitor, your Captain Shelley. Find the grave we put him in. Go kiss his bones and be damned!'

She knew her father could not forgive her. Three days and he had not spoken. He had locked himself in his room and only opened it to the knock of his servants. On that third evening she heard his soft padding down the stairs and into his favourite room, with the panelled beech and the view of Cork Harbour. She waited but he did not call. She went to the door, hesitated and went in.

He was in his armchair by the grate of a dying fire, in his dressing gown, with a shawl around his shoulders. He had not shaved nor combed his hair and he was barefoot. How small he looked, how gaunt and grey and shrunken, like a man crippled by life. A decanter of whiskey was on a table by his side. He held a glass, half full, in his hand.

He had been ordered back to England and he would leave in disgrace. A lifetime of endeavour, a half century of diligence and public service, annulled so swiftly, so finally, so unjustly.

Kate had wounded him but she had no way to heal him. She whispered to him but he heard only the screaming abuse of the snarling accusers and the secret revealed. His daughter conniving with the traitor shot dead for conspiring with England's enemies. Such treachery from his own flesh and blood. He who had loved her as dearly as her own mother.

'Father,' she said. He did not turn. He would not look.

'Father. I must tell you that …' He coughed and wiped away the spittle from the arm of the chair.

'Do not speak to me as your father. He no longer exists. You have lost all claim to him.'

He turned to the wall. He would not look at her.

'There is a sailing from Cork on Friday next,' he said. 'You will be on it. You will return to Lincolnshire and stay there until you hear from my lawyers. They will arrange an annuity, enough for you to live as you please and where you please. But not with me. Never more with me. That is my contract. Take it or leave it.'

'Father, you know nothing of that night. You do not know ...'

'I know enough to send you to prison. Enough to have you hanged.'

'I have done nothing. You judge me without ...'

'Quiet! Silence! Do not speak. I have indeed judged you and know now what you are and why. It's your blood, your mongrel blood. This is your mother's doing.'

'My mother is dead.'

'Dead, yes! Your mother died because ... because ...'

His voice was fading. She waited, afraid of what he might say next. He sat quite still. The only sounds were his breathing and the rustle of the curtains at the open window. He looked at her directly for the first time, the anger gone. He looked captured, defeated, lost. When he spoke again it was in a whisper.

'I sent her away. That was the sin of it. To send her off, away from me and away from you.'

Kate went down on her knees by his chair. 'Tell me Father, tell me. I will listen.'

He spoke as if he did not want to be heard. It was his confession, the secret he had kept hidden within himself all those years.

'I sent your mother away and you were never to know why. That was how I thought I would protect myself. To tell you would have been to lose you. Now everything is lost. I have lived with this secret all your life, a guilt eating away like a weevil

gnawing at my soul. I had no right to you. You belonged to her. I
denied you your mother.'

The light was leaving the room. His face was silhouetted, soft,
blurred, frail. Once he had been handsome. There was a portrait
of him as a young uniformed officer hanging in the hall. He
had brought it from Lincolnshire. As a child she would often
pretend to be a soldier and march back and forth in front of it.
He had taught her how to salute.

'Your mother was nineteen when I first met her. The most
beautiful girl I had ever seen. I was in my twenties, well set up,
a bull of an officer and I knew what I was worth. But I was an
empty husk and she nourished me. I wasn't much of a romantic
but I knew what I wanted and I wanted her. She loved me back
as fiercely as any man could wish for.'

He emptied his glass and filled it again to the top.

'But she was a Catholic. Yes! A Catholic. They say that love
cannot be reasoned with and so I thought it would be with us. But
it was impossible for us to marry. My family would have cut me off
without a penny and I could not have remained in the regiment.
How could we have managed? But she loved me and to marry me
she had to renounce her faith. Can you imagine what that meant
to her? I knew nothing then of her Church, nothing of its supersti-
tions and the way it holds a person prisoner. I did not know that
what she had promised me was not in her power to fulfil.

'So we were married in the Church of England and were
blissfully content. We travelled together to most corners of the
Empire and no mention was made of it again. Within two years
she was heavy with you, and it was then that I began to lose her.
I would find her fretting and weeping, talking to herself, and I
could find no way to comfort her. When you were born she did
not hold you or look at you. It was as if you did not belong to
her. So you were weaned by another. You were never wanting
of love and care, I can vouch for that. But it was not from her.
Never from her.'

He was silent again. He turned his head, resting the tumbler of whiskey on his knee. He looked down at it, the glow from the fire's embers reflecting the gold of it on his face. It was as if he was looking into a crystal ball, waiting for the images of his past to show themselves. Kate wanted to touch him, to comfort, to give him strength. But she could not. He was elsewhere and she was not with him. She leant nearer as he began again.

'She started riding out on her own and would not tell me why. I waited some time, some weeks I think, until I was curious, perhaps even jealous and one day I followed. She made no attempt to hide her tracks. She never looked back. There was no cunning. She rode some miles beyond our village, somewhere I'd never been before and stopped at a church. For a long time she stood between the gravestones and I wondered if she had a relation buried there, one she had not talked of to me. Or perhaps she had come to find a little peace, to be alone, away from me, away from everything. I could understand that. Then, just as I was about to turn to my horse, I saw him. I could see her plainly but his back was to me. She was pleading. I could see the anguish in her face and I saw him shake his head. She was on her knees, crying. I was in a rage. Had I brought my gun I would have shot them both, then and there, without hesitation. Deceived, I thought, cuckolded by the only one I had ever loved. How God must have struggled to hold me back and I've thanked him ever since that He did. For as the man turned I saw his face. She was kneeling before him, he touched her head and crossed himself. He was a priest.

'It was you, Kate, that turned her. You were the conflict within her. She had renounced her faith because of her love for me. But she could not commit you as well, for that would have been a double sin and she could never live with that. And, God help me, nor could I.

She did not stay. I would not let her. I arranged for her to go to a convent in Italy, near Lucca in Tuscany. The demons tore me

apart, my mind seemed no longer any part of me, but I vowed
I would not contact her ever again. God only knows how I did
it. Less than a year later, I received a letter that told me she was
dead. They said she had lost her mind. Then came the cruelty
of what I had done, the sleepless nights of torment, the days
and weeks and months of guilt. Punishment, yes! Never-ending.
What a cruel and sinister Church it is that makes a man spurn
the love I had and condemn the one I adored to die in such a
way.'

He stood and held the arms of the chair for support. Kate
stood with him and held out her hand. He did not take it.

'You share our blood but hers is more potent than mine. How
I prayed it might wash out of you! But now I see you are at one
with her, through and through. She mocks me. And now this,
the final torture.'

He walked slowly, hesitantly towards the door, still clutching
his tumbler. Without turning, he said, 'Goodbye Kate. If there is
a God, let Him keep you safe.'

The door opened and she saw him briefly in the light from
the hall. Then he was gone and she was alone, the child of a
ghost, searching in the dark for the image of a mother she had
never known.

∞

Perfumes, creams, powders and lotions once littered her dressing
table. Her wardrobe had been full of dresses and petticoats and
shoes of a dozen styles and colours. Silver caskets overflowed
with jewellery. The mirror now reflected a stranger to them all.
She went quietly down the stairs, past her father's bedroom to
the pantry and filled her saddlebag with pies and biscuits and a
small stone flask of water.

She led her mare out of the stable and saddled up. It would
be another hour before the sun rose and she would be far away

before the stable boy raised the alarm. Her father would guess where she had gone and would send men after her. Perhaps soldiers, too. But she knew the country well and she would be there long before them. Una had told her where to go. Now it would be for Sir Robert Fitzgerald in Youghal to decide her fate.

૭૨

'It's a dangerous thing you're doing, Kate. And it's a doubly dangerous thing you're asking of me. I'm a magistrate and my duty tells me I should hold you until your father's men arrive.'

They sat in the kitchen. Sir Robert had brewed tea.

'But the real business, Kate, is where to hide you. Maybe I can put them off for a day or two but your father will have them scouring every inch of bog and hill until they dig you out.'

'My father has disowned me,' she said. 'If I'm caught, he'll put me on a ship for England. Have you heard what happened in Dublin?'

'Kate, who hasn't? What shenanigans. You're a feisty girl.'

'I must get to Moran.'

'And where would you find him? Provided he's still alive and the odds are against it.'

'He's riding with Coburn. With the Young Irelanders.'

'I know of them and they're dangerous people. They're not for you.'

'I have no one else.'

'You are determined?'

'I am.'

'There'd be no going back.'

'I'll never go back.'

'Never is a long time.'

Sir Robert poured more tea. He took the cover from a dish of oatcakes. Then he said, 'I think I know a way, probably the only way. He'll not thank me for it but I'll send you to a friend of mine, a Protestant and a landlord too. His name is William O'Brien. Good stock. Descendant of King Boru, King of all Ireland. How's that, Kate? It's a great start to your adventures in the family of kings.' He laughed.

Kate did not smile. 'You tell me this is dangerous. Now you say it's an adventure.'

'So it is, Kate. An adventure while it lasts. A hanging when it ends. This is no game of make-believe. It is bound to go that way. Do you want a rope around that pretty neck of yours?'

'Would you have me go to England?'

'I just want you to know what it is you are doing, Kate. These rebels are violent, their heads full of wild dreams and many will not see their next birthday. They can fight for Ireland but you'll not show me a man who can win for Ireland. They will turn the English against us at a time when we need them most.'

'I have nothing to lose.'

'Except yourself.'

'That doesn't seem so important now.'

'You are important, Kate. There is only one of you and this life is not a rehearsal. The real world is beyond our shores and that world is yours.'

'Will you help me, Sir Robert? Yes or no?'

'Well if you won't sail to England, Kate, then we must find a way to keep you safe in Ireland. You will go to O'Brien and stay there until you make up your mind where you go next. But promise me, Kate, you will not get into this rebel thing any deeper.'

'I can't promise you that, Sir Robert. I've taken sides. I am my mother's child.'

They supped more tea and ate the cakes and she told him her father's story, word for word, as best she could remember. When at last she was done, Sir Robert leant and kissed her on both cheeks.

'You are your mother's child indeed. And Ireland's too perhaps. Jesus! This God of ours moves in the most cussed way but there's no mistaking it. This is His plan.'

He went to the door and called out to his yardman to fetch her horse.

'Now ready yourself, Kate. We've no time to dawdle. I'll scribble a note to O'Brien and then you must go. My man will go with you. Trust him. And remember, Kate, you are with friends. We'll not fail you.'

CHAPTER FOURTEEN

The tide of human distress was now in full flood. Ireland was emptying. The Irish were leaving their doomed land in droves, like refugees escaping war. Thousands filled the roads to the ports of Dublin, Limerick and Cork and the smaller harbours of Baltimore, Ballina and Tralee. Those who could walk no further watched the procession of the stronger move on without them and waited to die. There was no pity.

The landlords accelerated the mass evacuation. It was the quickest, cheapest way for them to clear their estates of unwanted, unproductive human weight. They hired the ships and paid the fares on vessels already condemned as unfit for the Atlantic crossing. Timbers were rotten, seams uncaulked, sails shredded and their masters lied about the ration of food and water aboard. They were called the 'coffin ships'. The port inspectors took their bribes and said nothing. There was much money to be made from misery.

The first ship to sail from Westport in County Mayo was grossly overloaded. Over four hundred emigrants were crowded into the hold. Despite a calm sea, the ship foundered on rocks and sank within sight of the land it had just left. All aboard were drowned, watched by those onshore who, only an hour before, had bid them farewell.

America was the dreamt-of destination, but only the fit and healthy were allowed to disembark there. Congress quickly passed emergency laws to bar the sick and diseased. Boston even refused entry into its harbour to all ships from Ireland and the New York harbour authorities demanded a bond of one thousand dollars from captains for every sick passenger aboard their ships. Ship owners refused to pay, and, after the suffering of the Atlantic crossing, shiploads of sick and starving immigrants were forced to sail north to Canada and the St Lawrence River. Grosse Island at the mouth of the river became their landing station and for many, many thousands, their burial ground.

Lord Palmerston, the future British Prime Minister, paid the entire costs of nine ships to sail from Sligo carrying two thousand of his tenants. Those who boarded the *Aeolus*, bound for Canada, were packed like herrings in a barrel. Over one hundred died during the crossing from typhus fever and dysentery. The survivors were put into the quarantined sheds on Grosse Island off Quebec as soon they landed. Many were too weak to walk off the ship.

For the first time, emigration across the Atlantic continued throughout the winter and this was the most severe in living memory. When another of Palmerston's ships, the *Richard Watson*, arrived, the master reported that nearly half of his passengers had died en route and were thrown overboard. The survivors disembarked near-naked in a snow blizzard and there was ice on the St Lawrence River. Palmerston's agents had promised every family money and an acre of land to help them resettle. The immigrants discovered there was no money and no land and Palmerston denied all knowledge of it.

Trevelyan appeared unmoved by the reports he read. But then, emigration was saving him money. The more Irish who left at the landlords' expense, the fewer there were to gorge on English aid, and fewer still to fill the workhouses. He was also reassured by a letter sent to him by Earl Grey, Secretary of State for the Colonies.

The desire to reach America is so exceedingly strong among the Irish emigrants that they are content to submit to very great hardships during the voyage.

How many thousands sailed with new hope to the New World only to perish in the coffin ships will never be known. But it was written at the time that a road of drowned skeletons drifted back and forth with the tide, from the shores of Ireland to the coasts on the far side of the Atlantic Ocean.

There was a quicker, cheaper, less hazardous way to escape Ireland. Many more thousands went east across the Irish Sea to England, Scotland and Wales. A crossing that would take not months but hours.

The steamer *Faugh a Ballagh* was packed on its twice-weekly journey from Drogheda to Liverpool, a journey that cost only five shillings. Other shipping companies on the Mersey joined the lucrative business and emigrants were soon arriving at the rate of a thousand a day. By midsummer 1847, over three hundred thousand Irish had settled in Liverpool, a city with a population only a little over half that number. There were not enough police to cope and twenty thousand civilians had to be rapidly sworn in as special constables. A battalion of infantry was hurriedly garrisoned at the docks.

Ships sailing from Cardiff and Swansea, carrying coal from the Welsh valleys to Cork and Dublin, no longer returned to their home port empty. Their owners filled the coal dust holds with paupers at two shillings each for the one-way crossing. Some were given free passage as human ballast. There was a regular ferry service from Belfast and Londonderry to Glasgow and there were sometimes queues of people half a mile long waiting for a space.

Once they had landed, the Irish poor knew they would no longer be hungry. Britain's Poor Laws would provide for them. In return, they brought with them the diseases of famine and within months, as they spread out across the country, they carried typhus and dysentery with them. The British people would now pay in kind for their government's indifference.

ↂ

William Smith O'Brien was a handsome man who lived on his brother's estate at Dromoland Castle in County Clare. He was a Protestant, a member of the Westminster Parliament and an active participant in the Catholic Association, dedicated to the repeal of the Union with England. Whatever the political contradictions, he was first and foremost an Irishman.

He was known as a benign and benevolent landlord and was serious in his politics. He passionately believed that only by political negotiation could peace and Irish independence ever be achieved. Violence would hinder change rather than hastening it. He believed that whatever new freedoms the Irish might enjoy, they were only England's to give.

He changed his mind one day in his ancestral town of Cashel. The square was packed. It was a political meeting, the first for many years. Such meetings were prohibited but there was not a Redcoat nor a peeler to be seen. Two men stood astride a statue of a saint. One was a tall, well-built young man with auburn hair that all but touched his shoulders. The second man was a priest. Draped around the statue was a string of green flags.

O'Brien was curious. He was not in town for politics. Wheat and its weekly price were his business that day. It was the voice that held him. A gentle coaxing voice that made men move closer and cup their ears to hear it better. A voice with sudden strength that rose loud with such venom and anger that men clenched their fists and tightened their jaws. They had not heard its like since Daniel O'Connell, the Great Liberator himself. The crowd pushed nearer. They cheered loudly as the man paused and were silent again as he spoke. But these were not O'Connell's words. The young man with the bright eyes had a different manifesto. His was a call to arms.

'We have been conquered not once but many times. Our lands confiscated, our churches razed, our people brought to the very verge of extinction. We were once beautiful people, our men famous for their strength, our women for their beauty. Our land was a beacon of learning, our poets, bards and music known and loved here and beyond. Our monasteries were the hubs of learning, full of light and culture. Look at us now. Our earth and our people exist for English profit. Only when they rid this land of us will they be content. The English sent fifty thousand pounds to help the starving Irish. They've sent twenty million pounds for the Negro slaves in the West Indies. Such are our masters' priorities.

'I defy anyone to exaggerate the misery of our people. Look at yourselves. You are like famished sheep. Will you let your Ireland perish like a lamb? Or will she turn as a baited lion turns? Let us unmuzzle the wolf dogs! They are here throughout the land fit to be untied and they become more savage every day they are kept caged. Let us together push the English back into the sea. Curse the tyrants that suck our blood. Fight! Fight for Ireland. Let our blood flow. Fight for liberty!'

That day, an Irishman was preaching rebellion, insurrection and revolution for all to hear in the streets of Cashel. It fired a passion in O'Brien, descendant of the king who had defeated the Vikings. The eight-hundred-year-old bloodline was suddenly rekindled. He resolved that hour to seek out the tall man with the auburn hair, the one called Daniel Coburn.

∽

'He does not ride with women, Miss Kathryn. He is very selective. He has to be. I think you are a very doubtful recruit.'

They sat facing each other at the end of a long oak table in the hall of O'Brien's castle at Dromoland. He had placed a tall candelabrum midway along it and a platform of light walled off the far end of the room. Kate had not seen a servant or any person since she had arrived. O'Brien provided bread and a round of cheese and filled two mugs from a jug of porter. He passed one to her.

'Mind you,' he said. 'We could make splendid capital out of it. Just think. The daughter of a knight of the realm, the former Relief Commissioner himself, creating havoc and gallivanting around the country with a ragged band of Irish revolutionaries. What wonderful propaganda!'

'Why do you mock me?' Kate said. 'I am already disgraced and my father is no longer anyone's favourite except his enemies'. I've come to you for help. I cannot go to anyone else. If they find me I shall be sent to England. I don't think I could bear that.'

'So you want to help Ireland?'

'I want to help the Irish who are suffering.'

'There are good Irish ladies already doing that. Why don't you join them? Anna Parnell of the Ladies' Land League will find you a place, I've no doubt.'

'My father will drag me from them. I can only bring them harm.'

'Then what help can you be to us?' O'Brien asked.

'Whatever help you need.'

'To cook and sew? Woman's work?'

'Whatever you want me to do, I will do.'

'Are you fit to do it?'

'I am fit.'

'This is men's work.'

'And I am a woman.'

'Yes, and you are untried in what we do.'

'Then you will teach me.'

'You are very cocksure of yourself, sitting here comfortably, eating my cheese. But life would be very different once you rode with us, very different indeed.'

'I'll bear that difference. That's why I am here.'

There was the sudden sound of a chair scraping the floor and movement at the far end of the room. A voice said, 'Would you steal? Would you kill?'

Daniel Coburn entered the pool of light and sat on the edge of the table close to her. How often, despite herself, had she conjured up a face to match the eyes she remembered from that evening by the river at Fivemilebridge, when he had ridden away with Moran? How often had she dreamt of it since he had fired his pistol and saved her from the hands of the mob on that day riding with Una? Now he was so close she could feel his breath on her forehead. His nearness was suffocating. It frightened her. It intoxicated her. She trembled as he spoke.

'Tell me, Miss Kathryn, if you came with us, would you select the role you'd want to play? Pick and choose according to the time of day? Whether the sun was out or not, whether it was warm or cold? Would you wear gloves to protect your dainty English hands so that guilt did not stain them?'

'I would not wear gloves,' she said. 'You mock me too.'

Coburn laughed as another man moved from out of the dark. A priest stepped forward.

'Don't, Daniel. We know who she is and what she has done.'

He held out his hand to Kate. 'I'm Father Kenyon from Tipperary. Silly people call me the Patriot Priest.'

He turned to Coburn. 'She has done much for our people, we know that well enough. If we cannot enlist her, the least we can do is show her some gratitude and good manners.'

He reached over the table and drank porter from O'Brien's jug.

'Miss Macaulay…' Coburn said.

'I am Kate,' she interrupted. 'I have no other name.'

'Yes, I know,' he said. 'Indeed I do. I have read Sir Robert's letter and it makes sad reading. But then Ireland is brimming with sad stories, enough I think to sink her. Yours is just one of a million.'

'How much did Sir Robert tell?'

'That you have mongrel blood.'

'Enough of that,' said Father Kenyon. 'Stop your blather, Daniel. It wouldn't do for any one of us to inspect our pedigree too closely. Now stop it!'

'Sorry, Father,' said Coburn. He was still smiling. 'And sorry to you too, Kate. I'm not used to company of your sort nowadays. But I do seem to remember that it was you who was prickly the last time we met.'

'It was a very frightening time. You must forgive me.'

'I forgive you. I do, really. In his letter, Sir Robert says you have crossed sides.'

'I had no choice. I am my mother's child.'

'But I think you turned long before your father put you out.'

'Why do you think that?'

'Can I guess when it was? And where?'

She waited. She did not answer.

'Was it Limerick?' he asked. 'When you said goodbye to the Keegans?'

'How did you know?'

'I was there. Only yards from you.'

'You followed me?'

'Not exactly. I had other business there that day. But I knew you'd be coming. You have become a friend of our people and I wanted to see you again. I think we owe you something, Kate. You have your story. One day I will tell you mine. All of us here have things to tell. Our stories explain everything. What we are and why we are here. They are our credentials.'

'Will you take me?' she asked.

'What are your credentials, Kate?'

'Only my story and you know it now.'

'We mean to change things, Kate. Change Ireland. Kick the English out. Your own people. You will join us in that. Fight with us against the English?'

'They are not my people. How many times must I say that to convince you? My people are not the English nor the Irish. They are the people who are suffering so dreadfully.'

'What you have seen restores your pity?'

'I am not wanting in pity. I ask you again. Will you take me?'

For some minutes Coburn said nothing. The priest emptied O'Brien's jug of porter, refilled it and cut himself a slice of cheese.

Coburn came and sat beside her. He did not look at O'Brien or Father Kenyon. He looked directly into her eyes. Then he took her right hand and shook it.

'Yes! You can ride with us. All the way to the gallows. Ride with us, Kate, and you and I will hang together.'

'Do not tempt the Lord,' said the Patriot Priest. 'He is aggravated enough already. But may luck ride with you both.'

He kissed his fingers, crossed himself and touched their heads. It was his blessing.

৩৯

She rode with them as hard and as long as any man among them. She asked no favours. None were offered. If two of the more prominent Young Irelanders were suspicious of her, it did not last. In the months that followed her introduction, Thomas Meagher, son of the Mayor of Waterford, and Gavan Duffy, a grocer's son from Monaghan, tried many times in many ways to test her. She did not fail.

When the snows came early that November, she had ridden with them to all but a few of Ireland's counties. From Donegal north to Bantry south, from Wicklow in the east to Mayo in the west. It was there, in the shadow of the Connemara Mountains, that Coburn took Kate to the place where he was born.

It was desolate country, a narrow corridor of camouflaged greens and browns, dividing the two vast loughs of Mask to the north and Corrib to the south. The towering Maamtrasna Mountain, its plateau mostly hidden in mist, sloped down to flooded plains and there was not a tree to be seen from Cornamona to Clonbur. It was as if all living things had fled from the place. Or that life had never come to it. Coburn stood by the water's edge.

'This was my home, Kate. The stones you see scattered here were once my family's home. I was one of many, nine of us, maybe more. The cottage was always full of children coming and going from other families, so I never did know how many were ours. My mother was always carrying, every year there was another baby. Some died soon after they were born and were buried at night so we wouldn't know.' He pointed towards the foot of the mountain.

'They're out there somewhere, along with the others.'

Kate followed his gaze.

'What others, Daniel? Who else is buried there?'

'I don't know them all, Kate. Only a few of them belong to us. There was so much dying then. You've only seen this famine but it was almost as bad then, twenty years ago. Many went down, starved to death, frozen to death, black and bloated with the fever.'

'It's hard for me to think of it that way when we stand here,' Kate said. 'There's a grand beauty about it, as if it has never been touched.'

'Maybe it's been given new life by the blood of the dead.'

'It's horrible to say that.'

'I think of it no other way. I never stop thinking about it.'

He paused. 'We shouldn't have come here, Kate. Not to this place. I have been many times before but I should not have brought you now. All my good memories have long been drenched by bad ones.'

'I asked you to bring me here' she said. 'You promised. It's a part of you I wanted to see.'

'There is nothing to see, Kate. Only the mountains and the loughs and they are no longer mine. They're nobody's now. Do you see the ripples along the slope of the mountain? You might think them the scrapings of a glacier sliding its way down the valley all those millions of years ago. A stranger might think them nature's own work. But they are the potato beds, dug by man and woman, husband and wife, child and child, generations of them, year on year for hundreds of years. How much work is that, Kate? And for what? Twenty years ago the potato failed them as it has failed again and they died of hunger just as we are dying now.'

'There was no other way?'

'No, Kate. We knew no other way. There was no other way. See that pile of stones just beyond the stream? My ancestors carried them down from the mountain, one by one, to build their home. Now the mountain has taken them back. For centuries, my people worked this land and they wanted nothing more. In all his sixty years, my father barely travelled beyond Cornamona, a few miles to the west or eastwards to Cong. Can you believe that? My mother never ever left the plot. She never wanted to. She wouldn't have known how to. They were simple people asking for very little, always ready to welcome a neighbour or give a bowl of broth to any traveller who happened to wander off his path.'

'Were there many families here?' she asked.

'There must have been a few dozen hereabouts but I can only remember some of the names. The Philbins, the O'Sullivans, Joyce, the O'Donnells. We all kept our distance but if there was a fight between them, we'd all join in, even if we didn't know what it was all about. But if a family was in trouble they hadn't to wait long for help and a bit of comfort.'

'What did you do with yourself?'

'I spent my time mostly alone. Sometimes days away just wandering and no one missed me. The best of it was on top of Maamtrasna, up on that plateau. There's a lake up there – Nafooey it's called – and it was mine. I'd spend days there, swimming, living on tiny fish and birds' eggs. It was grand place to be for a little boy, on top of the world. On top of Ireland.'

He splashed the shallow water between the reeds.

'I had a friend called Murdoc. He was a wild one, always making mischief, but a grand fisherman. He would go out onto the loughs with his curragh and nets and poach for trout and sometimes salmon. He sold them as far away as Ballinrobe and Clifden. I would dig worms for him and he would cut off a couple of fish heads and mother would make a soup that lasted all of us a week or more. I remember how we had to make for the boat quickly because of the thunderflies.'

'Thunderflies?'

'Biting midges that could make your life a hell. And the mosquitoes too. We called them buzzers because of the sound they made. But it was grand once we were out there on the water. I remember the evenings best, at dusk, the whir of bats, the drumming of the snipe, the curlew and the clack of the ducks being chased by otters.'

'You must have been a happy little boy.'

'I don't think we knew what happiness was, Kate. Not that I've ever really known it. We wanted very little from life, but we were content, hard-working, shying away from violence and deceit. All we asked for was enough to eat at the end of the day, some pennies for father's tobacco and decent put-ons for the children's Sunday best. It was our lot until somebody bettered it.'

'Where are they now, Daniel? Your family?'

Clouds quickly hindered the sun and the bright greens of the valley became sullen grey. A cold breeze came off the Corrib and she felt its sharpness on her face and hands.

'Where are all my dead now?' he answered. 'Where are their plots? There are none. They have no graves, Kate, no tidy mounds of earth, no settled peat, no headstones above the heather. You ask me where my dead are. They are hereabouts, hiding themselves. On every rock there sits a ghost who nods its head and whispers quietly as I pass.'

He walked away and turned his back to her.

She wanted to go to him, to touch him, to mourn with him. He stood by a scattering of stones that had been his home. She watched him pace the spaces between them. He stopped and knelt and stroked them as he would the neck of his horse. Then he stood and faced her.

'Why, Kate?' He was shouting. 'What had they done to finish this way? Were they not good Catholics? Did they not keep the faith? Didn't they bow their heads and give thanks to their invisible God morning, noon and night? And when they lay shrivelled and filthy and dying here among these stones, did they not ask themselves why? Why us? Maybe they did ask but they were never given an answer.'

He went away slowly towards the mountain. She did not follow. They were still too far apart.

∞

She had become Coburn's constant companion, at his side at every rally, with him at every speech. The crowds that came to hear him were fired by his passion but it was not his words alone that gave them hope and new resolve. It was the young woman with him, the Englishman's daughter who had deserted her own to become part of them. With her shining black hair, tied up with green ribbons, she had become a legend of their own making. The one they called the 'Dark Rosaleen'.

British newspapers eagerly grasped at it. The Young Irelanders rarely featured in their coverage but this was something extraordinary and they made it more so in the exaggerated fashion of their trade. It was magnified so that Kate, not the rebels and their aspirations, became the story. Cartoons in *The London Times* and the *Illustrated London News* caricatured her with fire in her eyes and snakes, not ribbons, streaking from her hair, like Medusa. She was held responsible for acts of violence they had not committed, attacks on landlords where there had been none. She was reported to have been seen in Kerry on a white stallion at the head of a hundred armed riders. In another report from Wicklow, she had charged and trampled under hoof an entire platoon of carabineers. The newspaper proprietors and their editors knew well enough the value of the story and the insatiable appetite their readers had for drama.

How easily fiction became fact. How quickly truth was absorbed by lies, the lies themselves becoming accepted truths. The make-believe in print began to assume such substance that the government was obliged to take notice. A proclamation soon appeared in the *London Gazette*, stating that Kathryn Macaulay, daughter of Sir William Macaulay, formerly Commissariat General for Irish Relief, was indicted for treason. A reward of five thousand pounds would be paid for information leading to her arrest.

Since his disgrace and departure from Ireland, Sir William had lived the life of an exile in his house in the Lincolnshire fens. Except for his two manservants, he saw no one and nobody wished to see him. It is said that memories serve old men well, that their lives are given extra spice in retrieved fond and loving reminiscences. But all that had been good and dear in Sir William's life had been erased by the tragedy that was Ireland. So he spent his days sitting alone and filled the vacuum with whiskey and brandy.

News of the proclamation was posted to him from London. It was brought to his bedroom with his early morning coffee. When his manservants later returned to help him dress, they found him still in bed. He would not talk. They thought he could not. He lay perfectly still, looking at the ceiling, his eyes unblinking, unmoving, and they thought him paralysed. They called the doctor but he could not rouse him. He would not move. He would not eat his broth nor drink his medicines. On the seventh day his servants heard him shouting. As they entered his bedroom they saw him convulse, raise himself from his pillows and call out a woman's name. Then his heart stopped beating. As he fell back, the air gushed from his lungs and he called out her name again for the last time.

The servants closed his eyes, pulled the bedcover over him and
went for the undertaker. The name their master had uttered in
his last breath meant nothing to them. They had never known
his wife.

ಬಿ

It was Moran who told Kate of her father's death. Sir William
had been in the ground a fortnight, buried within the family
enclosure of St Botolph's church in Boston. The vicar was the
only one to witness the disgraced knight's departure and three
lines in the obituary column of *The London Times* were all that
marked a half century of devoted public service.

Kate sat with Moran in the refectory at Dromoland. He had
ridden that night from Tipperary with the news. He said people
were rejoicing at it.

'It grieves me, Miss Kathryn, to tell you of this. He should
not be dishonoured this way. He was a good man, forced to do
dreadful things.'

'Tell me, Moran. How should I mourn?'

'I cannot answer you, Miss Kathryn.'

'I disgraced him'.

'That is not for me to say'.

'There was no one at his grave?'

'So it was written in the newspapers.'

'I would have gone if I had known.'

'You would not have come back, Miss Kathryn. We know they
had agents at Fishguard and Swansea in case you did cross the sea.
In Boston too. They'd have caught and hanged you. Better he
was buried alone.'

He could not help her. He wanted to comfort her but he
could not touch even her hand. She was of them now, a rebel, an
outlaw, but in her company he would always be her butler.

Late that afternoon Coburn took her to Clenagh, a half hour's ride south of Dromoland. He knew it well. He had walked its beaches many times. He knew of the ancient ruin of a tower there that would serve as a chapel where she could mourn the memory of a father she had loved and barely known. He knew too that she would take her rosary with her, a symbol of the faith that had finally broken them apart.

Coburn sat at the foot of the tower and listened to her prayers. How often had he done the same? A young man mourning those he had lost, those who had had no burial, no grave, no cross, no evidence of having lived at all.

She came and sat by him. Across the Shannon, in the evening light, they could just see the blurred outlines of Coney Island and Inishmore and the promontory of Rineanna Point. A sea mist was slowly snaking its way up river. Soon it would cover the sands and creep up the headland and before long all of Clare would lay damp and hidden under it. Coburn pointed.

'Look, Kate. Over there to the left. Another one off to the promised land.'

A three-master edged its way into view, the wind on its beam, its sails stiff and full. They watched in silence as it moved slowly down river until it too was swallowed up in the blanket of mist. The hundreds aboard had glimpsed their last of the land they would never see again.

'I blame them, Kate, and yet I envy them too,' said Coburn.

'You read my thoughts, Daniel.'

'I think I often do.'

'If you envy those who leave, you must have thought of it yourself.'

'Many times. But to think is not to do. I could never leave. There is something too deep inside me, call it what you will.'

'I think it's called love, Daniel. There must be many kinds of love and to love what you have been born to might be the strongest.'

'Then you must love England still.'

'Yes! You would think so. Perhaps I did once. But not now and it's not England's fault. But you will never change, Daniel.'

'I love Ireland. Indeed I do. But I wonder if there is a stronger love.'

'I don't know,' she said. 'I have never loved. I have never been loved.'

He stood up. 'Maybe there's a way of not knowing love but feeling it. If it comes as a stranger you might not recognise it. Then you might lose what you might have loved.'

She watched him walk slowly to the edge of the cliff. It was as if he was ending their talk, as if there was nothing left for them to say, when she felt there was so much more. She did not want an ending. She had been with him, ridden at his side for over a year and yet he had never spoken this way to her before. She waited. He turned and beckoned.

'Kate, will you come to me?'

'Must we leave, Daniel?'

He shook his head.

'No! But read my mind, Kate. Read it and tell me what you see. Tell me what I feel.'

'Daniel, I cannot.'

'Try, Kate. Let me hold your hands. Put them in mine. What do you feel?'

'I feel your pulse, your heart beating. It's very strong.'

'Kate, have you never really loved?'

'No, never.'

'And no one has ever loved you?'

'No.'

He held her hands tight and brought them to his chest.

'I think I love you, Kate. I have never known it but what I feel for you must be love. It is stronger than anything I have ever felt. You must know it too. You felt my heart pounding.'

'Is it stronger than your love of Ireland?'

'I do believe it is.'

He smiled and kissed the palms of her hands. She leant up to him and kissed him lightly on the lips. Then she kissed him again. He picked her up in his arms and walked back slowly towards the tower. He put her down in the soft ferns that ringed its walls and lay beside her. The air was still warm. The first wisps of sea mist circled above them. The only sounds were the soft rattle of waves along the sands below and the call of a distant curlew.

'Let me woo you with your own poem, Kate. The one they've named you after.'

She rested her head against his shoulder and felt his warm breath on her face. She closed her eyes as he spoke.

I could scale the blue air, I could plough the high hills.
I could kneel all night in prayer to heal your ills.
One smile from you would float like light
Between my toils and me,
My own, my true, my Dark Rosaleen.

'A little boy from Kinsale taught me that,' she said. 'A million years ago.'

'What was his name?'

'I knew him only as Eugene.'

'Where is he now?'

'Buried only a short walk from where he was born. That was as much as he knew of this world and he had such a yearning to learn more. I was so proud of him, he might have been my own child. He lost his family in the first year of the famine.'

'I was that same little boy,' Daniel said. 'One of thousands of children left to survive as best as they could on their own.'

'Tell me.'

'I was eleven years old, but so small and thin that people thought I was six. It was just another year of many hungers but the worst of it was in my own Mayo. It takes three months to

starve to death. Did you know that? That's a long time for a
little boy to watch that much suffering. And to think that only a
month before we had flowering potatoes with stems as thick as
that little boy's wrists.

'One morning, we woke and knew we had lost them just
by the smell. Father had seen it all before. He knew there was
nothing to do but sit and wait for the bailiffs and the tumbling
gangs. So he went off to the whiskey dens and never came back.
I looked for him and my sisters and brothers searched too. But
mother knew he was gone.

'I tried to feed them. I stole turnip tops and at night I milked
the udder of a rich man's cow. Sometimes I would cut a vein in
its neck and draw out the blood and mix it with the milk. But
everyone was doing it and men sold their cows before they were
bled to death. I searched the beaches for dead crabs and rotten
fish and when a storm fetched up seaweed we ate that too. Once
I found a cockle but I never found another. Do you know that
there wasn't a bird flying, not a frog or a snail to be found anywhere? The land had been scoured clean of life.

'So we sat by the peat fire and ate blind herring. Do you know
what that is, Kate? It's a fish that isn't there except in your mind.
We sat eating fish that wasn't there and we wasted away. They
died, slowly, one after the other. It must have been the fever.

'So the little boy sat, not knowing what to do, not having the
strength to bury them on his own. So he set fire to the hovel
he had called home. I buried them in fire, Kate. My flesh. My
blood. All of them. Remember that day in Connemara? You
asked me where they were buried and I didn't answer? They
were under the stones, Kate. That little square of stones I walked
around. That was their grave. All my family, together.'

She wrapped her arms around him and began a story of her
own. Of another boy she had seen one night in the fire of her
Lincolnshire home. A child encircled by flames, his small face
cursed by innocence, wondering who was to blame for the pain

of dying so young and forgotten. His image had scorched her with a scar as vivid as any wound from a firebrand.

She told of how often that boy had entered her dreams, of the night when she was in the final throes of her fever and how he had held out his hands and saved her.

'Am I that little boy, Kate?'

She did not answer. She pulled him tight towards her and kissed him again many times and, cloaked within the soft warm mist, they were joined.

CHAPTER FIFTEEN

Daniel Coburn was a man of many colours, a revolutionary mired in contradictions. Like all Irishmen, the '98 rebellion was scorched into him like a branding iron. Wolfe Tone, O'Neill, Emmett, Monro, Fitzgerald and Father Murphy were among his many martyrs and the slaughter at Vinegar Hill and the barbarity of the Gibbet Massacre were the founding of his deep hatred for the English. When he was eighteen he had walked thirty miles from Connemara to Daniel O'Connell's monster meeting in Clifden. Like the many thousands there that day he was inspired by this man of fine words and grand vision. It was the young boy's baptism.

Coburn the child had survived one famine. Coburn the man was now living through another far more tragic one. It swept aside all past values. The whole pyramid of Irish life had been precariously balanced on the potato crop. That base had collapsed and a whole new way of life had to be devised.

He had a vision of the peasantry rising as one, raising the green flag in armed rebellion, an agrarian revolution that would herald the birth of a new social order. Up and down the country he had preached it again and again. The future of Ireland lay in the absolute possession of the land, the Irish sole owners of Ireland's soil. He took to it with a passion, as fervently as a man adopts a new religion. It was his shibboleth and he never wavered.

He was encouraged by events beyond both Ireland and England. The dawn of universal liberty was now being trumpeted throughout Europe and Continental governments were falling like dominoes. The French ruling elite had been overthrown yet

again. In a bloodless revolution, another republic had been pro-
claimed, and King Louis Philippe had fled across the Channel to
Dover in disguise. Insurrection in Sicily had forced the monar-
chy to concede a new and democratic constitution. There was
mass rioting and barricades in Vienna and Prince Metternich
was obliged to become another exile in London. The people
of Milan drove their Austrian rulers out of the city and raised
improvised banners declaring its autonomy. Further south, the
Venetians had fought their own military, seized their garrison
and arsenal and demanded self-rule.

The republican victories throughout Europe were seen as
Ireland's own and the Irish cheered them all and none cheered
louder than the Young Irelanders. Bonfires were lit on the highest hilltops from Donegal to Munster, from Wicklow to Killrush.
Crowds in the streets of the towns and cities carried banners
celebrating the triumph of Europe's dispossessed.

Coburn was convinced it would set off an Irish explosion,
certain that the fuse that had been burning imperceptibly for
centuries must now detonate. He decided that his tour of the
counties, his meetings and his speech-making were over. The
message had been spread far and wide and there was not a
man or woman in Ireland now that did not know of the Young
Irelanders and not one among them who said they would not
rally to the cause. Now was the time for deeds. The providential
hour should not pass if the people were to be liberated.

The landlords would be targeted. They would be made to live
in fear. If some had already fled to the safety of England, then
their bailiffs would suffer on their behalf. Their lordships' man-
sions would be torched, their livestock slaughtered and taken as
food. No estate would be safe and there would be no exceptions.

Coburn made ready his campaign. English newspapers would
no longer ridicule the Young Irelanders and their aspirations
with cartoons and make-believe stories. They would now have
something real and harsh to report.

ɷ

The ship was a clear sharp silhouette against the moon's light on the water. She was out from Wexford, bound for the French port of Cherbourg, carrying a cargo of corn and flour. At the mouth of the river Slaney the wind failed, and her sails dropped. So her master decided to bottom her on the South Slob mudflats and wait for the tide to rise.

Word of it came quickly to Coburn from men who had loaded her the previous day. Three hundred and eighty sacks of grain were in her hold.

'We take. We give,' said Father Kenyon. 'We are the men in the middle. A few sacks will keep more than a few alive. It's a gift from God.'

'We'll need carts,' said Duffy.

'I'll get the carts,' said Meagher.

'And curraghs,' Coburn said.

'I'll have them, too.'

'Daniel. Will we kill?' asked O'Brien.

'Only if I kill first,' Coburn replied. 'You will wait for me to strike. It may not come to that.'

'We will take a gun each then?'

'No! I will take only mine. If I have to use it, then we are lost. They'll hear it on shore and we'll have no time to escape them.'

'Haven't you forgotten something?' the priest asked.

'Tell me,' said Coburn.

'I shall,' said the priest. 'What will you do if you can take all you want? Where will you hide sacks of grain hereabouts? The Redcoats will take every cottage apart, even the tumbled wrecks. They'll turn every sod of turf and every stone too. Have you thought of that, Daniel?'

'Then don't hide them on land,' said Meagher. 'We can drift the curraghs to Gerry Cove on Beggerin Island. Only our own people know of it. Let's keep the sacks there until the searches are over. Then we can give the grain out to the people, little by little.'

'And we will hold off the day,' said the priest. 'Well done, Meagher.'

'You will not come on this one, Kate,' said Coburn.

'I will,' she replied.

'You will not come.'

'I will too!'

The tide was flowing out to sea. Soon it would be slack water and an hour later the water would begin to rise again and soon the ship would be on her way. There was no time to haggle. What they had to do they had to do quickly.

The current turned on itself under the lee of the mudflats and carried the three curraghs out without effort. Only light pulls on the oars were needed to bring them close to the ship. Its black tarred hull towered above them. Its sails were tied and there was no movement on deck, only the soft rattle of the rigging and the slap of water against the planking. At the stern, her name was painted in large white letters: *Jackdaw*.

Coburn, Meagher and O'Brien pulled themselves up on the aft anchor line. Duffy and Kate followed them.

'Who's there?' They saw a lantern swinging and the shadow of a man standing by the hatchway. He shouted, 'Have you come to take my ship?'

'No, sir,' Coburn replied. 'We have come for a little of your grain. Our people are starving. I'll ask you not to resist. We will not cause you harm. Just a few sacks is all we need. You'll not miss them.'

The captain came towards them, a short, broad man with a beard flecked with grey. He was wearing no topcoat or cap. He held a mug of tea in one hand, the lantern in the other.

'Is your gun loaded?' he asked.

'Why else would I carry it?' Coburn replied.

'You will get ten years transportation for that.'

'And death for you if you try to take it from me.'

'I have men asleep below. I have only to shout.'

'Then I will shoot you,' said Coburn.

The captain hung his lantern on a hook at the mast. 'Must I die for a few sacks of grain?' he asked. 'Must you hang for it?'

'We can both live,' Coburn answered. 'You are taking food from our land, food from our people.'

'What use is raw corn to you?'

'One ear of corn, one handful of flour will save a life. What I've come to take will save a hundred families. It belongs to them. Think of them, Captain. Think of them'.

He needed no reminding. He had been sailing to ports along the Irish coast all his working life and had never been far from the wretchedness of the poor. He was no stranger to their miserable lives. In this past year of famine he had been forced to witness what no decent man should be asked to bear. The images would never leave him. The howling of the hungry in Tralee as they watched barrels of herring and sacks of barley being loaded, bound for a foreign port. How bodies were left rotting in the snow in Westport because the ground was too hard to bury them. How he had shot the dogs eating them until he had no cartridges left.

He needed no reminders. He held out his hands, palms open.

'I have no gun,' he said. 'Put yours away and take what you want. As much as you can carry.'

'You trick me,' said Coburn.

'No trickery, my desperate friend. Take it. The rats will take more than you can carry by the time we get to France.'

'I will want twelve sacks,' said Coburn. 'We have three curraghs at your side.'

'Then pull back the canvas and open the hatches. Send two men down and two to haul.'

'And when we're down there, you will call your men?'

'No! But the choice is yours. And make it fast. There's a breeze up and I'm waiting on the tide.'

He unwound the rope and threw the end into the hold. 'Do it now or go.'

O'Brien and Meagher went into the hold. Duffy took the line.

Coburn called to Kate. 'Take my gun and pray the captain is a cautious man.'

She stepped into the light of the lantern. Only then did the captain show surprise.

'Lord above!' he exclaimed. 'So this is the lady all England is talking about. And here you are, on the deck of old *Jackdaw*. Will anyone believe me when I tell my story? I doubt it. But here she is, the Dark Rosaleen.'

'My name is Kate,' she said. 'I go by no other.'

'Whatever name you go by, you are exactly how they say you are.'

He moved a step forward to see her better. She stepped back out of the light.

'Captain. Stay still. Don't let me use this.'

'You'll have no cause to. I'm not an Irishman, Kate. Like you, I'm from England, from Kent. But I'm pleased to have met you and I wish you luck.'

Twelve times the rope was lowered and twelve sacks were lifted from the hold. Soon the curraghs were full and low in the water.

'Why have you done this, Captain?' Coburn asked.

'Must you ask?'

'Do you have a name?'

'Not one you have to know. But *Jackdaw*'s my ship.'

'How do we thank you, then?'

'You have no need. But go now. Once you are away, I will have to send a man ashore to raise the alarm. I'll say there were twenty of you, each with a gun. I'll have my story.'

'You are a Christian man, Captain. You have saved many lives. They will not know of you but I will never forget.'

The tide had turned and the current was flowing inland by the time the curraghs were within sight of Beggerin. The rebels heard the ship's horn and a gunshot. The captain had raised the alarm, as he said he would. Now he would have to wait for the military to come aboard and he would have his story and many of their questions to answer. His sailing would now have to wait another day and another turn of the tide to take him and his cargo to France.

ಣಣ

It was Meagher who brought it to Coburn. He had torn it out of the *Cork Examiner*: a newspaper report on yet another series of brutal evictions. It might have passed unnoticed by them except for the name of the landlord.

'Kate,' Coburn called to her. 'I think you know this man.'

'And who might that be?'

'Edward Ogilvie.'

He held out the newspaper cutting. She took it and her hand was not still. It was a name from another age, swallowed up in the mishmash of the past where fond and hateful memories jostled with each other. Could she ever forget him, the repugnant half-sir and his bullwhip, the jeering face, the smell of whiskey on his breath, the stench of his sweat, Eugene and blood on her skirt?

'I see he's still remembered, Kate,' said Coburn. 'You're in a bit of a tremble. Sit by me.'

She read the report. Then she let it drop to the floor.

'What is he to you, Daniel?' she asked.

'He is a landlord to me. He is the enemy to me. Did you not read it all?'

He picked the cutting off the floor. Meagher and Duffy, who were sitting across the large kitchen in Dromoland, came closer.

He read it aloud.

From the estate of Mr Edward Ogilvie, MP.

This past week, three villages of Castletown, Coppeen and Enniskeen were tumbled and all tenants evicted with the help of a company of the 49th Regiment. They were turned out in the depth of winter, being denied clothes to carry or any provisions. It was a night of high winds and storm and their wailing could be heard from a great distance. They made shelters of wood and straw but Mr Ogilvie and his drivers pulled them down. They stood bewildered looking at the ruins of their homes and their few possessions being trod into the mud. They pleaded with Mr Ogilvie but he ordered the soldiers to drive them off. Three hundred persons, including pregnant mothers and their children in various stages of starvation and nakedness, wandered away not knowing where they were going. Some were too weak to crawl. They were dead by morning.

'Meagher brought it to you,' Kate said. 'Why?'

'Do you need to ask?'

'Will you go for him?'

'I think we will. He was not meant to be first on the list but he's put himself there.'

Meagher spoke. 'Daniel, think more on it. Let's not be hasty. He's a member of the English Parliament. It's a high risk for us. Let's go for a lesser man. He can wait. We'll have him when we're better at it.'

Coburn looked across at Duffy. 'And you? Is he too big for us?'

'I think Meagher's right,' Duffy replied. 'It's a good distance away and remember we can't be sure what help we'll have there. It's not a place we know.'

'Shall we wait for O'Brien?' Meagher suggested.

Coburn looked to Kate. 'And what of you, my Rosaleen? How soon do you think we should pay Mr Ogilvie a visit?'

She took his hand. 'If we are together, Daniel, we must decide together.'

'Yes!' He nodded. 'That's right, Kate. We'll wait for William.'

ோ

O'Brien returned and it was agreed. Ogilvie was indeed a big
target and a dangerously important one but Coburn argued that
that was exactly why he should be the first to be attacked. It would
be a sensational coup for the Irish and a shock to the English.

Meagher started on his journey to Ogilvie's estate the next day.
He would find out how close the nearest military garrison was
to it, map out its geography, establish how well it was guarded,
how many servants lived in the mansion, and how often Ogilvie
was in residence.

He would take soundings of his tenants and gauge what support he could expect from them. They would be suspicious of
him. Strangers were not welcome anywhere now. Too many
were paid informers or agents of the landlord and the constabulary. But Meagher had his ways. He was a handsome young man
with a ready wit and persuasive charm and the maid servants
in the mansion were also young. He would need his guile. He
would need to be patient.

Within the week, he returned to Dromoland. He sat with
Coburn, Kate, O'Brien and Duffy at the long oak table.

'He's been busy doing a lot of clearing. The three villages are
bare and there are more tumblings to come. They say he means to
turn his land over to sheep and bring in Scottish shepherds and
that by the end of the year, there'll not be an Irishman left there.'

'Did you find out if he is there every day?' asked O'Brien.

'They say he stays in the house all weekdays but he's away on
Saturdays and Sundays. No one seemed to know where.'

'He's not on his own?' said Duffy.

'He has two girls serving in the house. There's a man, his but-
ler-cum-groom and a fetch-and-carry young lad. They all live in.
That's all. His agent lives some miles away at Macroom.'

'What of the military?' O'Brien asked. 'Did you see them?'

'I saw their barracks. About two miles from the house, towards Enniskeen. Fusiliers. I'd say about fifty of them.'

'You've done well, Meagher.' Coburn shook his hand. 'Tell me, do the servants ever leave the place?'

'Not when I was watching. The gates are some way from the house and there's only one path to it. I never saw them on it.'

'Then we can't torch it,' said Duffy. 'Not if they're inside.'

'We'll find ways,' Coburn said.

'The problem is how we put in the fire,' said Meagher. 'There are shutters at every window. It's a fortress. Ogilvie knows he's at risk. I watched his man put up the boards every day just before dusk. If we're going to torch him it'll have to be while it's light and that's not a good thing.'

'When is dusk?' Coburn asked. 'What time will that be?'

'It will be dark around four.'

'Then that will be the hour. In the half light.'

'You said you want the servants out,' Kate said. 'But they'll not leave if Ogilvie is there. How can they? We can only do it when he's away.'

'You're a fine lieutenant, Kate.' Coburn took her hand and kissed it.

'Don't mock, Daniel. You've only got two days of the week to do it, Saturday and Sunday.'

'Don't the servants go to Mass?'

'I wasn't there on a Sunday.' Meagher answered. 'They might well do. There's a small chapel in the village. I suppose it's …'

Again Kate interrupted. 'Daniel, you say we must attack just before dusk. The servants might go to Mass but they'll not be in church all Sunday.'

'Then I don't know how we can empty the house,' said O'Brien.

'We'll have them out,' said Coburn. 'Fear will do it. Sunday it is.'

&

The sun had sunk an hour before but its amber light still rose over the cedar trees and lit the rooftops of the house. It was large, built by the Georgians, not of grey Connemara stone but red brick imported from England. An avenue of limes, a quarter of a mile long, led up from the wrought iron gates of the estate to a pair of lions carved from granite that sat either side of the massive oak front door. The immaculate lawn, with long regimented flower beds, stretched right up to the base of the tall front windows.

They dared not stay long. They were seen arriving as they rode through the ruins of the villages wrecked by Olgivie's tumbling gangs. Those who watched them go by would talk about these strangers and that talk might find its way to the police and then quickly on to the Redcoats two miles away.

Their torches of oiled peat were ready to be lit. It would not take long. The house would be well alight and beyond rescue long before the soldiers or any of the neighbouring landlords raised the alarm. That was the score of it. There was nothing to fault. It was simple, quick and safe.

They waited by their horses within the cover of the trees. Kate was their sentry. Coburn saddled up.

'I will go and call them out,' he said. 'Just the four of them, is it, Meagher?'

'Yes, Daniel! The four servants.'

Coburn lit his torch of peat.

'Wait until the four of them are on the lawn,' he ordered. 'Wait until they're well away from the house and I give the signal. Then come and ride in fast. And keep moving.'

He cantered to the house and hit the front door hard and loud with the flaming stick.

'Come out! All of you,' he shouted. 'I'm torching this house and none of you will be hurt if you come out now. I cannot wait long. Come and be quick with it. You'll not be harmed.'

He turned his horse again and rode along the line of windows, smashing the panes of glass, breaking the frames.

'You have minutes to get out. This house is going to burn. Come out now. Save yourselves!'

He heard a man shouting inside. Then the screams of the girls. A shot was fired. Then a second. The front door opened and a man came out bleeding. He staggered forward and clutched at the lion's head. He raised a hand towards Coburn and tried to speak as blood trickled from his mouth.

'The master ... The master ...' Then he fell onto his chest and did not move.

A girl and a boy ran out from the back of the house, past Coburn, and threw themselves down on the lawn behind him. He raised the flaming torch above his head and the three horsemen left the trees.

'In with it, boys, and fast!' he shouted to them. 'In at every window. The curtains first, then torches to the rooms.'

The maid and the boy lay flat on the grass, too terrified to move. They watched the horsemen with their flaming sticks, putting fire in through the windows and the open front door, spreading the flames. There was no delay, no moments of waiting for the fire to take hold. Within seconds, the rooms exploded with a roar and smoke blasted out in great black spirals. The heat burst up through the ceilings into the second floor and there was a mighty crash of timbers and another explosion. Balls of white hot splinters cascaded out as if they had been shot from cannons.

Coburn saw Kate riding fast towards him, raising her arm towards the roof. He looked up. Through the smoke, standing high on the parapet, he saw Edward Ogilvie.

'What's the bloody fool doing?' O'Brien brought his horse to Coburn's side. 'He's shouting at us. My God, Daniel. Look at him. He has someone in his arms. He's holding a girl.'

Coburn jumped from his horse, went to the boy and pulled him up off the grass. He shook him hard.

'Is it the maid? Did she not come out with you?'

The boy could not speak.

Coburn slapped him across the face. 'Talk boy, talk. Can he get down from there?' Coburn shouted again at him. 'Is there a way down? Quickly, tell me!'

The boy stuttered. 'At the back, sir! Stairs … The stable … At the back … Iron stairs.'

Coburn shouted to Kate. 'Take my gun. Ride to the gates. Fire one shot if you see any movement from the road. One shot. Go now, go!'

Coburn and O'Brien ran to the back of the house. There was much smoke but the fire had yet to reach there. A narrow cast-iron stairway spanned the stable to the first floor of the house above the kitchen. Coburn ran to it and began climbing. The rungs were already warm and blasts of hot air seared his face. Thirty feet up he came to a ledge where the iron stairway ended. A single wooden ladder continued up to the roof. As he held the first rung to climb again he saw Ogilvie standing on the parapet above him, the girl tight in one arm, a pistol in his other hand.

Coburn shouted, 'Give her to me, Ogilvie!'

'I'll have you first!' he shouted back. 'You've killed my servants and now you are trying to kill me.'

'Your servants are alive. You shot your own man.'

'He refused to bar the windows. He defied me.'

'Give me the girl and jump, you fool! The wall is collapsing.'

'Look at me, Coburn. Look up at me. Let me see your face.'

He swung his pistol towards Coburn and pulled the trigger but the shot that killed his butler had been his last.

Coburn shouted again. 'Let her go, you fool. Lower her down and then jump down to the ledge here. I can't wait longer. This wall is red hot.'

Part of it began to crumble. A shower of sparks shot out of a window and the wooden ladder was suddenly ablaze.

'Jump with her, Ogilvie … jump now.'

'I cannot. I will not reach it.'

'You will, you fool. Now, or you'll burn!'

'Why have you done this to me, Coburn?'

'Think, man. Think of all you did. Think of the thousand poor devils you shoved out of their homes. That's why we're torching yours.'

Coburn began feeling his way back down the iron stairs. The rungs now burnt his hands and feet. The heat was intense and the smoke began to choke him.

Ogilvie pushed the girl aside. 'Don't leave me here, Coburn. I'll jump. Catch me. I cannot do it on my own. Stay and catch me!'

Coburn stopped. But it was too late. Flames suddenly burst up through the roof and a mass of slates and bricks blew up into the air like an erupting volcano. The force of it lifted Ogilvie and the girl bodily off the parapet, spun them like a top and sucked them screaming backwards into the well of fire.

Coburn touched the ground as O'Brien came running to him.

'Hurry, Daniel. Kate has fired the shot. They must be coming … The Redcoats. Duffy and Meagher have gone to her. We must ride. Hurry, man!'

They met the others waiting at the gates. On the rise of a hill less than half a mile away, they could just make out the line of red marching towards them.

'This is as far as they dare come,' Coburn said. 'They don't know how many of us there are. They'll not push further.'

'Do we ride off together?' Meagher asked him.

'No! Go separately. But not directly. We'll meet at Dromoland in a week. Be in no hurry. We've done what we came to do and more. But once they know Ogilvie is dead, there'll be hell to pay.'

'Who will they blame, Daniel?' Duffy asked. 'Who will they go for?'

'They will blame us because I will let them know it's us. That's what this is all about. We've made the first strike and it's a bloody one. It is us they'll be after now. This is the beginning, boys. We have marked it this night.'

In turn they reached out, shook hands with each other, then rode off their separate ways. Coburn and Kate went together, side by side. They looked behind them. The sky was glowing orange.

CHAPTER SIXTEEN

Coburn did not wait to be named as Ogilvie's murderer. He announced it himself. Within a week he published a pamphlet declaring war on the landlords. Within days it was being read across all of Ireland.

Let them see their blackened piles, let us destroy the great wealth that lies between tyranny and liberty. Out of persecution comes a lust for revenge. Let them know vengeance is a pitiless obsession, and that we know well enough how to harness that. We will not get justice from the English by holding out an empty hand. Fill it with a gun or pike and if you have none, close your fist. Let our landlords threaten us and we will answer them with fire. Let us stop them now and not wait until caution clears our heads.

His call to arms was quickly answered. The cull of marked landlords began. Lists of those to be attacked began to circulate and they were not all of Coburn's making. Many were headed with the line: 'Your lives are not worth the paper this is written on'. Many killings were acts of individual vengeance.

Within two weeks, six landowners were shot dead as they rode from their estates. A seventh was blinded by grapeshot. Within a month, ten more had been killed and as many wounded. Such was the complicity and silence of the people that not one of the assassins was arrested. Of all the murders, it was Mahon's that angered the British government most.

Major Denis Mahon was a handsome, popular and well-intentioned young officer in the 49th Lancers Cavalry Regiment. He had inherited an estate in County Roscommon from his distant relative Lord Hartland. The old peer had died in a lunatic asylum and left a derelict estate and debts of over £30,000 in unpaid rents.

The young major began the new management by encouraging those tenants who would peaceably give up their plots to leave so that the land could be turned over to sheep farming. He hired two ships and those who wanted to emigrate to Canada and America could do so for free. He paid for extra provisions aboard the ships so that none would suffer in the crossing. Eight hundred accepted his offer. Three thousand more did not. They could not pay his rent and they would not leave. He felt he had no option. He gave them an ultimatum. They must pay or be evicted and evicted they were.

The parish priest of Strokestown denounced him publicly from the pulpit as a tyrant, the worst since Cromwell. Such words coming from a priest were encouragement enough. That November evening, Major Mahon having just finished chairing a meeting of the workhouse committee, was driving in an open carriage on the high road out of the town towards his estate. Three miles on, as he came to the crossroads, he was ambushed by two masked men on horseback. Before he could reach for his own gun they shot him twice in the chest. He died an hour later. As soon as it was dark, fires were lit on the hills in celebration.

Fear now spread fast among the landed gentry and those in their employ. Poor Law relief was suspended in many counties because officials were afraid to travel. Land agents and bailiffs were careful not to venture beyond the safety of their masters' estates.

At Carrick-on-Shannon, mourners who attended a funeral of a landowner all carried guns. The hearse was escorted by four armed policemen.

Landowners and their families hurried to leave for the safety of England. Lord Clarendon, the Lord Lieutenant, felt so threatened he quickly sent his children back to their London home. He also sent a letter to Prime Minister Russell, threatening to resign.

There is an open and widely spread conspiracy for shooting landlords and burning their properties. A flame now rages in a rebellious campaign and my fear is that it will become a general conflagration. The condition of Ireland is now that of a servile war. Distress, discontent and hatred of English rule are increasing everywhere. I receive murder threats daily and dare not go out without bodyguards and those I barely trust. I am a prisoner of the State, living in an enemy country. There are weapons in the hands of the most ferocious people on this earth. The time to suppress sedition has come. You will not ask me to remain here when I feel my power has gone.

He did not have to wait long for the Prime Minister to reply and he was heartened by it.

These outlaws must be caught. I will send you another regiment to do it. If they remain free to do as they will, there may soon be little room for us left in that accursed country.

But Russell hesitated. He had promised Clarendon the immediate dispatch of fifteen thousand more troops. Without explanation, they were delayed. There were demands that those caught in acts of rebellion should be charged with high treason and, upon conviction, the punishment was to be hanged, drawn and quartered. But Russell chose to ignore the clamour. His political opponents in Westminster accused him of cowardice. Others began to wonder whether it was, instead, cunning.

༚

Coburn and Kate were now never long in one place. Notices offering rewards for information leading to their arrests were nailed up in every town and market place in all the thirty-two counties. Caution being the wiser part of valour, Coburn sent O'Brien, Meagher and Duffy out to galvanise the people, and instructed Father Kenyon to establish the strength of support among the priests.

In March, a meeting was held in the Music Hall on Abbey Street in Dublin, where the Young Irelanders publicly announced the plan for national insurrection. Men of fighting age were invited to join a national guard with a target of fifty thousand volunteers. An Irish brigade was to be recruited in the United States for dedicated Irish-Americans willing to launch themselves across the Atlantic and fight for a free Ireland. Pamphlets were distributed in the hall with instructions on how to organise street fighting. Boiling oil was to be poured on soldiers' heads from windows, broken glass scattered in the streets to halt the cavalry, homemade ammunition, including grenades containing acid, would be made ready and lead, stolen from rain spouts and rooftops, would be made into bullets.

O'Brien reminded his audience that Irishmen made up a third of the entire British Army and ten thousand more of Irish stock were serving in the British constabulary. Would they ignore a call to arms to free their motherland? O'Brien told them that the French had pledged their support and he was about to leave for Paris to enlist the help of the revolutionaries who had so recently and bloodlessly deposed their king.

O'Brien, well tutored by Coburn, gave a final rousing speech. He addressed Lord Clarendon as 'Her Majesty's Executioner' and 'Ireland's Butcher'. He spoke of the holy hatred of foreign domination and the determination to rid Ireland of her oppressor, 'which glows as fierce and as hot as ever'.

He ended his speech draped in a green cloth.

'Rouse yourselves. Let us fan the embers and send care to the winds. Ignore English law, arm yourselves and be ready to march on Dublin Castle and tear it down. Let us shred English power forever.'

The cheering in Abbey Street could be heard all the way to St Stephen's Green. O'Brien and Meagher were immediately arrested but they were not, as expected, charged, convicted and transported to Botany Bay. Instead, to the surprise and disgust of all England, they were released on bail and O'Brien, breaking his bail conditions, promptly left for France for the meeting with his young rebellious counterparts in Paris.

Irish newspapers were now daily printing the full texts of public speeches up and down the country calling for insurrection. Unsigned pamphlets, detailing the easiest and quickest ways to kill English soldiers, were being handed out on the streets under the very eyes of the police and the soldiers themselves. And nothing was done to stop them. Only *The London Times* found space in its columns to protest.

In the wake of this Irish rebellion, English leniency, call it generosity, is hardly to be expected. The course of English benevolence is frozen by Irish insult. In no other country have men made treason and then come begging for sympathy from their so-called oppressors.

'What is happening, Kate? We push and they retreat. We go one step forward and they step back. What game is Russell playing?'

Following the attacks and murders of the landlords, Coburn had expected an immediate and brutal reaction. None came.

'Why is it, Kate? What are they planning? Could I walk in the streets of Dublin today and not be taken? Are they fools? Or are we?'

'They are not fools, Daniel. They are simply waiting.'

'Waiting for what?'

'For nothing to happen.'

'For nothing? Nonsense! It is happening. It's all around us. The landlords live in terror. Those who haven't left are making ready. O'Brien is in Paris, Meagher and Duffy are out there with the others and Father Kenyon is moving among the young priests. There's a swell of support across the country and it's rising.'

'Maybe the English don't think so. Maybe they think that only we believe it. Remember they've seen this all before and remember what they did to the people who fought them the last time.'

'There's not an Irishman who doesn't remember '98.'

'Perhaps they're just biding their time.'

'For what? What are they waiting for?'

'They do not want to make a martyr of you. If they catch you, if they catch us both, we will hang. You've said that yourself. With the two of us convicted of treason, they will have no choice. Maybe they're wondering what might happen if we hang. Whether Ireland will then find its courage.'

'How simple you make it sound, Kate. So, shall we surrender ourselves and then not live to see Ireland rise?'

'Perhaps I know the English mind better than you, Daniel. Don't you see? They have to keep us alive. Our deaths could just be the spark that ignites. Russell cannot have that happen until he is ready. Why do you think we have been left to ride so freely? The English are calling Russell a coward. I don't think so. I think he has a plan. He is waiting.'

'And must we play his waiting game? How can we do that? I've read that revolutions rise to a peak and you grab it at the hour or you lose it forever. Ours is rising fast. The people are preparing themselves, just waiting for our call.'

'Daniel, I love you. I love every part of everything you dream of, everything you are fighting for. But …'

'But what, Kate? Speak.'

'You talk of our people readying themselves. You and I have spent a year with them, speaking to them, rallying them. I've stood by your side and watched their faces as you spoke, heartened by their cheering. But every day, Daniel, every day, I have watched them grow thinner and weaker and hungrier and the crowds have dwindled and the cheering has grown fainter. Hunger has drained them. If they have no food in their stomachs, where's their fight? Russell knows it. Trevelyan knows it. They all know it.'

'My God! Is that what it's all about? Is that what you believe? Has that been their plan from the start? To starve us slowly into submission?'

'No! Not in the beginning, Daniel. I don't believe it was. I won't believe it. My father would never have been an accomplice to anything so vile. It has just become so. I remember Tom Keegan telling me of O'Connell's monster meeting at Clontarf when a million men there could have taken on the English troops and beaten them.'

'And so they will again, Kate.'

'No, Daniel. Clontarf's men were fit and healthy, not men already beaten. People have had their courage starved out of them.'

'Then what we have to do we must do soon. The longer we wait, the fewer our chances. We cannot be puppets of Russell.'

'Is it not already too late, Daniel?'

'Too late? Is that what you think, Kate?'

'I don't know what I think. None of us know.'

'Exactly, Kate. How can we know for sure? So we must gamble. I read once that revolutions are like the throwing of a dice. Nothing is certain until the end. If we're not prepared for the risk, if we're not ready to lose and die, then we are not the people to ask others to follow us. Kate, you cannot be with me if you doubt me.'

'I will not leave you, Daniel. I could never do it. That first day at Dromoland you said we would ride to the gallows together. I agreed to the terms and I've not changed. Nor will I.'

ಞ

There was no declaration by either side. Civil war does not begin by proclamation or by any curt exchange. Like a smouldering sheaf of straw, it takes only the random breeze to set it ablaze. Was it the sensational headlined story in *The London Times* that twenty thousand Irishmen armed with guns and pikes had taken the towns of Kilkenny, Clonmel and Carlow, blowing up railway lines and setting railway stations and post offices aflame? Was it the report that thousands of British troops had been mobilised and were rapidly embarking on warships in Holyhead bound for Dublin? Did one or both excite and encourage men to believe rebellion was already under way? But both reports were untrue. Fiction. Hoaxes. There were no fires in Kilkenny or Clonmel or Carlow and no British troops had left any of their garrisons that week. But the spark had been struck and the Irish were about to be propelled once again in bloody contest against their English masters.

Coburn planned to split his command four ways. Immediately O'Brien returned from Paris with the expected pledge of support from the French revolutionaries, he would tour the south to recruit and organise, taking in Tipperary, Cork and all of Kerry. Meagher and Duffy would rally support along the counties east of the Shannon as far north as Meath. He and Kate would ride west to Clare and Galway and Connaught. Father Kenyon would canvas those young priests who had already secretively pledged the support of their parishes. All that was lacking now was the call to fight and the weapons to fight with.

Prime Minster Russell knew otherwise. The information he was receiving told a very different story. As his predecessor William Pitt had done so cunningly in the 1798 rebellion, he had sent his own secret agents across the Irish Sea to mingle and listen. Those agents confirmed the surge of support for Coburn and his men and that there was a popular movement for rebellion. They reported that the Young Irelanders were being feted wherever they went and that there was much enthusiasm among the crowds. But the agents added vital addendum to their reports. They wrote that the rebels were grossly exaggerating the numbers attending their rallies, that support for them was ragged and spiritless, that there was no organisation in place, no headquarters, no preparations, no plan. And crucially, that the rebels had very few weapons and no stores of ammunition.

Russell then sent his agents a question that would decide his next move. He asked them if the mass of Irish were physically fit to fight. Were they collectively strong enough, man on man, to endure a lengthy war? He received their prompt and unanimous reply. The Irishmen were not strong. They would not stand and struggle for long. They would soon die from exhaustion. Their hunger would kill more than the Redcoats' rifles.

It was what the Prime Minister had wanted to hear, what he long expected. He would delay no longer. It was time for his planned offensive. Ireland was again about to be reminded of the futility of opposing England.

The fifteen thousand troops that he had promised Clarendon immediately set sail for Dublin. The Hussars with field artillery were sent to Mayo, five thousand troops were dispatched to Clonmel and another battalion to Limerick. The Enniskillen Dragoons were brought up from Newbridge to Dublin and two squadrons of Light Dragoons reinforced the garrison guarding Dublin Castle. The 75th Regiment, at the ready, bivouacked in nearby Phoenix Park. Moving columns of riflemen, light artillery and cavalry, able to move rapidly, were ready to scour the countryside. The fleet, anchored off Lisbon, was ordered to sail immediately to Cork and three warships, the *Dragon*, the *Merlin* and the *Medusa* were anchored off Waterford. Two more were within short-shelling range of Wexford. The Duke of Wellington, hero of Waterloo and of Irish birth from County Meath, volunteered to advise the government on further troop displacements.

The suspension of *habeas corpus* was rushed through Parliament. Dublin, Cork, Waterford and Drogheda were put under virtual

martial law. Irish civilians were no longer allowed to own weapons of any kind and anyone found carrying one was summarily
sentenced to one year's hard labour. If a landowner or government official was murdered, all men in the surrounding district
between the ages of sixteen and sixty were expected to actively
assist the police in the arrest of the murderer. Anyone resisting
or failing to cooperate would be sentenced, without trial, to a
minimum of two years' penal servitude. Over one hundred and
twenty people were arrested on various charges on the first night.

There was worse news from O'Brien. He returned from France
but not with the much hoped-for pledge of support in his pocket.
The exuberant reign of liberalism and idealism there had been
short-lived. Having deposed their king, the Republicans were
now fighting each other and barricades had once again been
erected in the streets of the capital. The Archbishop of Paris, crossing no man's land in an attempt to mediate, had been shot dead.

The Vatican took notice. Pope Pius IX immediately issued
a Papal Prescript forbidding his flock to involve themselves
in matters of State and politics. In a separate edict he directly
accused the Irish clergy of 'giving provocation to murder.' Father
Kenyon, the Patriot Priest, was summoned by his bishop, severely
reprimanded for his support of the Young Irelanders and suspended. That same day he came to Coburn and told him he was
returning to his parish and would remain there, obediently silent.

'I am condemned by my own Church, Daniel. I have no
option. I cannot help you.'

'Father, you have twenty parishes under your wing. That's over
a thousand men and boys and I need them all. You've given me
a list of a dozen priests who you say will follow us. I need everyone one of them too. Most of all I need you.'

'Do you not understand, Daniel? We priests are now forbidden by our Pope, our Holy Father, to involve ourselves. Do you
expect me to disobey him? If I thought we had a glimmer of a
chance, I would face the wrath of God for my love of Ireland.

But I will not lead my people in an act of mass suicide. You talk of rebellion, but go to the towns and villages, raise the green flag and see how many gather round it. See how little spirit there is left out there.'

'We can't surrender now.'

'This is not surrender. This is being wise. Go into hiding. Plan it better. Pick your time. You cannot beat the English now. They're too strong and too many. They're everywhere. Give way for a while.'

'I'm damned if I will.'

'You're damned if you don't. This is a bootless struggle.'

'Then I'll struggle on without you.'

'You're a fool, Daniel. You'll be drowned in blood.'

'Goodbye, Father.'

'No! Not goodbye, not yet. I'll be with you in the shadows watching and praying. That's as much as I can do. The moment you are really in need, I'll be there.'

Father Kenyon wet his forefinger and made the sign of the cross on Coburn's forehead. Then he left for Tipperary to watch and wait and help feed his starving parishioners.

ॐ

'It is betrayal. He obeys his Italian master and deserts Ireland. Every priest is pulling away from us now.'

Coburn had summoned O'Brien and Meagher to meet him in Wexford. Kate sat, as usual, at Coburn's side.

'Are the priests that important to us?' she asked.

'By doing nothing they do us much harm.'

'Maybe they'll keep their silence.'

'Silence too is damning.'

'What do we do then, Daniel?' Meagher asked.

'Father Kenyon says we should bide our time. Wait another year.'

'It will give us time to prepare ourselves better,' said O'Brien.

'People will be stronger then,' Meagher added.

'Only if there's food,' said O'Brien.

'And what if there's not?' asked Daniel. 'Do we fight the bloody British Empire with an army of skeletons?'

'Our revolution then hangs on the potato,' Meagher said.

'It does,' Coburn answered. 'If this famine stretches further, and there's not a decent crop next harvest, there'll not be an Irishman alive left to fight.'

'Then we have no choice,' O'Brien said. 'We do it now or we never will.'

'Kate?'

'You've always said that no one person can decide it, Daniel.'

'Tell me then, all three of you. Do we go or do we not?'

There was a moment of silence as if each was afraid to be the first to lead in such a decision. To do nothing would be tantamount to surrender. But to fight and lose? It was O'Brien who spoke first.

'We've come this far after a year of talking and a thousand meetings. If we go away from it now, will we ever return? It's with God now. We rise and win. We rise and fall. There is only one honourable course.'

Meagher stood up. 'I remember you saying, Daniel, that we must fan the embers of the fire. Leave it a year and that fire may well be out. I'm for it.'

Coburn clasped his hand. He looked across at Kate. She nodded.

'So it is then,' he said to them. 'We do it now or we will never do it. Are we agreed?'

'We are agreed,' they answered together.

'Then send your men out and get the people on the streets. Target Kilkenny, Callan and Carrick. Have them out and the green flags flying. We'll have two last rallies. Cashel is your town, William.'

'Indeed, Daniel. It's been O'Briens' for five hundred years.'

'And Waterford is yours Meagher. Arrange both meetings at the same time on the same night. Get out there and excite them. We have to make the people believe we can do it. Kate and I will come to both.'

'Is that wise, Daniel?' she asked. 'The military will be there.'

'So will our people and a thousand of them will give us cover enough. I have to be among them. They have to see me and hear me this one last time.'

'And what then?' Kate asked.

'Then we'll go at them ever so slowly, ever so carefully, attacking them in pockets. They are too big and we are too little to face them full on. But we'll hit them in small places, again and again, biting them like a thousand thunderflies.'

'Should we go for the railways?' asked Meagher.

'We will blow the lines,' Coburn replied.

'And the ships in Cork Harbour?'

'All targets now.'

'They'll up their patrols,' said Duffy.

'We'll make them helpless, however many troops they ship in.'

'This will be a different kind of war, Daniel.'

'It's the only one we're capable of fighting', he replied. 'We will be like the will-o'-the-wisp, moving at night, invisible by day. The English have their cannons but we have a better weapon. We have surprise, we have the unexpected. They have an army but we have patience and sufferance. Wars need not always be fought on battlefields; that much we have learnt. No soldier, no politician, no landowner will feel safe. They'll ever be looking back over their shoulders. We will snipe at them, have them jumping at every shadow. It's the fear that will get them, that little bit of constant terror. That's how it'll be. We'll fight them with terror! We will be terrorists. They will never have had to fight an enemy like us before.'

ಚಿ

The Rock of Cashel sat above the town, a towering mass of lime-
stone crowned by Cormac's chapel in the cathedral ruins. It was
once the shrine of ancient Ireland and the stronghold, five hundred
years before, of Brian Boru, King of Munster and William O'Brien's
ancestor. The moon, white and fully round, lit up the mass of stone,
making it appear translucent. Below spread all of Tipperary.

O'Brien thought he had prepared his rally well. Messengers
had been sent ahead days before with instructions to bring the
townspeople to the foot of the rock, light watch fires and fly
their green flags high on poles. He remembered his early time
as a Young Irelander, those thrilling days of idealism and revolutionary fire. When he had dreamt of entering his ancestral
home to be greeted by columns of sturdy men preparing for war.
In his vision, carts would be ready laden with supplies, black-
smiths would be hammering shovels and hoes into weapons, old
men would straighten their backs and women would throw off
their aprons and together pull the wreckage from their tumbled
homes and build barricades with the debris. Even the children
would be little mercenaries come the day of the great insurrection. Such were once his dreams and now they were an age away.

He rode in at dusk with thirty men and halted within the
ruins just below the peak of the Rock. He saw no watch fires,
no sentinels. No green flags flew from poles, no candles flickered
from any window. The town below him was silent and still. He
beckoned the nearest rider.

'Do you know O'Connor's house?'

'I do, sir.'

'He has the big corner one on the square.'

'I know it well.'

'Go down on foot and be careful. If the military are there they
are well hidden. Daniel will be coming any time now and it's

him they'll be after. Find out from O'Connor what it's all about. We'll not move until you signal us with a light.'

They watched him go down. There was no sound, no shouts or calls from sentries. They waited.

'Should one of us follow, sir?'

'No!' O'Brien answered. 'If he's caught, they'll have you too. We'll hold here longer.'

They moved deeper into the shadow of the chapel ruins.

'They say there are tunnels under here, Mr O'Brien.'

'And they're right. A great maze of them. I know them well.'

'We are safe here then? If the Redcoats come?'

'We are,' O'Brien answered. 'Now let's stop the talk.' He was anxious. Soon Coburn would come riding in with Kate and they would be expecting crowds. They were to be their cordon of safety. Without them they would have no protection.

'There's something going on down there, Mr O'Brien.'

There was a single dim shaft of light from the centre of the town.

'It's in the square. Must be O'Connor's. Our man's made it, thank God. We'll wait until he calls us.'

Suddenly there was commotion. More lights shone out. A man was shouting, then more shouts were heard and women were screaming. A shot was fired, then four, five, six muskets were firing together.

In the moonlight they saw soldiers running through the streets, some holding torches, spreading out from the town, left and right. At that moment O'Brien turned at the sound of hooves and saw Coburn and Kate galloping towards him. His own horse reared.

'Get away, Daniel,' he shouted. 'Go off. We're betrayed. They've been waiting for us.'

But Coburn did not turn. He brought his horse to a halt between the pillars of the chapel, out of the moonlight, and dismounted.

'Are they around us, William?'

'I don't know. But there's nobody above us yet. We've just come from the peak. Daniel, you must go while you've time.'

'William, I have all the time I need now. There is no hurry any more.'

'Why do you say that? What's happened? What news of Waterford?'

'I've heard nothing from Meagher.'

'And Kilkenny?'

'Empty except for Hussars.'

'And Callan?'

'Every door was shut. No one dared come out for fear of being shot. There was some fighting in Carrick but what could three hundred men with pikes do against three thousand Fusiliers. As soon as the shooting began they threw down their pikes and ran. The towns are silent. Youghal, Cork, Dungarvan, Limerick … They've all been scared off the streets. The army is everywhere. It's over for us, William. Over, even before we've begun. All this time they've had their own people inside ours. They've been too clever for us.'

'Mr O'Brien, sir, there are horsemen.'

A column of riders was coming towards them from the town, six Hussars in a single line. The leader was holding a white flag. The night air was clean and crystal clear and their tunics shone bright in the moonlight. They trotted slowly, almost casually, as if they knew there was no threat to them.

O'Brien held Coburn's arm. 'Daniel, go! Now! Kate, take him. It's him they want.'

'Daniel.'

'No, Kate. We will not leave. They've not come to take me, at least not yet. Not with six men. They've come to talk and I think I can guess why.'

The riders halted some fifteen yards away. The leading officer lowered his flag as the others brought their horses level with his in a line. He shouted.

'May I talk with Mr Daniel Coburn? I believe he is with you?'

'He is here. Speak and he'll listen.'

'Is that you, Coburn?'

'It is. What is it you want?

'I must tell you first that Thomas Meagher has been arrested. By the time the few came to listen to him, he was already in chains. Your people tried to stop us and barricaded the bridge but with good sense he stood on his carriage and forbade them to try to rescue him. It was wise. We have three warships in the harbour ready to reduce that pretty town to rubble within minutes. He is presently on his way to Newgate Prison to join your man Duffy. Within the week they will be transported on the convict ship.'

'I expected to hear no less,' Coburn replied. 'This is not our night.'

'Yet it may well still be, sir. I am instructed to make you an offer. It seems that my government does not want you alive or dead. Neither you nor your mistress. My government fears that killing you by English bullets or hanging on English gallows might well incense people who until now have remained mostly subdued.'

'Not subdued,' Coburn shouted back. 'Starved to submission.'

'As you wish, sir. But the offer remains. Would you hear it?'

'I'm listening.'

'It comes from the very highest office, from a gentleman whose word is final. To his mind, the Atlantic is more of a barrier to your mischief than the Irish Sea and he would prefer to export it elsewhere. There is a ship presently anchored on the Shannon soon to sail. That is our offer. Safe passage to America. I hope you agree that no pair of traitors can ever have expected such a generous settlement. And please do not expect help from the townspeople. My soldiers have orders to shoot on sight anyone who dares open their door.'

O'Brien leant towards Coburn and whispered, 'We could shoot them now and be done with.'

Coburn did not reply to him. Instead, he looked to Kate. 'Safe passage, Kate? To America. Is it a bargain? Nod if you think we should go the English way.'

Kate did not nod. She did not speak. Coburn waited. Kate shook her head.

Coburn urged his horse forward.

'I see you are a captain and a very young one at that. Well, tell this to your gentleman, whose word you say is final. I reject his generous settlement. Tell him it settles nothing for me or my people, for such I believe them to be. You say you will shoot them if they come to help me and I believe you. You offer me free passage to America but I'll not take it because I do not believe it to be an honest proposal. Nothing has ever come freely from you English except from the barrel of your muskets. Tell your master that we are defeated tonight but we will fight again another time and when we do, we will decide the place of it and the nature of it. You have been here for five hundred years but one day you will be gone and we shall still be here. Then you will understand why we hated you so much. And when you have gone we will hate you less and you will also know why.'

'A pretty speech, sir, and I appreciate your dilemma. I do. But the offer stands. Refuse it and you are drafting your own death warrant and that of your mistress too. Must you do that to her? Reject this and you are a selfish fool.'

'But not a trusting one.'

'You have weapons?'

'We are not fools enough to come here naked.'

'It doesn't matter. You are surrounded. Accept the offer. Agree and you and your mistress will be free to leave Ireland. Refuse and you both die.'

'No, sir, we do not agree. Now go your way and we will attempt to go ours.'

The young captain urged his horse a few paces closer until he was only a length away. He lowered his voice as if he wanted only Coburn to hear.

'You must listen to me, Coburn, listen to what I say. I will tell you my orders. If you will not surrender, I am to kill you and your mistress by whatever means. I am to burn your bodies and scatter your ashes. My masters want no martyrdom and no pilgrimage to your graves.'

'Thank you,' Coburn replied. 'So we will be nowhere but everywhere. It's a fitting tribute.'

The captain leant forward in his saddle and Coburn could now see his face clearly. How young he was! And how earnest he seemed. He hesitated, then spoke to Coburn again in a whisper.

'It seems as if you jest, as if you think this is part of some game of ours. But I urge you to heed my warning, seriously. I do not want to kill you or your lady; do not ask me why. But leave here, Coburn. Now. I will give you time but it cannot be long. Once I am back with my men I must give the order to advance on you.'

'Why? First you say you've come to kill us and now you urge us to leave, giving us time to escape. What kind of manoeuvre is this, what mischief? What is your trick?'

The young captain said nothing. To Coburn's surprise, he saluted him and then backed his horse towards his men and as a troop, they all turned together and went slowly back down the hill.

As if to close a chapter, clouds suddenly swarmed over the moon and the Hussars disappeared into the blackness below.

CHAPTER SEVENTEEN

The thunder was fierce and the lightning a blinding white, so they did not hear or see the first explosion. Then, as the orange ball of flame erupted from the town and the ruins rattled about them, they jumped from their horses and fell to their knees to shield themselves from the blast. The clouds turned bright orange.

'Have they fired the houses?' somebody shouted. 'Are the bastards torching us?'

Shrapnel hit the chapel walls and fragments of stone fell on their heads. Coburn crouched low and edged his way forward beyond the pillars. Below him, where the moor met the outskirts of the town, there was a blaze like no other he had seen since the burning of Ogilvie's house. Each explosion was quickly followed by another, like a volley of a thousand firing cannons. Gunpowder erupted and great mushrooms of white smoke billowed up; red streamers were propelled into the sky, narrow tracers rising in a long arc until they sank out of sight. Coburn saw soldiers running with buckets towards the horses trapped in their shafts, on fire and screaming.

'They've hit the army's ammunition wagons — two, three, maybe more — I can't see it all for the fire and smoke. O'Connor must have got the message.'

'He's done it to keep the army away from us,' O'Brien said. 'To give us time.'

Coburn eased himself back towards the shelter of the chapel. 'To do what?' he asked. 'There's no way out now. They'll be working up to the peak behind us.'

O'Brien caught his arm. 'Daniel, it's beneath us. The way out is under our feet. This is my place, remember? My family's cat-acombs are here and there's a tunnel where my ancestors hid when Cromwell was doing his murdering. It goes west from the town, out towards the Tipperary road.'

'Is that beyond the soldiers' lines?' Coburn asked.

'I've no idea. Maybe not. You will only know when you come out and see daylight. But what else is there? Do we have a choice?'

'No! No choice.'

'Then I will lead you as far as I need to. Then I'll come back and surrender.'

'You will not, William. If we go, you go too.'

'That's not possible and it makes no sense anyway. As long as they can see us and our horses, they will assume you're still here. Once I know you're well away, I'll go to them.'

'They will hang you.'

'No, Daniel, they will not. I am a Protestant, an aristocrat and once I was a member of the English Parliament, let's not forget that. I'll be looked after. Be assured.'

'Daniel, he's right,' Kate said. 'You cannot fight and if you sur-render they will do what the officer said he'd do. You will be shot.'

'Both of you,' said O'Brien. 'Yes! Kate too. Does that not per-suade you, Daniel?'

'It should but it does not. Kate, understand. How can I run away now? Wouldn't I prefer to die? Shouldn't I?'

'Daniel.' O'Brien was angry. 'Go kill yourself then. Go out there now and fire off a shot and start the whole bloody thing. They'll leave their fires soon enough for you. But don't let them kill Kate. You talk only of yourself, but for God's sake, remember there's two of you.'

'Not two,' Kate said. 'Three.' She turned away from Coburn. The dancing light from the fires reflected on her back.

'Three, Kate?' he asked. 'What is this nonsense? Why three?'

Still she did not look at him. 'Because, Daniel, I am carrying your child.'

There was another loud blast, another shower of splinters above their heads and in the vivid surge of colour, the three stood still and unspeaking, silhouetted against the ruins.

ຄຄ

The catacombs had been hewn out by hand, generations of hard labour. Either side of a long, low and narrow corridor were the coffins of the mummified ancestors of one of Ireland's most famous families. The air was dank and smelt of burnt ash. Dried brittle skeletons of bats lay in the crevices where they had died. Fine white dust, like flour, carpeted the floor. O'Brien lit a torch.

'Are you surprised how well I'm prepared? I have oil for the light and spring water feeds an urn further on. My father said it was a bolthole for many an O'Brien on the run.'

'How far does it go, William?'

'I once counted two hundred and eighty paces, say about three hundred yards. It opens beneath an outcrop that's well hidden. If the military is still around, you can wait there until it's safe to go on.'

'Safe to go where, William?'

'Listen to me, Daniel. Listen, Kate. When you look out from the tunnel you'll see below you a road going west. It takes you to Tipperary twelve miles away. Father Kenyon's church is there somewhere.'

'He will not help us, William. He won't disobey his Pope.'

'Oh yes, he will. He'll not turn away from you now. He's obliged to give you sanctuary and he'll give it willingly. You have to believe that.'

'I believe it,' said Kate. 'Daniel, he's the only one who can help us. There is no one else. He will know that. He won't refuse us.'

'I shall try and get a message to him,' O'Brien said. 'As soon as the military realise you've left Cashel, they'll have no reason to stay. Before they take me I'll somehow let O'Connor or his sons know you're on your way. With luck you will be there before them. They will help you, protect you. Trust me, Daniel. Trust them.'

'I trust them, of course I do. But then what? I suppose if we can make it to Limerick, we could hide up for a while. Then move on to Clare or even Connemara. We'd be safe enough there.'

'Whatever you decide, Daniel. What's important is that you disappear, you and Kate.'

'Do you give a nod to that, Kate? Does that seem right to you?'

'It does, Daniel. It's right for both of us.'

'You mean all three of you,' O'Brien added. For the first time in many months, he managed a smile.

୨୧

When they reached the opening beneath the overhang of rock, dawn was still three hours away. The wind had dropped but the moon remained hidden. They sat hushed, listening for any sound of talk or movement below them and waited for the light. They had taken water from the urn and it had made their hunger more painful.

O'Brien lay flat, reached out to the grass and pulled up a bunch of tall yellow weeds. He bit off the flowers and leaves and scraped the thick white stems and roots clean with a sliver of rock.

'Eat them, Kate. A mother should feed well.'

'What is it?' she asked.

'Wild fennel. Some cook it. Some have it raw. Just eat it.'

She did as she was told. 'It is delicious, William. You are a man of many surprises.'

'And with that compliment, my Kate, and you, Daniel, I must leave. Once the military have put out their fires they will come looking. I have to be there when they do. Go as soon as you know it's clear. Good luck to you both and pray that we'll meet again. You are dear, dear friends and there's much we might have done in different times.'

Kate embraced him. She said nothing. With the back of his hand he wiped away her tears.

Coburn held out his hands. 'William …'

'Say nothing, Daniel. It has all been said. Take care of Kate. She's carrying delicate cargo. One day, when your names are mentioned, all Ireland will praise you.'

೧೨

It was twelve miles to Tipperary, three hours walking. Was it too much to risk in the daytime when anyone might be stopped by the military or police simply for being about? Should they instead be patient and wait for the safety of night? It was Kate who decided it.

'We must go just as soon as we think it's clear. Once they discover we've left the Rock, they'll cover as much ground as they can. That captain cannot afford to lose us.'

'Only if he's intent on catching us.'

'Why do you say that, Daniel? He had orders to kill us.'

'Yes! That's what he said. A strange boy, and too young for trickery, perhaps.'

'Daniel, we must leave now.'

They could see clearly the road below them, the road they must take. It was empty as most roads were now. How easily they would be spotted.

'How far do you think we'd get, Kate, two people on a road like that?'

'Daniel, look! Just on the left of it.' She pointed to a deep, narrow trough that had once been a working peat cutaway.

'See how it dips deeper with the slope. If we could reach that and keep low, we'd be hidden until we are a long way off.'

'But it's open ground from here.'

'We must risk it.'

The morning light was grey and the air damp and cold. They came out from their hiding place, shivering, hesitant, and edged out slowly beyond the ledge. They listened. There was no loud army talk, no rattle of arms, no bustle of horses and no giveaway bright uniforms. Then they heard rifle shots and saw riders galloping at speed to the right, away from the road. And behind them, chasing them, a line of red and blue, a column of Hussars.

'It's William's men. He's sent them down as decoys to take the army away from us, to give us a chance to the road. Look at them ride. It's working. God bless the boys. Come, it's our chance. Run like you've never run before.'

৩৫

The mist was with them, the dense, heavy mist of the boglands. Its canopy covered the moors and gave them shelter all the way to Tipperary. When they had reached the outskirts of the little market town, the mist lifted and only then did they see the first of the morning sun. They thought it an omen.

The town square of Tipperary was deserted. Shopfronts had long been boarded up and the trees bordering the water troughs had been cut to pieces for firewood. Between the houses, in the narrow alleys that divided them, Coburn saw bodies huddled under sacking, asleep or maybe dead. Beyond the square, in what might once have been the main street, he saw a small stone church. It had no name-board. Perhaps that too had been used as winter fuel. They entered by the side door. It was empty. They sat and rested.

'You want food? You'll find no food here. There's nothing here. Best you go.'

The priest was loud and abrupt. He came from behind a screen and faced them. He was large and ugly, unshaved, unwashed and fat when all men thereabouts were thin. Coburn stood as he approached.

'We want directions, Father.'

'To go where?'

'St Olave's church. I'm told it is south of the town in the lee of the Galtee Mountains.'

'That's the church of Father Kenyon.'

'Yes! Father Kenyon.'

'He's what they call the Patriot Priest. Why would you want to see him? What is it you're after?'

Coburn hesitated. He looked to Kate. He read her thoughts. Trust no one.

She said to the priest, 'We would have him marry us.'

'Indeed? Well I can do that and save you the journey. Do you have money?'

'No!' said Coburn. 'We have nothing. But we must find Father Kenyon.'

The fat priest came closer. They could smell the sweat of his body and the drink on his breath.

'Are you from these parts? Do I know your face? And your woman?'

'No, Father,' Coburn replied. 'We are from Cashel.'

'Cashel, is it? Then you must be new for I know most living souls there.'

'We're on the move, looking for work.'

'There's not a person who isn't. Yet you look well fed and you're not in rags. Who are you? Haven't I seen you before?'

'It's Father Kenyon we're after. At St Olave's.'

'Yes! So you said. I could send a rider to fetch him.'

'No! That won't do. He knows we're coming. It would not be right to hurry him. I'm told his church is near Bansha Woods.'

'Do you think I don't know?'

The priest walked some paces to the altar steps. He seemed impatient. He spoke without looking at them.

'St Olave's is a good hour's walk away, if you walk fast, that is. From the square take the southern road towards Newtown. Beyond Brookville Bridge, you'll see a signpost to Rathkea. His church is a mile beyond that. Now leave me.'

'Thank you for your help, Father. May I give Father Kenyon your regards?'

'As you wish.'

'And your name?'

'Kennedy. Kennedy of Killaloe.'

ഇരു

The horses were resting and tethered. Their riders were standing by them, spooning from bowls of stirabout. Father Kenyon sat cross-legged on the low wall that encircled St Olave's. When he saw Coburn, he let out a great howl, ran fifty yards down the lane and collapsed in his arms. Then, gasping for breath, he grabbed Kate by her hands and swung her round in a circle, as a father does to a child.

'God bless you both, but I thought you'd never make it. I should have had more faith. The O'Connor lads here have just come from Cashel. O'Brien got a message to their father. They've told me everything. They are here to look after you both.'

Coburn nodded to them. 'Did they see William go?'

'Yes! The military took him away and with a bit of respect, so they tell me.'

'And the boys, the decoys? We saw the hussars after them. Did they get away?'

'Two of them were dead when they found them.'

'Two of O'Connor's boys. Killed because of me.'

'They'd have wanted it no other way. The two of you are precious to us. They wouldn't have done it otherwise. Now, are you both hungry?'

He led them into the annexe of his little church and fed them soup.

'Daniel, I really didn't think you'd get here, least of all in daylight. Did nobody see you?'

'The mist was as thick as your soup, Father. If anyone was out there on the moors, we didn't see them and they never saw us.'

'Then how did you find me? You've never been here before.'

'We asked a priest in Tipperary.'

'What priest?'

'He said his name was Kennedy.'

'Kennedy of Killaloe?'

'That's the man.'

'He knows you're here? By Christ, Daniel, you couldn't have chosen a worse one. Of all the people, you picked him.'

'I picked nobody, Father. The town was near deserted. Is there a problem?'

'Do you think he recognised you? Did he see Kate?'

'He saw us both.'

'He was suspicious,' Kate said. 'He didn't want us to leave.'

Father Kenyon walked hurriedly from the room and shouted to the O'Connors.

'Saddle up, boys, and hurry. Daniel and Kate are leaving now. They'll need horses, so two of you will have to stay.'

Coburn went after him. 'Father, what is it? What's the trouble? Is it the priest?'

'Yes, Daniel, it's Kennedy. A hateful drunkard of a man and an informer. He will have guessed by now who you are and he'll already be on his way to the constabulary. They'll pay him well. Now quick! We have no time to talk. You must be off. The O'Connors will take you to Limerick. Keep yourselves safe there until you decide what to do next.'

'We will stay there for a while and move on to Galway and Connemara.'

'Do what you think is right,' said the priest. 'But hurry off now. The O'Connors are waiting, the horses are ready.'

'Come, Kate.' Coburn took her hand but she pulled it away.

'Father.'

'Yes, Kate.'

'The Kennedy priest asked us why we were looking for you. I told him you would marry us. It was an excuse. I couldn't think of any other.'

'It's as good as any and probably the best.'

'Will you?'

'Will I what?'

'Marry us?'

'Marry you?'

'Yes! Here and now.'

Coburn stopped at the door. 'Kate, are you mad? The military's on its way and you want us to be married?'

'Exactly!'

'But I haven't asked you.'

She ignored him.

'Will you, Father?'

'Doesn't Daniel have a say?'

'Father, I am with his child and I will not carry a bastard across all of Ireland searching for a place to wean it.'

'Daniel?'

'Marry us, Father, and be quick with it.'

∞

The fat Kennedy of Killaloe sat in his vestry, sipping whiskey from a jar and pondering on a face without a name. It was the face of a well-fed and clothed man looking for work, travelling with a fine-looking woman with a strong trim body and raven hair. Here they were in Tipperary asking after Father Kenyon, the outcast, scolded by his bishop. What was it they wanted of him? Who could they be, these strangers, looking for the Patriot Priest? Only then, as he asked himself that question, did he realise he had just met the leader of the Young Irelanders and his lady, known throughout all Ireland and beyond as the 'Dark Rosaleen'.

He trotted as fast as his heavy body would carry him to the constabulary to report his discovery. The one policeman on duty then walked a mile to the small military depot on the Limerick road and within twenty minutes a column of forty foot soldiers from the 49th Regiment were fast-stepping their way to Bansha Woods and the church of St Olave's.

ର

The hurried marriage that made Coburn and Kate one now threatened to separate them forever. As they waved Father Kenyon their goodbyes and trotted away in the company of the O'Connor brothers, the men of the 49th were already passing Brookville Bridge. Soon they would be in sight of the church.

O'Connor's horses heard them first, the tramping of military feet, the rhythm of marching men. The lead horse shook its head and tried to turn. Its rider reined it back. Then he too heard them.

'Back, Mr Coburn, back,' he shouted. 'It's the military already. Ride for the woods, we'll hold them here as best we can.'

The horsemen jumped from their saddles and ran either side of the lane for cover. They cocked their weapons and waited for the column to round the corner. Five men with flintlocks and a single blunderbuss about to face the advancing forty fusiliers armed with quick-loading rifles.

The O'Connor brothers waited until the first line of red tunics were only twenty yards from them and then opened fire.

Five soldiers fell. But it would take another fifteen seconds for the brothers to recharge and reload their pistols. By the count of ten, three were already dead. For a full minute the fusiliers swept the undergrowth with so much fire that saplings were cut in two, tree bark flew like shrapnel, leaves and grass were scorched and began to smoulder. It was as if a vast scythe had cut it clean. When they were done, they dragged three perforated bodies onto the road and went further into the tree line, firing blindly as they hunted for the other two.

Coburn saw the brothers up along the ridge that bordered the woods. If they did not turn into the cover of the trees they would run straight into the soldiers and be shot on sight. He ran towards them up the slope, waving his arms. The brothers saw him, stopped and began their way down. Then there was a volley of shots and Coburn fell to the ground and did not move.

Kate and Father Kenyon came running from the church as the two brothers began dragging Coburn towards them.

'Lift him onto my shoulder, Father,' Declan, the older one, shouted. 'Help me with him into the trees. That was a stray shot, for sure they haven't seen us yet.'

Coburn was bleeding badly. Only the pressure of his body, heavy against that of the big man, helped stem the flow.

'I know a place,' said Father Kenyon. 'It is well inside the woods. Can you make it?'

'I can and I will,' said the big man.

'God give you strength.'

'Where is it we're going?'

'It's the ruins of an old church towards Slievenamuck.'

'I know it.'

'We will be safe there, I think,' said the priest.

'We will be safe,' said the big man.

Declan was strong. No lesser man could have done it. With Coburn across his shoulders, he laboured for nearly an hour barging his way through the thick armour of Bansha Woods, unhindered by man for thousands of years. When finally they came to the ruins, he laid Coburn gently on the ground and, without resting, turned to go.

'Will you not stay with us?' Kate asked.

'No! We must go back. I think my brothers are dead but I must know for sure. I must tell our mother.'

'Thank you, Declan, thank you,' said the priest. 'And may God be with you both.'

The big man nodded. He took his brother's arm and together they returned the way they came.

The bullet had hit Coburn in the elbow, run up under his arm and lodged itself in his shoulder blade. When he had fallen, the bone had snapped. He was still unconscious.

'Help me, Kate,' said the priest. 'He's bleeding badly but I don't know how to stop it.'

'I do,' she said. 'Let me see his shoulder. Hold him to you as tight as you can. I must first get to the bullet.'

She untied the scarf she wore around her neck, tore it into strips and rolled them into hard balls. She split open his shirt and, as his blood swamped her hand and arm, she felt for the wound. It was not deep. She touched the bullet. With her little finger she massaged it and slowly eased it out from between the folds of flesh until she felt it slip into the palm of her hand. Then, one by one, she wedged the balls of cotton into the hole, prodding them in with her thumb, harder, deeper, tighter. Slowly the bleeding eased and saw the blood begin to congeal.

Father Kenyon cradled him, unconscious, in his arms.

'You are remarkable, Kate. I would not have believed it if I hadn't watched it with my own eyes. He owes you his life.'

'Not me, Father. I learnt it from somebody he never met. A dear friend who was a doctor. He owes it to him.'

'Dare we move him?'

'If we do he will bleed again. And his arm is broken.'

'There is only one doctor in town I can trust. Joyce is his name. I know he's still there. I must go to him. We cannot cope on our own. If the soldiers are out there they will not suspect me.'

'Go then, and be quick, Father. If the wound breaks open again there's nothing more I can do.'

Father Kenyon passed through the military cordon with the bravado he was famous for.

'Have you caught the treacherous rebel yet?' he asked the sergeant.

'No, Father, but we will soon,' was the answer.

'Do you think he is still around here?'

'No doubt of it,' the sergeant replied. 'We have him sur-rounded. There's no other way out.'

'But there is,' said the priest. 'Beyond my church there is a new track, cleared a year ago by the Public Works but never recorded and never used. Didn't you know of it?'

'No, sir, I did not'.

The sergeant immediately split his column in two and sent twenty of his men on a track that led nowhere.

Father Kenyon saw the three bodies that had been dragged out of the undergrowth onto the lane. They lay encircled in their blood. When he returned with Dr Joyce half an hour later, they were still there. It meant Declan and his brother were still free.

ରୂ

Dr Joyce would hear no argument. 'You cannot move this man now that I've bound him. He will need rest. He has lost much blood and he'll be too weak to walk or ride. Try it and you will kill him. You did well, young lady, to stop the bleeding, but I've taken out what you put in and treated him with my own remedy, sphagnum moss. It grows on the peat in the woods and bogs and it's the best healer nature can provide. I'll leave

some with you. If any blood appears, use more of it. His arm is
in splints of a sort. It's the best I can do. I doubt he'll ever use
it again. When he wakes up dose him with a little of this. It's
laudanum, a small tincture of opium. It'll help take away some
of the pain and coax him back into deep sleep. And take comfort. Had that shot settled an inch or so lower, we'd be burying
him now.'

Once Dr Joyce left, Kate and Father Kenyon kept vigil until
it was dark. None of the local people would dare to enter
Bansha Woods now, believing, as they did, that banshees wandered there at night. Kate lay close to Coburn to give him
warmth.

'We are trapped again,' she said. 'First Cashel and now here.'

Father Kenyon nodded. 'Yes! And you will escape from here
just as you did from there.'

'How?'

'That I don't know. Remember I'm a man of much faith.'

'How long can we can stay here?'

'Again I don't know.'

'Will the soldiers come in this far?'

'Probably not. Or maybe in time. But they can know nothing
of this old church. We are deep inside. Would you have found it
without me?'

'Never.'

'It is an old Penal church from the times when we Catholics
were forbidden to build churches with stone, only with wood
and thatch, nothing permanent. And they had to be beyond the
sight of the roads so as not to offend any Protestants who might
be passing by. That's why this one is here, well away from everything and everyone. That big flat rock by the door was the Mass
rock, our altar. This your hideaway.'

'It's a gift from God, Father.'

'Indeed it is and I shall thank Him for it presently. But let
us think of tomorrow. In the morning, Kate, I will leave you. I

must be seen about my own church. They'll be suspicious otherwise. I'll get a little food and some water and I'll be back around
midday. Now you must sleep and I must pray.'

There was still some light. She watched him go to the altar
rock and kneel on a carpet of dry leaves where once there might
have been a holy rug. She lay still and for many minutes listened
to the soft whisperings to his God. Soon she was asleep by her
wounded husband.

ର

He was awake but he could not move. Pain engulfed him as if
a red-hot iron had been plunged into him. Yet his mind was
sharp, uninjured and detached from the bloody mess around
it. He could think clearly. Kate's face was close to his. He felt
her breath on his cheeks. Her lips were bruised and there were
cuts across her forehead where streaks of blood had dried. Dead
leaves were caught in her hair. She was his wife of a day and a
night.

He knew he could not move from here. He knew too that
he dare not let her stay. He would not argue. She could escape
even if he could not. When she had gone she would be carrying
something of him inside her. That was why she had to go. How
simple it was. How terrible. When he had had nothing but his
own life he could be brave and reckless. Now he had her and,
within her, his child. How could he lose them both? For the first
time he experienced fear.

He heard footsteps. He closed his eyes. He would listen to
them talk and plan. Kate stirred by his side. Father Kenyon called
her name.

'Wake up, wake up! I've a little food and water for you and a
sip of brandy for the patient. Don't ask me where I got it but it's
medicine enough. Has he slept well?'

'I don't think he's moved. I've tried not to touch him.'

'Difficult enough for a new bride!' He smiled but crossed himself in an apology. 'Forgive me, Kate, but I'm in need of some humour.'

'What's happened?'

'They've taken away the three bodies of the O'Connor brothers. But there's nothing of the other two. I've been praying all night that they're still alive. It's the older one, Declan, who'll know what to do. There's nothing we can do without him, nothing! I can't go to town for help. The army is everywhere. By God! We need those boys and we need them now.'

∽∾

Declan was the eldest of the O'Connor brothers, Tomás the youngest. They had seen their three siblings stretched out in the lane as soldiers kicked their bodies and spat on their dead faces. All that night they had lain hidden in a culvert behind St Olave's, covered in moss and bracken, not knowing what they should do next. Had Coburn survived? Was he already dead? How would they know? How long could they remain? Should they surrender, or show themselves and fight and die as their brothers had done?

Then, at first light, they glimpsed Father Kenyon leaving his church by the rear door, carrying food and water into the woods. This answered their questions and settled their doubts. Coburn must still be alive. At a distance they followed the Patriot Priest.

Declan and Tomás had been within fifteen paces of Father Kenyon all the way to the ruins of the Penal church and he had not known it. That was their way, their skill, and none did it better than Declan. He was a thief and a poacher, living on his wits to keep his family from starving, tracking his prey and outmanoeuvring those who came hunting for him. He was a large, strong man and no other man dared cross him, but all men knew they could trust him. He had no match in all of Tipperary.

As Father Kenyon crouched over the sleeping Coburn, Declan touched him lightly on the shoulder.

'Jesus Christ! And Lord forgive the blasphemy. Declan, you frightening man. Did I hear a thing until you were on top of me? If you'd been a Redcoat, we'd all be done for. Don't ever do that again. Holler next time.'

'Sorry, Father. I wasn't wanting to wake Mr Daniel.'

'No matter, Declan. You're with us and that's what matters now. We need you to tell us what to do, man, where to go, how to get them both away.'

'Father, we will never get them away together and time is not with us. I watched the soldiers all last night and they're spreading out. More will be brought here. It will take a regiment to scour these woods but scour them they will.'

'We're depending on you, Declan.'

'That I know, Father, which is why you must do as I ask. Tomás here knows these parts every bit as well as me. He must take Kate away and there can be no argument. I'll be with Mr Daniel until he is fit to ride.'

'I will not leave without him,' said Kate.

'Kate, you must do as Declan says.'

'Father, I will not leave until he's ready to go too. That is final.'

'No, it's not, Kate,' Coburn opened his eyes. 'You will do as Declan says.'

'I will not.'

'Come here, my sweetheart.' He raised his good arm. The blood drained from his face with the pain of the movement. She sat down by his side and nestled his head in her lap. She combed his hair with her fingers.

'Kate, I am your husband now and the father of your coming child. If they catch the two of us they will hang all three of us. They will not care that you are carrying. Don't you see? You must go. Tomás will look after you and see you through. Isn't that right, Tomás?'

'Indeed it is, sir. We'll make for Limerick. There are many paths to that city and I know them all. We have family there. My mother will know what to do.'

Coburn reached to touch her face. 'It is for the best, Kate, and there's no arguing about it. You must go. Say yes.'

She looked at him and said nothing. His face was shining with sweat. She could feel the heat in him and the trembling of his body. She leant down and kissed his forehead. She had often said that he read her thoughts and so it was then.

'Yes! I will go, Daniel. When I was a baby, they took me from my mother. They will not take my baby from me. Our child will never know the things we know and the things we have seen and it will be better for not knowing. I will go and wait for you to follow.'

Coburn heard her words and closed his eyes. She felt his body relax. He was asleep again.

'You had better leave soon, Miss Kate,' Declan said in a whisper.

'How far is Limerick?' she asked.

'About twenty-five miles as I know it. Tomás is a fast walker. Five hours, perhaps six.'

'The military will be on the roads.'

'There are no roads the way I go,' said Tomás.

'Declan, how will you get Daniel away?' asked Father Kenyon.

'Once Miss Kate is safe in my mother's house, Tomás will come back and meet us at Rathkea. It's a small village a few miles from here, tumbled and deserted except for a family of tinkers. He'll bring the horses there. He knows where to steal them.'

'How long will you wait here?'

'No longer than we have to. Two days, maybe more. I must wait until Mr Daniel is ready for it.'

'You will watch for the military.'

'I will watch.'

'And then you'll make for Limerick?'

'I shall.'

Kate came to him. 'Declan, I'll be waiting there. Promise you will bring my man safely to me.'

'That I promise. We will have you both together soon enough.'

CHAPTER EIGHTEEN

Coburn slept through the day. He woke that evening. Declan was a shadow by his side.

'Is Kate safe away, Declan?'

'They've been gone six hours, Mr Daniel. Tomás will have her in the Limerick house by now.'

'How long do we have here?'

'Not long, sir. They'll have more troops up by now.'

'We must move, Declan.'

'I'll not shift you, Mr Daniel, until I have to. I know a bit about bleeding – I've seen enough of it – and you're not ready yet to go anywhere. We must wait until the wound begins to close.'

'How will you get us away?'

'A little gap, a tiny escape hollowed out by men many years ago.'

'Tell me, Declan, so I can ready myself.'

'The Protestant landlord who owned these woods forbad the building of this church. But my people did build it and they hid it here, deep inside the thick of the trees so they could come to Mass. To get here and out again they dug a deep path and wove the saplings together over it so that it was like a tunnel. No stranger found it then, nor will they now. No soldier could ever know it's there. That's our way out, Mr Daniel.'

'I'm in good hands, Declan.'

'You are, sir. I'll be with you all the way and hope I live long enough to tell the story one day.'

'I'm thirsty, Declan.'

'A good sign.' He held a water jug to Coburn's lips.

'And hungry.'

'Even better. Father Kenyon is bringing more food.'

'What chance do we have?'

'More than half a chance if Tomás brings the horses. He knows where to get them.'

They heard a noise outside, a rustle in the undergrowth. Declan drew his pistol. Then came Father Kenyon's warning call, the thrice repeated call of the thrush. Declan put his pistol back down on the floor beside him. The priest entered carrying the bundle of food.

'I've got this for you, Daniel. From Dr Joyce, God bless him. Some more of his wonder moss. And a little more opium to help you sleep.'

'What of the soldiers, Father?'

'Too many, Daniel. The town's full of them and they're spreading out across the lower slopes of the woods.'

'Declan says Kate was away in good time.'

'She was. Well away, Daniel. She's in safe hands now.'

∞

Mother O'Connor's house in Limerick was close to the Shannon in a narrow alley off Bell Tavern Lane. From the top garret window Kate could see ships passing in and out of the docks and the endless flotilla of barges scurrying among them, carrying their cargoes to the mass of stevedores working on the warehouse quays. That morning she had watched a ship sailing downriver, westwards towards the Atlantic, its decks crammed with silent, motionless people. Not one of them waved goodbye to the Ireland.

She had been welcomed into the family and this was her third day. She had washed, fed and given the safe sanctuary of the room at the very top of the house.

Mother O'Connor, like her eldest son Declan, was strong and large with a shining dome of a forehead and a thin covering of ginger hair pulled back tight in a bun. Living so close to the docks, in a slum of strangers, she was careful and cautious, living by the maxim that nothing and no one was quite what they seemed.

From the day her husband had deserted her for a younger woman in Cashel, seven years before, she had lived on her wits and by them she had prospered. She knitted cotton jerkins for visiting seamen, sold jars of homemade illicit rum and lent small amounts of money at a pawnbroker's rate of interest. She kept to herself and those who did business with her knew it was wise not to argue over trifles.

She lived cheek by jowl with inquisitive, suspicious and troublesome neighbours and it worried her that some might have seen Kate's arrival. They would ask themselves who she was, this handsome young woman taking a room in the O'Connor's house, with such clothes and a clean head of shining black hair. They might suspect she was a fugitive running from the constabulary or a wife from her husband. Whatever her secret, they knew there might well be some profit in discovering who she was and why she was hiding in such a place.

Mother O'Connor was anxious, which was not her nature.

'I had thought of cutting off your hair, Kate, and giving you some old rags to live in. But if you've been seen, and I think maybe they've already spied you, that would only make them more suspicious. We just have to pray you won't need to stay long here.'

'When is Tomás leaving?'

'Tonight. He's taking some horses from the coach yard after dark. They'll not be missed until morning. You mustn't worry. Leave that to me. You'll have your man with you by this time tomorrow.'

'I've no way of thanking you. You are risking so much for us.'

'And willingly so. I heard him speaking here in Limerick, not a year ago. I've never thought things could ever change in Ireland, but when I listened to him and all his fine words, I really did begin to think we were ready for something better.'

'And now?'

'It will come, my dear. I do believe it will come one day and I thank him for that. I thank you both.'

ণ্ড

Tomás had picked the three sturdiest mares from the coach depot on the far side of Wellesley Bridge. He waited until the night-watchman was long asleep and the horses had finished their oats. They made no fuss. He would have to ride them without sad-dles, but the rendezvous at Rathkea, where he would wait for Coburn and Declan, was barely twenty miles as the crow flies. It was no hardship to ride bareback.

He was close to his mother's house when he saw movement in the shadows. There were no gas lamps and no moon, but there was no mistaking them. He had dodged too many soldiers in his time.

They were less than a hundred yards ahead, about a dozen, but he guessed there were more beyond the turning that led to the back of the house. They must know about Kate. Someone had informed. He led the horses further back and tied them to a bol-lard on the quayside. Then he began climbing.

When he reached the top of the first house, fifty feet up, he took off his boots and swung them round his neck. Then, step-ping ever so gingerly, he went from roof to roof, treading the tiles as if they were made of porcelain, until he came to the roof he recognised as his mother's. He leant over the guttering and tapped on the window of Kate's garret.

'Kate,' he whispered.

He tapped again. 'For Christ's sake, Kate, wake up. The mili-tary is here. Open up. It's me, Tomás.'

Kate lit her candle. Tomás's face was looking at her through the window. She opened the fanlight and he squeezed himself into the room.

'They're on their way. I saw them. We're done for, Kate, there's no way out. And by Christ I had the horses ready too.'

Mother O'Connor knew what to expect before she heard the knocking. Alarm was no stranger. As she feared, the neighbours had told on her. A fist hit the door hard. A man shouted.

'Open this door! I am an officer of the Queen's army. Your house is surrounded by my men. Open and you'll not be harmed.'

Mother O'Connor did what she had to do. The officer entered, a young man, so young to be a captain. A soldier stood either side of him. They held their rifles aimed at her.

'You can put your guns away,' she said. 'There are no men in this house and you'll have no cause to shoot at me.'

The young officer beckoned to his men and they lowered their weapons.

He said, 'I have come to arrest a woman hiding in this house.'

'There is no woman here but me, young man. This is a clean and respectable house so I'll ask you to search elsewhere.'

'I know she is here,' the officer said. 'Her name is Kathryn Macaulay. I demand you give her up.'

'I'd give her to you if she was here but I've never heard of …'

'My name is Kate and I go by no other name.'

Kate came into the room from the stairs, wrapped in a blanket.

The officer stepped towards her. 'You are Kathryn Macaulay, daughter of the deceased Sir William Macaulay?'

'I was his daughter once and I repeat, my name is Kate.'

'Whatever name you prefer to go by, I am here to arrest you. You are charged with treason and I am to escort you to Newgate Prison in Dublin. You are to prepare yourself for that journey. And it is a long one.'

Mother O'Connor shouted at him. 'You'll do nothing of the kind. You cannot take her all that way. Do you not see she is carrying a child? It will kill her and her baby too. Have pity. In the name of our God, let her stay awhile. Take her now and you will kill both of them.'

The officer looked stunned. He paused, seeming not to know what to say next. Then he mumbled his words.

'I did not know this. I was not told. But I must obey my orders.'

'May I dress?' Kate asked.

'Of course.'

The officer turned and ordered his men out of the house. But as Kate went to climb the stairs back to the garret, the officer closed the front door behind him, locked it and stepped back into the room.

'Kate.' He said it quietly. It was almost a whisper. 'Come here, Kate. I have little time. My men will expect me to leave soon.'

'You call me Kate? Why?'

She came back, hesitant, confused and stood close to Mother O'Connor.

'Do you not recognise me?' the young officer said. 'It was I who came to you in Cashel with that offer of a pardon and free passage to America.'

'It was dark,' she replied. 'I would not have known it was you. Why should it matter now?'

'There was no such offer. It was deceit. A trap. They wanted a quiet killing of you both. If you had surrendered I had orders for my men to shoot you.'

'This we knew. Of course we knew. But what are you saying? You come to arrest me and now you tell me this.'

'Kate, you will find this hard to believe. But I have come to help you escape.'

'Mother of God!' Mother O'Connor collapsed on her stool.

Kate did not move.

'You trick me,' she said. 'Why do you trick me?'

'Look at me, Kate. Look at me. Do I not remind you of somebody, somebody you knew years ago, somebody who was your friend when you had none? Was he not your ally?'

'You are not he. He is dead.'

'What was his name, Kate? You cannot have forgotten him.'

'I shall never forget him. His name was Shelley. Captain John Shelley. And I loved him as a brother.'

'Kate, I am Richard Shelley, captain in the Hussars. I am John's younger brother.'

She looked at him again, his pale face, his high cheekbones, his fair hair and his eyes, grey-green and full of sadness. And she knew it to be true.

Captain Shelley went to the front door and unlocked it.

'Sergeant, bring all the men to the front and have them lined up in column for escort.'

'Even the men at the back, sir?'

'I said all the men to the front, sergeant. Now.'

He closed and locked the door again.

'Kate, it is not by accident that I am here. I have worked on it, planned it. When I knew for sure that you were alive, I manoeuvred my way towards you again, planning it day by day, asking favours, bribing, switching regimental orders, doing everything that was necessary to make it certain that I would be put in charge, the one officer whose responsibility it was to hunt you down. Now I've found you, Kate, and I have made preparations. I have a way out for you and it will succeed, trust me.'

He looked to Mother O'Connor. 'You will help her?'

'I will, sir. Just as fast as these legs will carry me.'

'Once my men are lined up outside, you will escape through the back alleys. You will make for the port. There is a ship there named *Pegasus*. She's a three-masted square rigger, a white and black hull, moored on pier eighteen. Have you got that, Mother?'

'I have, sir. *Pegasus* on pier eighteen. I know the way well enough.'

'The master is Robert Howard, an Englishman, a good friend of mine and once my brother's too. He knows all about you, Kate, and you'll not want for anything. It sails tomorrow evening. Captain Howard will hide you until you're safely up the Shannon beyond Loop Head and out to sea.'

Kate said, 'I cannot go.'

'You must. You have no choice, Kate. I have no choice. If you refuse I must take you to Dublin. Please, you must go.'

'I must wait for Daniel.'

'There is no time. Say yes! Now. Otherwise I must unlock this door and take you away.'

'I promised I wouldn't go without him.'

'You are waiting in vain, Kate. We know where he is. The 49th has surrounded the wood he's in and there's no escape. They will burn him out if they have to. They will not stop until they have him, alive or dead. You must believe me'.

'Why are you doing this for me? Tell me.'

'Kate, you know why. They killed my brother. He wrote to me about you and what you had both planned to do together. He told me of the things he had seen here, all those terrible, terrible things. But I did not believe him, I could not. It seemed impossible that so much was happening, so many evils and the powerful in England were turning their heads from it. John was so disgusted by what he had seen, so full of despair and so desperate to help that he defied his own country, the country he loved. Then they executed him as a traitor, killed him in cold blood. Mown down by English rifles.

'When my regiment was commissioned to come to Ireland I saw it all for myself. My very first duty in my first week was to protect a tumbling gang as they destroyed an entire village. I was helping them when I should have been protecting the families. I was only nineteen, fresh from England, and I saw it all, the screaming, the beatings, the children. I see it still and I cannot bear to see more.

'Kate, if you do not go they will hang you and your child and God help me because I will be party to it and my brother's ghost will haunt me until the day I die.'

Mother O'Connor would hear no more. She pushed Kate towards the stairs.

'No Irish babe is going to die on English gallows. You will go, Kate, even if I have to carry you away myself and I'm bloody well capable of that. Now go, get your clothes and be quick with it.'

Kate said nothing. Then she nodded and quickly climbed the stairs.

'What will happen to you, sir?' Mother O'Connor asked the captain.

'I don't know. I have thought it all out so carefully, every little detail except for this, the final bit. Perhaps, inside me, I never thought it would come this far, that I'd never get to her in time. I'll probably tell them you tricked me or some such story, but they'll not believe me. So now I shall do what is expected of me, surrender to my sergeant and wait for my regiment to do what it must do. The punishment will be severe, perhaps even final. I'll not expect mercy, nor should I. But it doesn't matter now, it really doesn't. Once Kate is away and *Pegasus* is out of the Shannon I shall at last be at peace with myself and with my brother. The debt will have been paid. He will have been avenged and all the wickedness wiped clean from both of us.'

Mother O'Connor said nothing more. She crossed herself, reached for his hand and kissed it.

Tomás, hidden in the garret, heard it all. When Kate had gone he sat still, listening for any movement by the officer below. Then he heard him unlock and open the front door. From his window, he saw him hand his pistol and sword to the sergeant. Then they marched him away.

The horses were still tethered where he'd left them. He whipped the lead mare and cantered away, not caring if the clatter of hooves on the cobbles as he crossed John's Square wakened the constabulary. There was no one to stop him now. Soon he would be well away from the city and deep into the country he knew so well, there to find his brother and Daniel Coburn waiting in Rathkea. It was still some hours to dawn and he knew he had done well.

೧೪

The tinker family in Rathkea brought them a jug of boiled tea and they drank it scalding hot. On the horizon, beyond the layer of heavy black clouds, a thin stream of sunlight caught the tree-tops that outlined the distant Bansha Woods.

'Tell it again, Tomás. As you heard it.'

'Mr Daniel, I've told you twice already.'

'I want it again, word for word.'

'The officer said it was called *Pegasus*, sailing from pier eighteen. I remember that clear enough.'

'What time does the ship sail, Tomás?'

'The officer didn't say a time. Just in the evening.'

'Did Kate say anything when she left?'

'Not a word.'

'But you're certain she went for the ship?'

'No, Mr Daniel, how can I be sure? But the officer said it had all been arranged. He said it was well planned and the English master would look after her.'

'And the officer was marched away by his own men?'

'Yes! I heard him tell my mother he would surrender to his regiment and that he would be punished. I saw them march him away under guard. I saw it clearly.'

'Did he say why he did it?'

'He said the English had killed his brother, but I couldn't make out what that was all about.'

'Did you hear the officer's name?'

'No. My mother was making such a fuss I couldn't listen properly.'

'Tomás. Close your eyes. See the dark. Think back. Listen again.'

Tomás did as he was told. Coburn waited.

'Think, Tomás. Listen to the voices'.

'I'm trying sir. But it's all a jumble. I was scared. I thought they'd come up the stairs. I thought they'd have me.'

'Ease yourself, Tomás. Slowly now. Remember. You are up the stairs, listening. The officer gives his name. Now, give me the name.'

Tomás pressed the palms of his hands hard over his eyes, slowly rocking his head from side to side.

Then, 'It's coming, Mr Daniel. I think it's coming. I remember it sounded like … Kelly. Yes! That was it. It was Kelly.'

'Tomás. No! Think again. Would an English officer have a name like Kelly?'

'Well that's what it sounded like. Or was it …?'

'Shelley?'

'Shelley? Christ! That's the one, Mr Daniel. That's the one for sure. It was Shelley. No mistaking.'

'Thank you, Tomás. Now I understand. Now it makes sense. Captain Shelley joined the boys some years back and the English outlawed him as a traitor. When the boys raided the depot at Kinvara, the Redcoats were waiting. It was a trap. They killed the lot of them. It was Martineau that planned it.'

'The one we hanged?'

'Yes, Tomás. The one we hanged.'

He raised himself slowly onto his elbows. 'Declan, get me to that ship. Get me to the *Pegasus*.'

'You dared not go to Limerick.'

'I know that. Find another way. There must be another way.'

'There is only one other way, Mr Daniel.'

'Tell me, Declan.'

'There are the hookers, the sailing boats that bring the river pilots off the ships mid-channel of the Shannon, close to Inis Cathaigh'

'Where's that?'

'The English call it Scattery Island, off the Clare coast.'

'Declan, this is nonsense. *Pegasus* leaves Limerick this evening and Clare is days away. I'll have bled myself dry with Kate already out in the Atlantic.'

'I know that well enough, Mr Daniel. But when the sky's as black as it is now and with a southerly wind blowing, the pilot boats will tie up on the Kerry shore. They leave their moorings a good two hours before the ships come level.'

'How do we get on to a pilot boat?'

'I've done it before, Mr Daniel. It's a way of getting certain people out, people who wouldn't dare leave under the eyes of the English in Limerick.'

'How far must we go?'

'Near to Ballylongford, about fifty miles from here, maybe more, and it's rough going, sir.'

'Then that's where we go, Declan, now!'

'But if your bleeding starts again, Mr Daniel, how far can you ride?'

'Never mind. I'll make it, Declan. Just get me to it.'

'I will, sir. I will get you there.'

ඉ෴ඉ

Father Kenyon arrived with oatcakes, a fresh bundle of moss and a small bottle of laudanum.

'This is goodbye then, Daniel. Did we ever think it could end like this?'

'No, Father. We once dreamt of a different ending. Can you tell me why it had to be this way?'

'No, I cannot. Nor can any one of us. But everything that is done is done for a reason, whether men realise it or not.'

'Even the famine?'

'Even the famine. There is a purpose, Daniel, somewhere there is always a purpose, though I do not pretend to know what it is. Each time I anoint a dying child, or give my blessing to a good and decent man dying, I ask God, "Why?" And He never answers. It is the greatest test of my faith.'

'Faith in a God that condemns us to this. No, Father. We are abandoned people, as helpless as thistledown in the wind.'

'But how is that, Daniel, since thistledown's purpose is to carry its seed? All we can do is to wait for the seed to settle and prosper.'

'You hoped it was me.'

'Yes! We hoped it was you.'

'Must I blame myself?'

'There is no blame.'

'It was the people who betrayed us.'

'Nonsense,' said the priest. 'Who are you to condemn them? Shouldn't we have known that a belly empty of food has no fight in it either?'

'We came to them too late.'

'Or maybe too early.'

'This was not the moment to turn history and I was blind to it.'

'Oh, Daniel! Why are men so severe with themselves? Like two sides of a coin, always at odds. Comfort yourself. You were not cast as the Great Patriot. You are a fighter and we know that the great men sit at the rear. You must now let others do the fighting and the dying.'

'You were ever the optimist, Father.'

'Yes! Daniel. Optimism and faith. They live together.'

'God grant you survive.'

'We will. We shall survive the famine, we will outlive the fever and finally outrun the English. One day they'll be gone and we will still be here and our children will live to see our land prosper. Have no fear. This is not the end by any means. The winner will always be he who refuses to lose. And remember my words, remember them when you think of us. Never regret what is gone, Daniel. The past is just a prologue.'

'I will remember, Father. They are wise words'.

Father Kenyon knelt by Coburn's side, leant down and kissed his forehead. Then he went quickly to the door, turned and crossed himself.

'God speed you to the New World, Daniel, and take the love of Ireland with you.'

కాు

They stopped many times. A fit horseman might canter fifty miles cross-country in six hours with a stop or two. But Coburn was half drugged on laudanum, without stirrups and with only sacking as his saddle. He could not trot his mare, every step jarred his bones, every stumble threatened to break open his wound. They stopped at streams for water and rest the horses but Coburn would not have them stop long, and urged Declan to go on. The wind cut his face and his wound burnt as if the bandages were on fire. But he thought only of her, knowing that every hour of pain brought her nearer.

It was almost dark when they came to the shores of Ballylongford. A sharp wind carried a cold drizzle from the sea and, behind it, the threat of fog. A line of oil lamps lit up a long, narrow wooden jetty where half a dozen small boats were tied up. Men sat smoking pipes, huddled beneath a shelter of an old discarded sail.

Declan shouted to them.

'Which one of you is meeting the ship *Pegasus* tonight?'

'Who is it who wants to know?'

Declan went closer to the man who had answered.

'Is it you?'

'It is. What is it of yours?'

'Because we're coming with you.'

'You are not. You have no authority.'

'See here, friend. Is my pistol authority enough? Tell me, which is it to be?'

Within the half hour they had lifted Coburn into the boat and tucked him under the small fo'c'sle wrapped in a blanket and sheltered him from the spray with a tarpaulin cover. His wound was seeping blood. Declan took molten candlewax from the lanterns and, rolling it in his palms until it was warm and supple, smeared it, layer upon layer, across the bandage until the dressing was tight. Soon the bleeding stopped.

'You have much pain, Mr Daniel?'

'I feel nothing, Declan.'

'Be brave with it, sir. We are at last on our way.'

It began to rain hard and the wind smacked at the sails as the helmsman tacked slowly out towards mid-channel.

Declan shouted to him above the wind.

'When will we sight her mast light?'

'You'll not see it yet,' he answered. 'Not for a while.'

'How will you know it's her?'

'I've been ferrying pilots on this river for over forty years and I can tell a ship by the smell of her. I'll give you warning when I sight her. And you'll not need the pistol now. I know who it is you are carrying and I've much respect for him and I can see he's very sick. The waters are rough, it's wind against tide and it's rising but I'll do my best to keep it easy. Tuck that tarpaulin tighter. Keep him warm and keep the water off him.'

Declan held the lantern higher to the man's face.

'What's your name?'

'Brennan.'

'When this is all over, Brennan, people will remember you.'

'It's a small part I'm playing but I'll have a hell of story to tell.'

'How will we get him aboard the ship?'

'The master will turn into wind and we'll heave to on the lee side. The water will be steadier there for the pilot to get clear. It will not be easy but there'll be plenty of muscle to haul him up. You must trust me.'

'I trust you,' said Declan.

The helmsman tacked his boat deeper into the blackness that was the Shannon, without compass, without stars or river lights to guide him, sometimes running with the wind, sometimes fighting it, but all the time getting closer to his rendezvous with the great sailing ship. The rigging shrieked in the wind, the short mast bent under the blow and they stood ankle-deep in bilge water. The boat twisted with the force of the waves, rising on a crest and then plunging down into the trough in great dizzying sweeps with the white huge back breakers rising behind it. Declan spread his large body over the tarpaulin covering Coburn to protect him from the storm.

Then he heard the helmsman shouting. He was pointing out beyond the bow and as the boat rose again, there, cutting through the rain and spray, Declan glimpsed the glistening black hull and white sails of *Pegasus*.

ঞ

She stood on the deck, shivering in the cold heavy sea fog. It hid the coast from her, teasing her, tormenting her, vague outlines of a land she would never to see again. The salt from the spray mixed with the salt of her tears and she turned away from the wind and wiped her eyes.

Along the shining deck she saw the prow climbing and dipping, ploughing through the waves, torrents of water gushing through the scuppers. She knew she was looking west, towards the vast Atlantic Ocean, west to Canada and America, places that promised her safety, a new life for herself and the child she would bear in the New World. And in return, there would be emptiness, the dread of a lifetime of loneliness, praying for the tides and the winds and another ship to bring him to her.

She heard the moan of a fog horn ahead and men shouting. Were they familiar voices she was so desperate to hear? She heard the thud as the rope ladder hit the hull's side. The river pilot was leaving. She saw the glow of a lantern held on a pole high above the gunwales. As the bow parted the fog, she saw a small boat with a single sail and the shapes of men beneath tarpaulins.

'Another's coming aboard.' She heard the shout above the roar of the wind. She strained to see. She might even have believed it was him. She sighed and wept at her fantasy and recited out loud yet again the words of the poem she had heard for the first time from a little boy in a land near dying.

I could scale the blue air,
I could plough the high hills,
I could kneel all night in prayer
To heal your many ills,
My Dark Rosaleen.

She closed her eyes and turned her head once more into the wind. When she opened them again, Ireland was already a shadow.

Sebec Lake
Maine County
So ends their story as told to me. It was Ireland that first called them together, Ireland that forged them into one and delivered them to the New World, where they lived long and happily, as I can vouch. Daniel and Kate Coburn are buried here in Maine, side by side in the foothills of the Appalachians. Forever in America and I thank God for it.

– THE END –

HISTORICAL NOTES

Daniel Coburn is based on John Mitchel, an attorney and journalist, founder of the nationalist newspaper *Young Ireland*.

He was an early follower of Daniel O'Connell, and the leader of the Repealers. Coburn rejected O'Connell's policy of non-violence and founded the Young Irelanders, campaigning for direct action against the landlords and insurrection against English rule. 'Irish soil for the Irish.'

After the failed uprising in 1848, he was charged with sedition and treason, convicted and sent to the penal colony in Bermuda. He was later transferred to a prison on Van Diemen's Land (Tasmania).

Coburn escaped to America and founded the Irish-American newspaper *The Citizen*.

He supported the South in the American Civil War, based in Richmond Virginia. Three of his sons fought for the Confederates.

He returned to Ireland in 1875, and was elected Member of Parliament, but this was invalidated because he was a convicted felon.

Mitchel County, Iowa, is named in his honour.

He died in 1875, aged 60.

William Smith O'Brien was born of an aristocratic family in Dromoland in 1803, a descendant of Brian Boru, an eleventh-century king of Ireland. He was a Protestant and an MP, and also an ardent Irish nationalist, co-founder, with Mitchel, of the Young Irelanders.

Convicted of treason after the failed uprising of 1848, he was sentenced to be hanged but this was later commuted to life imprisonment and he was sent to Van Diemen's Land, where he met Mitchel again.

He was released in 1856 on condition that he would never returned to Ireland.

After a stay in Brussels, he was allowed to return to Ireland.

O'Brien never involved himself in politics again and died in 1864, aged 61.

Thomas Meagher was born in 1823, the son of the mayor of Waterford.

A member of the Younger Irelanders, he was convicted of sedition following the failed 1848 uprising. He was sentenced to be hanged but this was commuted to transportation for life to the penal colony in Van Diemen's Land.

In 1852, he escaped to America, and lived and worked in New York as a journalist.

During the American Civil War he supported the Union, and recruited and led the Irish Brigade, where he was promoted to brigadier general.

After the war he was appointed acting governor of Montana Territory.

Meagher drowned in 1867, after falling from a steamboat in the Missouri at Fort Benton, aged 44. His body was never recovered.

Gavan Duffy, son of a grocer, was born in Monaghan in 1816.

Journalist and later attorney, he founded *The Nation*, an Irish nationalist newspaper. He was a follower of Daniel O'Connell and the Repeal Association, but he left along with Mitchel, O'Brien and Meagher to form the Young Irelanders.